"This couldn't have worked out better if I'd planned it,"

Jake said happily.

Brittany laughed. "Shame on you. Are you saying you're happy that the movie theater was crowded and that we can't sit with your children?"

"Damn right. Even a father needs time off for courting once in a while."

"Are you courting me, Jake?" She meant it to be a lighthearted remark, but it came out sounding hopeful.

His grin faded. "Couldn't we just pretend for a while that I am?" His tone had lost its teasing lilt. "We have so little time left together. What would it hurt?"

It could hurt us both very deeply, Brittany thought....

Dear Reader,

Happy New Year! May this year bring you happiness, good health and all that you wish for. And at Silhouette Special Edition, we're hoping to provide you with a year full of books that are chock-full of happiness!

In January, don't miss stories by some of your favorite authors: Curtiss Ann Matlock, Myrna Temte, Phyllis Halldorson and Patricia McLinn. This month also brings you *Far To Go*, by Gina Ferris—a heartwarming addition to her FAMILY FOUND series.

The January selection of our THAT SPECIAL WOMAN! promotion is *Hardhearted* by Bay Matthews. This is the tender tale of a woman strong enough to turn a gruff, lonely, hardhearted cop into a true family man. Don't miss this moving story of love. Our THAT SPECIAL WOMAN! series is a celebration of our heroines—and the wonderful men they fall in love with. THAT SPECIAL WOMAN! is friend, wife, lover—she's each one of us!

In Silhouette Special Edition, we're dedicated to publishing the types of romances that you dream about—stories that delight as well as bring a tear to the eye. That's what Silhouette Special Edition is all about—special books by special authors for special readers.

I hope that you enjoy this book and all the stories to come.

Sincerely,

Tara Gavin
Senior Editor

Please address questions and book requests to:
Reader Service
U.S.: P.O. Box 1325, Buffalo, NY 14269
Canadian: P.O. Box 1050, Niagara Falls, Ont. L2E 7G7

PHYLLIS HALLDORSON

A HAVEN IN HIS ARMS

SPECIAL EDITION®

Published by Silhouette Books
America's Publisher of Contemporary Romance

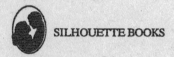

SILHOUETTE BOOKS

ISBN 0-373-09863-4

A HAVEN IN HIS ARMS

Printed in U.S.A.

Books by Phyllis Halldorson

PHYLLIS HALLDORSON,

at age sixteen, met her real-life Prince Charming. She married him a year later and they settled down to raise a family. A compulsive reader, Phyllis dreamed of someday finding the time to write stories of her own. That time came when her two youngest children reached adolescence. When she was introduced to romance novels, she knew she had found her long-delayed vocation. After all, how could she write anything else after living all those years with her very own Silhouette hero?

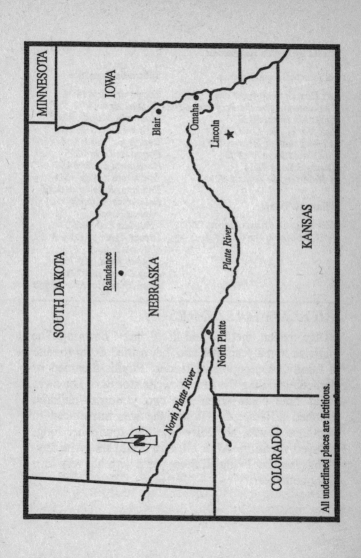

All underlined places are fictitious.

Chapter One

Brittany Marie Castle's heart raced with apprehension as the taxi pulled into the loading zone at the Independence, Missouri, airport.

She carefully surveyed the area in all directions while the driver got out and went around to remove her luggage from the trunk. The coast seemed to be clear, but just because she didn't see Ronny didn't mean he wasn't lurking somewhere nearby where he could see her.

When the driver opened the door for her she let him help her out and hoped her trembling knees wouldn't buckle. Her hands shook as she paid him, then she picked up her suitcases and walked into the terminal.

She spent the twenty minutes between the time she finished checking in her luggage and the time the plane was due to start boarding by hiding in the women's rest room, hoping she'd been clever enough not to arouse Ronny's suspicions.

She'd been so careful, but Ronny Ralston was far more cunning than the ordinary man. He wasn't easily fooled, and if he caught up with her...

She shivered with remembered revulsion.

At the appointed boarding time she eased out of the rest room and tried to lose herself in the crowd of milling passengers. Still no sign of Ronny, but she wouldn't be safe until she was on the plane and it had lifted off.

Fifteen minutes later all the passengers were aboard and seated, and the heavy doors had been shut and locked. Brittany had become an expert on furtive surveillance in the past few weeks, and not a nook or cranny on the airplane had escaped her vigilance. Her nemesis was not on the aircraft.

She was free of him at last! Now maybe she could relax, and possibly even sleep for a while.

The sky above Omaha was overcast with heavy dark rain clouds later when the pilot landed the big jet at Eppley airfield. Despite the weather, Brittany felt rested and eager as she gathered up her purse and carry-on luggage and prepared to disembark.

It had been seven years since she'd graduated from high school in the small town of Raindance, located in the northwestern part of Nebraska. Life had been so exciting then. She'd been a straight B+ student, a cheerleader and queen of her senior prom.

She still had a picture of herself in the blue-and-silver robe, being crowned with the sparkling tiara, her naturally curly blond hair cascading down her back and her wide hazel eyes shimmering with excitement.

A few weeks later she'd kissed her grandparents, who were also her legal guardians, goodbye. She'd driven her beat-up little compact car toward Independence, and the community college where she'd enrolled to study to become a veterinary technician.

Ah, yes, life was one big adventure and anything was possible when you were eighteen.

She'd been back only once, and that was five years ago when Gramps had died suddenly of a stroke. Gram had followed three days later. The doctor said it was a coronary thrombosis, but Brittany knew it wasn't a clot that had killed the loving woman who was more of a mother to her than her own mother had been. It was a broken heart. She and Gramps had been married sixty years.

Brittany walked into the terminal and stopped to look around and get her bearings. First she had to go downstairs and retrieve her luggage, then she had to find the car-rental counter. Her plan was to rent a car and stay in Omaha for a few days until she could find a good secondhand one for sale cheap—although that was probably a contradiction in terms—then drive on to Raindance. She'd stay there until her class reunion at the end of the month. Surely by then she'd have calmed down enough to make intelligent decisions about where she wanted to relocate.

Damn Ronny Ralston! That maniac had terrorized her and turned her entire life upside down, and there hadn't been a thing she could do about it!

Her gaze found a sign indicating the way to the luggage area, and she started in that direction, when she noticed an elderly woman several feet away, leaning heavily on a cane. The woman seemed to be arguing with an impatient young man.

A swift jab of horror, as strong as a physical blow, knocked the breath out of Brittany in a shuddering gasp. That man! He looked like—

No, it couldn't be. He was partially turned away from her, for heaven's sake. It could be anybody. She was just still seeing evil and danger lurking in every shadow.

Then he turned, and the horror escalated. It was! It was Ronny! She couldn't mistake the short blond curly hair, or the blue eyes that twinkled when he laughed but turned cold and cruel when he was crossed. The woman still held his attention. He hadn't seen Brittany yet.

Something in her panic-fogged mind registered the presence of a motorized luggage cart passing by, and purely by reflex she scrambled onto it and crouched behind a stack of boxes.

The startled baggage handler who was driving it gasped. "Lady, what are you doing? You can't—"

She turned her head to look at him and murmured, "Please, don't stop. Just get me away from here."

She must have appeared almost as scared as she felt, because he continued down the concourse and in seconds had taken her out of Ronny's viewing range.

"Are you all right?" he asked when he stopped at the freight elevator.

Brittany didn't move but managed a deep breath to draw oxygen into her starving lungs. "I... Yes, I'm fine." Her tone was reedy. She cleared her throat and tried again. "I... uh... I saw someone back there waiting for me who I don't want to talk to. Please let me go down in the elevator with you."

Just then the doors opened, and he shrugged and wheeled the cart inside with her still crouching on it.

What was she going to do now? Obviously Ronny was here at the airport to meet her plane, although it seemed impossible that he could have known she'd be coming to Omaha on that flight. Or that he could have arrived here before she had. She'd been so careful not to let anyone know she was leaving Independence or where she was going.

She wouldn't dare go to the luggage area to pick up her suitcases. That's the first place he'd look for her when he realized he'd missed her coming in. Maybe the baggage handler could help....

"Sorry, ma'am," he said, interrupting her thoughts, "but I've got to unload these boxes, and I can't take you into the storage room."

She looked up and realized that they had paused in front of a door on the ground floor. She'd been so wrapped up in her fear and her disjointed thinking that she hadn't even noticed when they'd left the elevator.

She nodded and climbed off the cart. As he opened the door she unfastened her purse and reached inside. "Thank you for being so understanding," she said. "Would you...that is, could I impose on you for one more favor? I'll pay you, of course."

He hesitated. "Well...I guess that depends on what you have in mind."

She pulled a ten-dollar bill out of her wallet and held it out to him. "I need you to pick up my luggage and bring it to the taxi stand outside. I'll be waiting in a cab."

He looked at the money, then at her and nodded. "I guess I could do that as soon as I get rid of these boxes."

She thanked him, gave him the money and her claim check and told him her name and how to identify her two suitcases, then breathed a little prayer that her trust in him wasn't misplaced.

Fifteen nerve-racking minutes later, as she sat huddled in the back seat of a cab with the meter running, she saw him coming along the walkway with her Pullman cases, and asked the driver to signal him.

She hadn't noticed any further sign of Ronny, but kept her face turned away from the window until the luggage had been stored in the trunk and they were out of the vicinity of the airport. Then she told the driver to take her to a car-rental agency in town.

By the time they arrived there it was dark, and a brisk cold breeze had sprung up, bringing the sweet, clean smell of rain. Brittany chose a gray two-door car that was nearly indistinguishable from the hundreds of other compact cars on the road, and asked for directions to highway 275.

In her panic, she'd discarded her plan for spending a few days in Omaha. Now her only thought was to get out of the city as quickly as possible, and highway 275 was the road to Raindance.

As she drove through the unfamiliar streets, listening to country music on the radio, her thoughts again centered on Ronny, and doubts began to surface. Was that really him she'd seen or just someone who looked like him? She'd only glimpsed the man. Maybe her subconscious was playing tricks on her.

If he'd caught up with her at the airport in Independence she wouldn't have been surprised. He'd been stalking her for weeks and knew every move she made. That's why she'd been so careful when she had decided to disappear. She hadn't even notified her employer or her landlady.

Only a handful of police officers knew where she was going, and that was because they'd made the arrangements for her. A warrant had been put out for Ronny's arrest, but he'd been too wily to be caught.

One of the officers had bought her airline ticket, and he'd agreed to wait a few days, then notify her landlady and employer that she'd decided to relocate but was all right.

As she drove along she belatedly realized she'd been so immersed in her troubled thoughts that she wasn't paying attention to where she was going. She was almost out of the city, yet she still hadn't seen the entrance for highway 275. Slowing down, she tried to read the road signs, but they were difficult to see in the dark. She'd never driven in Omaha before and had no idea how the streets were laid out.

Several minutes later, when none of the guideposts she'd been told to watch for materialized, she faced the fact that she'd taken a wrong turn somewhere and was hopelessly lost.

Not only that, but the rain which had seemed nonthreatening in its early stages, was now accompanied by claps of thunder and jagged bolts of lightning that kept coming closer as it was blown in on the escalating icy wind.

With a shiver, she stepped on the gas and kept going. She reached the outskirts of the city and then found herself all alone on a rural road with no light except her headlights, and no idea where she was going.

But rather than turn around and head back toward the city, Brittany decided to continue on until she happened on civilization again. As she drove along her mind returned to the man who pursued her with such determination.

Brittany hadn't known Ronny long, only a little more than four months, but she'd been immediately attracted to him. He not only looked like a Greek god, he had an Ivy League education and was a perfect gentleman.

She'd been so enchanted by his good manners, his impeccable breeding and his overall Old World courtliness that it was some time before she could accept the fact that he had a dark side, too.

Such as a compulsion to have his own way and a vicious display of temper if he didn't get it.

When he'd asked her to marry him she'd been tempted, but her wariness had won out. She'd told him she wasn't ready for marriage yet, and his carefully hidden simmering rage had exploded in violence directed at her.

Outraged, she'd told him to get out and never come near her again. It was then that he'd begun a systematic reign of terror that had made her life a nightmare of fear and foreboding until there was no safe place for her.

* * *

A brilliant bolt of lightning cracked just a few yards off the road, jolting Brittany out of her grim reminiscence. A long, deafening rumble of thunder actually shook the ground as the skies opened and the rain became a downpour so heavy that the windshield wipers could barely keep up.

To make matters worse the humidity inside the car caused the windows to fog over, and when she finally found the defogger and turned it on it didn't work. Frantically, she wiped at the windshield with her bare hand, only to have it fog over again within seconds.

Brittany was trembling with dread. She couldn't even see the blacktop in front of her. If the wild lightning didn't strike her first, she'd probably go off the road's edge and roll the car.

She should stop, but she was afraid that if she did she might not get the engine started again. She knew nothing about the mechanics of an automobile, but if the defogger didn't work maybe there was something wrong with the electrical system. She pulled over to the side, slowed the car to a crawl and drove on.

After what seemed like hours the road curved, but she was halfway through the turn before a streak of lightning revealed that the two-lane road she'd been on continued on straight, and the road she was now on was a branch. She felt like screaming with frustration, though she had no choice but to follow it, since trying to turn the car around in the middle of this deluge was almost certain to land her either head-on into another vehicle or top down in a ditch.

The thunder was earsplitting, and the jagged rods of lightning were coming closer. These forces of nature alternately offered brilliant flashes of illumination, like a light show from hell, then total blackness. The wind and rain were so strong as they pelted the little car that they threatened to overturn the vehicle.

Brittany's wrenched shoulders ached as she fought to keep the lightweight vehicle on the road. The DJ on the radio had just announced that it was eight minutes before ten o'clock when a screaming gust of wind rocked the car. She overcorrected and sent it careering down an incline.

There was a jarring crash and she was thrown forward against the restraining seat belt just before a burst of pain ignited fireworks behind her eyes.

Brittany was stunned, but aware of the noises around her. It was a piercing sound of splitting wood that revived her enough to react. She pushed herself up, to see that lightning had struck a huge old tree just a few feet away and split it down the middle, although both pieces were still standing.

A wave of dizziness enveloped her, and she put both hands to her aching head in an effort to stop the whirling sensation. The lightning was dangerously close, but she was relieved to see, by the almost constant flickering illumination from the storm, a large house only a couple of hundred yards to her left.

She was terrified that the car would be hit by the all-encompassing electrical display, but she was equally afraid to leave its dubious protection to make a dash for the house with no cover at all.

Then there was another hit, so close it shook the car. Brittany shrieked as panic ripped through her. By blind instinct she scrambled out of the car and ran toward the house.

Twice she stumbled in the darkness between lightning bolts and landed on her knees in puddles of water, but each time she managed to pull herself up and keep going.

At last she reached the steps and staggered up onto the large covered porch. The house was dark both inside and out, and she heard the threatening bark of a big dog nearby.

Dear God, what if there was nobody home?

Her head was pounding, she was soaking wet and her breath was coming in gasps when she finally found the heavy oak door. She banged on it with her fists, screaming hysterically, "Let me in! You've got to be home! Oh, please, let me in!"

The door was flung open so suddenly that it threw her off-balance. She had only an impression of the tall husky man with dark hair and eyes, who stood just inside. He carried a lantern in one hand and caught her around the waist with the other arm as she lurched forward and fell against him.

He was strong and warm, a bulwark against the unleashed forces of nature, and she threw her arms around him and clung like a frightened child as she buried her face in his solid chest and sobbed uncontrollably.

Chapter Two

The antique grandfather's clock in the living room of the big old country farm home started bonging the hour of ten while Jakob Luther was making his way cautiously from room to room through the darkness.

This spring storm was shaping up to be a real gully-washer, he thought, as a gust of wind whipped the heavy rain against the house with a force that rattled windows and tore branches off the big old elm trees surrounding the property.

The electricity had gone out, and he was crossing the kitchen on his way to the utility room, where they stored their battery-powered emergency lamps, when his foot hit something solid in the middle of the floor. He stumbled, sending the object crashing noisily against the wooden cabinet.

He grabbed the throbbing knee he'd twisted and uttered an angry oath.

"Jake, are you all right?" called his mother, Dagmar, from the living room.

"Yeah, Mom, I'm okay," he replied as he tested his considerable weight on the damaged leg, "but I'm going to have words with those kids of mine in the morning. I don't know why they can't remember to put their toys away when they're finished with them."

"Don't be too hard on them, dear," Dagmar said as she appeared in the doorway, a lighted candle in her hand. "They had no way of knowing the electricity would go off tonight."

"That's not the point..." Jake started to argue, then thought better of it. She was right. He should have brought the candle with him. Even so, you'd think that after being born and raised in this house and spending all but twelve of his thirty-eight years here, he'd be able to find his way around in the dark without stumbling.

He took the candle she handed him and limped into the laundry room to look for the lanterns. They had four, one for each of them—his mother, his small daughter, his pre-adolescent son and himself. Power failures were a fact of life in rural Nebraska. Especially during a howling storm such as this one. It paid to be prepared.

He found what he was looking for in the cupboard over the washer and dryer and carried them back into the kitchen. "I'll leave a lamp in here," he said as he flipped the switch and blew out the flame on the candle. "You take this one." He turned on another and handed it to her. "And I'll take the other two upstairs and put them in Kurt's and Heidi's rooms in case they wake up and need them."

As he reached out to pick up the lanterns, an especially brilliant bolt of lightning illuminated the whole outdoors. It was followed by a vibrating roll of thunder that seemed to shake the ground.

"Daddy! Daddy! Daddy!" The terrified voice of his six-year-old daughter Heidi rang through the house, and both Dagmar and Jake rushed out of the kitchen and through the dining room to the stairway in the entry hall. The child flew down the stairs and threw herself into her father's arms. Her brother, Kurt, older but still young enough to be frightened by such a storm, was right behind her.

"It's all right, baby," Jake said soothingly as he squatted and reached out to draw Kurt into the circle of his embrace, also. "It's only a bad storm. The lights went out, but that's happened lots of times before. I was just coming to bring your battery lamps to your rooms when you called."

"I want to stay down here with you and grandma," the little girl wailed as she drew back to look at Jake.

"Me, too!" exclaimed Kurt.

"Fine," Jake agreed. "There's a fire in the fireplace. We'll all sit in the living room and tell stories till the storm is over."

Dagmar had her light with her, so she led the children into the front room while Jake went back to the kitchen for the other lamps. He'd just picked one up and turned it on when Dakota, the black Labrador retriever who had been snoozing in front of the fireplace, suddenly barked and leaped toward the entryway. Seconds later someone started banging on the door and yelling, but Jake couldn't distinguish the voice or the words.

"I'll get it," he called to his mother as he hurried to the front of the house, carrying the lamp with him. Who on earth would be out in this storm in the middle of the night? Was there an emergency at one of the neighboring farms?

"Quiet, boy. Down," he commanded the excited dog as he reached the door and pulled it open. A blast of frigid wind staggered him, and he had only a fleeting awareness of a medium size figure lurching toward him. Spontaneously he reached out with his free hand to ward it off, but it fell against him and he caught it in a one-arm embrace.

It was then that he knew it was a woman. Dripping wet, muddy and hysterical, but definitely a soft, nicely rounded woman.

Pandemonium broke all around Jake as the dog commenced barking, Dagmar and the children rushed in demanding to know what was happening and the lady in distress sobbed noisily as she clutched him in an unbreakable grip of panic. Her whole body shivered and her teeth chattered from the cold.

"Close the door," he yelled over the noise as he handed the lamp to Kurt and swept the sodden, thoroughly-chilled figure up into his arms.

Carrying her into the living room, he headed for the fireplace. He wouldn't get much information from her until she'd calmed down, yet there was one thing he had to know. He forced her to stand on her feet in front of the fire, but put both his arms around her and held her close as she continued to cling frantically to him.

"Is there anyone with you?" he raised his voice to ask. "Anyone who is still outside somewhere?"

She seemed to understand what he said, because she shook her head even as she continued to sob plaintively.

His mother brought a woolen blanket and wrapped it as best she could around the young woman, who showed signs of possibly going into shock. Had she been injured? He couldn't tell, because she'd buried her face in his chest and wouldn't move far enough away from him so he could look at her.

Finally, when she continued to cry and tremble, Jake picked her up again and carried her over to his big comfortable leather chair, then sat down with her on his lap. In that position he was able to wrap her completely in the blanket.

He cradled her in his arms and held her quietly, as he did with Heidi when she was frightened.

Who was this woman? Where had she come from and what had scared her so badly? How long had she been out in the storm?

These questions and many others tumbled over in his mind, but he couldn't ask them while she was hysterical. Dagmar had apparently taken the children and the dog, as well as one of the lights, and gone into another room.

He smiled. His mother was a wise person. She knew that the noisy dog and kids would traumatize this waif he'd found on his doorstep all the more.

Jake remembered the times his mom had soothed him when he was small and upset. She'd always been a full-figured woman, and her well-padded frame had felt soft and warm as she'd rocked him and sang lullabies in German, the way her mother had sung them to her in the old country.

On the other hand, this was no child he was holding, and he sure as hell wasn't going to sing a lullaby to her. In fact, it was high time he pulled himself together and got on with the task of finding out who she was and what had happened to her.

As the wind died down, the thunder and lightning became a distant rumble, and the rain settled into a steady patter on the roof. The woman's sobs also quieted, and she relaxed her grip on him.

"Oh, God, I'm ... I'm so sorry," she said mournfully as she pushed away from his chest and started to sit up.

"Sorry for what?" he asked, but instead of answering she groaned and put her hand to her head as she fell against him again.

Oh, damn, she *had* been injured!

"Does your head hurt?" he asked anxiously.

"Yes," she gasped. "It hit against something when my car plunged into the tree."

Jake's anxiety escalated. "You were in an accident? Where? Was there another car involved?"

Again she tried to sit up, but he held her in place with his hand against her cheek. She didn't resist, but once more relaxed against him. "I'm so sorry," she said again. "I'm being such a bother. I'm behaving like a baby and getting you all wet and muddy—"

"Never mind that now," Jake interrupted impatiently. "Just tell me about the accident. Was anyone else involved?"

"No, I wa-was alone." Her voice shook. "The road was slippery and the wind blew my car off the side. It went down an incline and ran into a tree. The lightning..."

She shuddered, and Jake tightened his arms around her. "Where did this happen?"

"N-not very far away. I was so... so afraid the lightning would s-s-strike my car. I could see your h-h-house...."

She was trembling again, and Jake tried to calm her. "Hush," he said softly. "Don't try to talk about it now." He moved his hand to run his fingers through her wet hair in search of an injury. "Just tell me where your head hurts."

"Here," she said, and turned so she could put her hand to her forehead.

He drew in a quick breath when he saw the angry-looking lump over her left eye. She'd hit hard against something. "Were you wearing your seat belt?"

"Yes, and it held," she said, "but I was thrown forward when the car hit the tree. I blacked out. I must have banged my head into the steering wheel. Is it bleeding?"

Jake touched the swelling gently. "No, the skin's not broken, but you've got a real goose egg there. I'd better get you into some dry clothes and take you to the emergency clinic."

Her pretty hazel eyes widened with dismay. "Oh, no, please. I'm so embarrassed about being such a bother. I'll be okay. I'm just a little dizzy, but that will go away when I get up and move around."

He frowned. "Don't count on it. You could have a concussion."

He slid one arm under her legs and stood, then turned and sat her in the chair. "You stay right there while I get my mother. She'll know what to do better than I."

He picked up the lantern and strode out of the room and across the hall to the den at the back of the house.

Dagmar was telling Kurt and Heidi a story when he interrupted. "Excuse me, Mom, but I need your help. That girl has been injured, but she doesn't want to go to the emergency clinic. Maybe you can convince her."

Dagmar herded the children along ahead of them as they all returned to the parlor. The young woman still sat slouched in the chair where he'd left her. Jake went over and hunkered down beside her.

"Miss," he said. "We haven't gotten around to introducing ourselves yet. I'm Jakob Luther, and this is my family. My mother, Dagmar, and my children, Kurt and Heidi. Can you tell us your name?"

She looked around, acknowledging each with a glance, then smiled weakly. "My name's Brittany Castle. I'm from Independence, Missouri, and I just arrived in Omaha this afternoon. I... I got lost in the storm and have no idea where I am."

"Do you have relatives in the area? Someone we should contact?"

"No," she said. "I'm on my way to Raindance, but they aren't expecting me there for a couple of weeks."

Jake was familiar with the town. "Oh, yeah, I know Raindance. Northwestern part of the state on the rim of the Sandhills. Great area for hunting pheasant. I go up there almost every year."

Dagmar approached and touched the swelling on Brittany's head. "That's quite a bump you've got there, Brittany Castle," she said briskly as she examined the young woman's eyes, "but you seem to be focusing all right. We'd better get you out of those wet clothes and into a warm bath. Then we'll decide about medical attention. The bathroom is just down the hall. Can you walk?"

Brittany nodded. "There's nothing wrong with my feet or legs, but I am a little dizzy. If you could help me to stand I think I'll be okay."

Jake rose and assisted her to her feet, then held her around the waist as she swayed. "Take it easy," he told her. "Lean on me and I'll walk with you, but let me know if you're going to faint. I don't want to let you drop."

She seemed a little unsteady, but they made it as far as the bathroom door. Dagmar took over from there, leaving Jake wet and muddy with two kids to be put back to bed, plus a myriad of unanswered questions.

Brittany leaned back in the tub water and sighed. She'd been so cold she'd doubted that she'd ever be warm again, but after getting her soaked clothes off and settling down in the steamy tub of water Dagmar Luther had drawn for her she felt toasty all the way to her bones. In fact, she was content enough to fall asleep right where she was.

She knew it was dangerous to put her trust in strangers, but she had no choice. She was out in the middle of nowhere with her car wrapped around a tree. Besides, this was a multigenerational family. Mother, son and grandchildren. Jakob hadn't mentioned a wife, but since he had children there must be one around somewhere. Maybe she was sleeping through all the commotion, although that seemed unlikely.

Surely these people weren't harboring any evil intent. Jakob seemed like an average family man, mid- or late-thirties, and though not exceptionally handsome, he was nice looking. His gentle concern for her—a stranger who'd practically forced her way into his house—indicated the innate kindness of a decent, law-abiding man.

A hot flush of humiliation swept through her. Dear God, what must he think of her? She'd banged on his door and howled like a banshee to be let in; then, when he'd opened it, she'd fallen into his arms and clung like a child being chased by demons.

Well, maybe she was. Not a child, certainly, but demon was a pretty good description of Ronny Ralston. And no one could deny that he'd been chasing her, although *stalking* was a more exact term.

Still, it wasn't Ronny who'd finally sent her over the edge emotionally. She could have handled the fact—or was it only a delusion—that he'd tracked her to Omaha before she'd even arrived. It was getting lost in the dark in an unfamiliar area, the intensity of the electrical storm and finally the car plunging off the road and into the tree, all piled on the original shock, that had unnerved her so completely.

That didn't make her behavior any less embarrassing, though. How could she ever face these people again? Especially Jakob? She'd gotten him wet and dirty, trailed mud through his house, upset his dog and his family and made herself thoroughly obnoxious by her childish behavior. He must think she was a real nut case!

Her musing was interrupted by a knock on the bathroom door and a voice calling, "Brittany, are you all right?"

It was Dagmar—Brittany had recognized the slight accent of Jakob's mother's voice. She'd surely committed another faux pas. She'd been hogging the bathroom, and for all she knew it might be the only one they had.

"I'm fine, Dagmar," Brittany called back. "Sorry I've taken so long. I'll be right out."

"No hurry," Dagmar said. "We were just concerned because of your head injury. You mustn't fall asleep. Come to the kitchen when you're finished. It's the room to your right."

Again Brittany reassured the other woman, then stood and reached for the thick fluffy towel beside the tub.

Several minutes later she'd towel-dried her hair and dressed in the long flannel nightgown and heavy blue wrap-around robe, both several sizes too big, which Dagmar had brought her. There was also a pair of hand-knit stretch slippers.

Brittany left the lighted lantern in the bathroom and stepped out into the hall. There was a faint illumination and the sound of voices coming from the room at the right end. She walked toward it.

Jakob and Dagmar were seated at a large round oak table under the corner windows of the roomy old country kitchen. In spite of the shadows she could see that it was a comfortable place, with plenty of space for both cooking and eating. The floor was covered with linoleum, the counters were tile and the cabinets were made of walnut. Yellow ruffled curtains at the windows created an impression of sunshine, and the appliances were modern and spotlessly clean.

Jakob stood as Brittany entered, and she saw that he had changed out of the clothes she'd gotten all wet and muddy. Again she felt the flush of embarrassment. She couldn't meet his eyes, so she lowered her head. "Mr. Luther, I don't know how to apologize—"

"Call me 'Jake,'" he interrupted, "and there's nothing to apologize for. We're just glad we were close enough for you to seek help."

He motioned with his hand. "Come on in and sit down. Have some hot chocolate and cookies before I take you to the clinic."

"Oh, that won't be necessary," she assured him as she walked across the room and sat down in the sturdy wooden chair he held for her. "I'm feeling much better now. The dizziness is gone and there's only a dull ache in my head."

Jake sat next to her, while Dagmar poured fragrant hot chocolate from a carafe into a cup and handed it to her. "Are you hungry? There's chicken and corn bread left over from supper. It wouldn't take a minute to warm it up."

"No, thank you. I had something to eat on the plane—"

"The plane?" Jake asked. "Did you fly from Independence to Omaha?"

Brittany took a homemade cookie from the plate Dagmar handed her. "Yes, I did. The car I was driving when the accident occurred is rented." She shivered. "I'm afraid to think of what the rental agency is going to say when they find out."

"You must carry insurance," Jake reminded her.

She nodded. "Yes, I also took out extra from the agency."

"Then you should be fully covered. You'll stay here tonight, and I'll take a look at the car in the morning. It might not be too badly damaged."

Brittany was torn between gratitude and regret. "I... I really appreciate your hospitality, but I'm sorry for being such a nuisance. Are you sure it will be all right with Mrs. Luther?"

"Of course it's all right with me," Dagmar said, and once more Brittany was engulfed in a wave of embarrassment.

"Oh, I-I'm sorry," she stammered. "I meant Jake's wife, the children's mother."

There was an uncomfortable silence before Jake spoke. "The children's mother doesn't live here," he muttered. "We're divorced." He pushed back his chair and stood. "If you're finished with your chocolate I'll show you to your room."

Now she'd done it, Brittany thought as she also stood. She'd apparently blundered onto a painful subject without ever meaning to. Couldn't she do anything right tonight?

Deciding she'd be wiser to keep her mouth shut, she followed him silently up the stairs as he lighted her way. At the top landing they turned left and stopped at a door. Jake opened it and went in first to set the lamp on the bedside table.

"I'll leave this with you," he said briskly. "The bathroom is next door on your right, and my room is the one to the left. The kids and Mom are on the other side of the stairwell. Is there anything else you need?"

Brittany looked around. It was a nice room, somewhat austere but neat and clean, with white sheer curtains at the window and a rose-colored spread on the brass bed.

"Nothing I can think of," she answered, "but you'll need the light. I can manage without it."

"That's not necessary. I have a flashlight in my room. I can use that. Please don't hesitate to call out if you need anything or if you don't feel well during the night. I'll hear you. I'm used to listening for the kids."

Brittany wondered why Jake's wife would let a man like him get away from her. He was thoughtful and generous and seemed to be reasonably well fixed financially.

And sexy! She could certainly testify to that. Those strong muscular arms that had held her against his broad chest had stirred desires deep inside her. She'd felt safe and cared for, as though nothing could hurt her as long as she was protected by his embrace.

"Thank you," she told him, and heard the quiver in her voice. "But I'm sure that won't be necessary. That bed looks so comfortable that I'll probably sleep like a baby."

Jake laughed. "Don't say that. Don't you know that babies never sleep at night? They cry and fuss and keep their parents in a constant state of alert. Then, when the alarm rings in the morning, they drop off and sleep peacefully all day."

Brittany laughed, too, delighted by his sense of humor. "I'll remember that," she told him, "if I ever get the urge to start a family."

He was once more serious. "Are you married, Brittany?"

Her smile faded. "No. I thought I was in love once, but he turned out to be all wrong for me. Thank goodness I found out before I made the mistake of marrying him. I'll be more careful about giving my heart away next time."

Slowly Jake reached out and caressed her cheek with his knuckles. "I'm sorry you were hurt," he said, and she knew he wasn't talking about the bump on her head. "Don't judge all men by one bad experience."

As though just realizing what he was doing and saying, he dropped his hand and turned. "Good night," he said gruffly as he walked away.

By the time Brittany awoke the next morning the sun was high in the sky. She was curled up in a strange bed in an unfamiliar room with roosters crowing under her window and cows lowing in the distance.

She blinked and looked around the room. The walls were papered in a pink floral pattern, and there were a couple of hand-hooked throw rugs on the hardwood floor. The maple dresser had a large mirror framed in matching wood hanging on the wall behind it, and on the bedside table was a clock radio, a lamp and a battery-operated lantern.

Brittany frowned and rolled over, then gasped as a wave of pain assailed the muscles in her upper back and shoulders. What was wrong with her? And where was she? She'd never been in this room before. Why did she feel so...so befuddled? Why couldn't she remember how she'd gotten here?

She heard the unfamiliar sound of machinery—possibly a chain saw—in the distance, and the persistent cackle of chickens closer at hand. Clenching her teeth against the soreness in her back, she pushed herself up to a sitting position and was assailed with a throbbing ache in her forehead.

She put her hand up and felt a large lump over her left eye.

Now it was coming back to her. The accident. Her car had gone off the road and hit a tree, but where was she? Not Independence. She remembered boarding a plane there yesterday and landing in Omaha.

Stiffening with alarm, she remembered seeing Ronny in the terminal and running away. Then she was driving a car and got lost. It was dark, there was a storm, then the crash....

After that her mind was a blank. She'd obviously hit her head. Maybe that was responsible for her partial amnesia.

She threw back the covers, then eased out of bed and stood, but swayed as a wave of dizziness caused her to grab for the brass headboard. The solid contact steadied her, and the wooziness receded. Her gaze focused on the clock and she was dismayed to see that it was nearly noon! Good heavens, how had she managed to sleep so late?

She noticed a rather faded blue robe lying at the foot of the bed and put it on over the granny-type flannel gown she was wearing. On the floor was a pair of slippers, but where were her own clothes?

Brittany pulled on the slippers and walked across the room to the window, where she parted the sheer panel curtains to look out. She was on the second floor of a house overlooking what seemed to be a farm. There was a lawn and flower gardens surrounding the house, but past that were several outbuildings, including a big red barn and a pen filled with cackling chickens. There were also several pieces of farm machinery about.

In the distance, as far as she could see, were fields of what she recognized from her years spent in Raindance as foot-high cornstalks. She could also see signs of destruction from last night's punishing storm everywhere. Water stood on ground too saturated to absorb more. Tree limbs, wrenched from their trunks by the gale-force wind, littered the land-scape.

Her memory was returning bit by bit. It had been too dark for her to see her surroundings last night, but she couldn't understand how she'd forgotten, even for a short while, running through that dreadful lightning and deluge to the safety of the house.

It had been like a footrace through Hades. When she got up on the porch she'd banged on the door and pleaded to be let in, but there she drew a blank again.

Well, obviously someone had taken her in, and now she'd better go downstairs and see if that kind soul was anywhere around. She'd also have to find her car and get some clean clothes. The ones she'd been wearing had probably been ruined. First she needed to find the bathroom.

That proved easy—it was right next door. After she'd washed her face in warm water and rinsed her mouth, she felt more alert.

When she stepped out into the U-shaped hallway that was built around the stairwell, she realized that this was an aw-fully big house. She counted six doors that opened onto the hall.

The bottom of the staircase put her into an open entry-way at the front of the house, with a living room on her left and a dining room on her right, both large and roomy. Since it was nearly noon she chose the dining room and turned toward it. No one was there, but on the far wall was an open door, and she heard sounds of someone bustling around on the other side.

Her slippered feet made no sound as she crossed the carpeted floor and stepped through the doorway. A rather heavyset woman in baggy denim slacks and a bulky sweater worked at the sink, her back to Brittany. She remembered the kitchen, and when the woman turned a bit she recognized her, too, and her memory of the previous night returned in full.

"Good morning, Dagmar," she said, startling the woman. "I'm so sorry I overslept."

Dagmar turned fully around and her look of surprise was quickly replaced with a smile. "Brittany. Good morning. I heard you moving around upstairs so I knew you were awake. How are you feeling?"

"Pretty stiff and sore. I can't imagine why I slept so long. I never stay in bed this late."

Dagmar wiped her hands on a towel. "You didn't oversleep. You were exhausted. I've been checking on you at intervals. After all, you had a nasty time of it last night what with the storm and the wreck and all."

She motioned toward the coffeemaker on the counter. "Pour yourself some coffee and sit down. I'll get your clothes. I washed and dried them, but couldn't get all the stains out—they were too muddy. And your shoes are a total loss."

Tears of gratitude stung the back of Brittany's eyes. She hadn't been this well looked after since she'd left her grandparents in Raindance and gone away to school. She'd forgotten how hospitable farm people were.

"That was nice of you," she said in a wavering voice, "and I do thank you, but you shouldn't have gone to so much trouble. I have suitcases in the trunk of the car. If you can tell me how to find it I'll go get them."

Dagmar shook her head. "You can't go out there. You'd be ankle deep in mud. I'll send Emmett for them. He's our hired man who helps around the place."

When the wizened little cowboy with the leathery wrinkled face and the shy smile returned with her purse and the weekender Brittany had asked for she took them upstairs. She dressed in jeans, a navy blue sweatshirt and a pair of sturdy leather loafers. Though the sun was shining, the temperature hovered in the low fifties and the breeze was cold. Even though she could hear the furnace running and knew the electricity must be back on, the house was still chilly.

After cleaning her teeth, giving her long curly blond hair a thorough brushing and applying a touch of lipstick, she hurried back down to the kitchen to help Dagmar prepare lunch—or dinner, as folks around here called it. Brittany remembered that when she'd lived in Raindance everyone had referred to meals as breakfast, dinner and supper.

As she neared the kitchen she smelled the aroma of chicken fried steak and found Dagmar mashing potatoes with an electric beater while fresh string beans simmered in a pot on the stove.

"May I help?" Brittany asked, pushing up her sleeves.

"You can set the table if you like," Dagmar answered. "The dishes are in the cupboard to your left. There'll be four of us. The kids have a hot meal at school."

Brittany opened the cabinet door and took down four heavy ironstone plates decorated with a strawberry pattern. "Do you eat in here or in the dining room?"

"We always eat in here unless we have company." Dagmar said as she turned off the beater. "It's more comfortable. There's bread in the bread box and butter and cream in the fridge."

Butter and cream were exactly what she meant, Brittany found when she located the items. Real churned butter, and thick cream probably fresh from the cow that morning. Murder on the arteries and waistline, but oh, such a delight for the taste buds.

"Here come the men," Dagmar announced as the sound of approaching male voices wafted in from the yard. There was a lot of stomping on the stoop outside the back door that opened into the utility room. They lingered in there for a few minutes, taking off their jackets and caps and muddy boots and washing up.

Brittany's heart pounded with excitement as she tried to appear busy while waiting for Jake to make an appearance. Was he as sexy in broad daylight as he'd seemed in last night's dimness? What would he think of her now that she was clean and dry and wearing clothes that fit?

She looked up when he and Emmett finally entered the kitchen. There was enough light to see him clearly. He was tall, well over six feet, and looked husky in his plaid flannel shirt, faded jeans and stocking feet, but she had good reason to know he was all muscle underneath.

Jake's expressive deep brown eyes immediately sought her, and his glance roamed from head to foot with honest appreciation but no hint of lewdness as his broad face split into a big grin.

"Well, I'll be a son of a gun," he said with a touch of awe. "It looks like the half-drowned, terrified little urchin I found on my doorstep last night has been transformed into a beautiful, self-assured young woman. How are you, Brittany? You look great, except that the lump on your forehead must be awfully sore. Is it? I can still take you to the doctor."

Their gazes meshed and held as she answered. "Thanks, Jake. I disgraced myself by sleeping till almost noon, but except for some pretty stiff muscles and a slight headache,

I feel much better today. I'll call the rental agency right after lunch—uh, dinner.''

Jake laughed as Dagmar finished putting the food on the table. "Get with it, city girl," he teased, as they sat. "You're in farm country now. We get up with the dawn and put in a full day's work before noon. We need a hot *dinner* to stoke our energy so we can put in another day's work before dark.''

He spoke lightly, but Brittany knew he wasn't exaggerating about the long hours of hard labor that farmers endured in order to make a living. Her grandparents had lived in town, but Gramps had owned a farm-implement business and they'd known all the farmers for miles around.

"Unless you're in a tearing hurry, why don't you stay with us until tomorrow?" Jake continued. "That would give Emmett and me a chance to check the car and see how much damage there is. It looks extensive, but at least we can make sure the garage doesn't overcharge you. It's always a good idea to have your own mechanic's opinion when dealing with insurance cases, and Emmett, here, is a real whiz with the insides of an automobile.''

That sounded reasonable to Brittany, but she hated to be even more of a bother. She turned to the hired man. "Would you mind, Emmett?"

"No, ma'am. I wouldn't mind a-tall," he said emphatically. "Be happy to take a look at it.''

"It would also give you more time to recuperate," Jake pointed out. "Raindance is better than two hundred and fifty miles from here, and you really shouldn't drive that far so soon after a head injury. Besides, you told us you aren't expected there for a while.''

"Did I?" Brittany was still a little fuzzy about the details of last night.

Jake's offer was extremely tempting. Who was she kidding? It wasn't just tempting—it was irresistible. She was still a little shaky, and the slight headache persisted. Why not stay with this nice family for another day?

Jake must have been sincere in his invitation. He certainly didn't owe her any more consideration.

Chapter Three

When Brittany hesitated in answering Jake's invitation Dagmar spoke up. "Why don't you stay, *Liebchen?* Jake's right, you shouldn't be traveling yet, and we have plenty of room."

That capped it. If both Jake and Dagmar wanted her to remain over until tomorrow she was certainly willing. They were right about it being unwise to drive so far with the sluggish ache in her head. The pain was distracting and would only get worse with the strain of traveling.

"There's nothing I'd like better than to spend another day here with all of you," she admitted, "but I don't want to be a pest. I can go to a motel. I'd originally planned to stay in Omaha until I could find a good secondhand car to buy, so it wouldn't be a problem."

"Don't even think of it," Dagmar said. "The room you were in isn't being used, so we won't be inconvenienced. Besides, Kurt and Heidi will be delighted. You made a bang-up entrance last night, and they were so disappointed when I wouldn't let them stay home from school this morning so they could hear the story firsthand.''

Brittany laughed, convinced that she really was welcome.''I'll be happy to tell them when they get home.''

Jake swallowed a bite of steak and looked at her. ''I won't be here when they come home, so why don't you tell me now? I'm as curious as they are. Why were you out in that storm?''

''There's not much to the story,'' Brittany replied as she buttered a thick slice of homemade bread. ''The storm was coming in when the plane landed at Eppley Field last evening, but I didn't expect it to be such a bad one. I rented the car and got directions for getting around, but somewhere along the line I got lost and wound up—''

She stopped abruptly, then chuckled. ''Now that you've asked, I've no idea where I ended up. All I know is I was out in the country, with no streetlights, when all hell broke loose. Lightning, thunder, wind, rain.... I was all alone and scared half to death. You know the rest.''

She put down her knife and looked around the table. ''Where are we, anyway? I don't know whether I was traveling north, south or west. It couldn't have been east or I'd have run into the Missouri River.''

''You were traveling north,'' Jake told her. ''We're about halfway between the outskirts of Omaha and the town of Blair. Our mailing address is Blair, and we're not far from the river. If you'd turned east at one point instead of west you'd have crossed it and ended up in Iowa.''

Brittany groaned. ''Oh, boy. I guess I really blew the 'keeping cool under pressure' test, didn't I?''

Emmett took a second helping of potatoes and spoke up. ''Don't be so hard on yourself, little lady. I can ride the range blindfolded, but I've lived in this area for over ten years and I still get lost in Omaha. They keep changin' the danged streets.''

Everyone laughed, then Jake changed the subject. "Do you have relatives in Raindance?''

Brittany shook her head. "Not anymore, but my mother was born and raised there.''

"Oh, really!'' Dagmar exclaimed as she set her mug of coffee down. "Did you live there, too?''

"Not until later. Mom met my dad and married him when she was at the university in Lincoln. He was a career army man, so we traveled a lot. I was born in Germany.''

"You were!'' Dagmar gasped, her face glowing with surprise and pleasure. "So was I, only I was a German national. I was five years old when my family immigrated to America.''

"I thought I recognized your accent,'' Brittany said, "although not from having lived there. Dad was transferred back to the States when I was two. I went to school in several parts of the country until I was thirteen. Then Mom and Dad were divorced and Mom married a man from Brazil. That's when she sent me to live with my grandparents in Raindance and went to Buenos Aires with Jorgé.''

Brittany hated the fact that it still hurt to remember the way her parents had rejected her. Neither had wanted to be bothered with a half-grown teenager once they were free of the restraints of an increasingly unhappy marriage. She'd been fortunate to have loving grandparents who'd taken her in, and she'd adored them, but she'd never been able to shake the feeling that she must be unlovable if her own parents didn't want her.

Both Dagmar and Jake looked confused, but it was Jake who commented. "Then you must visit her frequently down there. I understand it's a beautiful country. And your father? Is he still in the army?''

Brittany seldom talked about her childhood, but she owed these people who had taken her—a stranger—in and sheltered her.

"No, I've never been to Brazil. Mother writes now and then, but I've only seen her once since she remarried. That was when Grandma and Grandpa died within a few days of each other. As for my dad...I haven't heard from him in years, but last I knew he was still in the army."

Jake frowned, and Dagmar shook her head in disbelief. Brittany knew they were shocked by parents who would desert their child the way hers had. Dagmar didn't comment, but Jake's reaction was succinct and to the point. "That's a hell of a way for parents to treat their child! At least Tina drops by every few weeks to see Kurt and Heidi—"

"Jakob," Dagmar murmured, and he immediately stopped talking and looked sheepish.

"Sorry," he said to Brittany. "I'm afraid the subject of child abandonment is a rather volatile one around here. Maybe we better change the topic. Will you be visiting friends in Raindance?"

Apparently Jake's divorce wasn't an especially amicable one. She'd seen the pain and frustration in his expression before he'd managed to suppress it. Did he feel that his wife had abandoned their children?

"Yes, I will," she said in answer to his last question. "My high school graduating class is having a reunion the last weekend of the month, and I'm going back for that."

He looked at her and smiled. "You don't look old enough to have been out of high school for five years."

She felt herself blush, delighted by his compliment. "Actually, I graduated seven years ago, but through some sort of foul-up we didn't have a reunion at the proper time so we're having it this year, instead."

"You must have a lot of vacation time saved up," he remarked, referring to the fact that the reunion wouldn't take place for three weeks. "Or are you a teacher who has the summer off?"

Darn. Now the questions were getting difficult. How much did she want to tell this family about her plans? Maybe she should just sort of skirt around the real problem.

"Actually, the answer is no to both questions," she said. "I'm not a teacher, I'm a veterinary technician, but the animal hospital where I worked has been sold and the new owners have their own staff, so I'm temporarily unemployed. I decided to come to Nebraska early and spend some time here before deciding where I want to relocate."

"You're not going back to Independence?" Dagmar asked.

Brittany shook her head and lowered her gaze. She couldn't look the other woman in the eye and lie to her. "No, there's nothing to keep me there, and I guess I developed a wanderlust when I moved around so much during my childhood. I enjoy experiencing new places and making new friends."

That was an outright falsehood and she knew it. She'd hated being uprooted so often as a child and having to leave her school and her classmates to start all over again somewhere else. She'd loved Independence, gone to college there, made lots of friends, and had expected to live there for the rest of her life...until Ronny Ralston had made that impossible.

But she didn't want to discuss Ronny and his terrorizing tactics with the Luthers. She didn't want to talk about him with anybody. She just wanted to forget he existed!

When Jake didn't answer she looked up at him. His smile was gone, replaced by a mask of cold indifference that sent a chill through her. Now, what had she said or done to upset him?

"It must be nice to be a vagabond, free of encumbrances," he said brusquely, "but I hope you'll think a long time before bringing children into the world. Someone will have to take care of them, and your parents don't sound to me like the kind of loving grandparents who would raise them for you."

He pushed back his chair and stood all in one motion, then stalked out of the room.

Dagmar gasped, but Brittany couldn't even seem to breathe. She sat there staring, with her mouth open and Jake's scathing words ringing in her ears.

Jake slammed the door behind him and strode across the lawn and into the barnyard. Damn it to hell! When was he going to learn not to take women at face value? They weren't interested in being wives and mothers anymore. They wanted to be dedicated career women whose whole lives revolved around making it to CEO before they were forty, or else they were free spirits with their heads in the clouds who blithely went their own way, leaving their responsibilities for others to assume.

Take his ex-wife, Tina. She looked like a pixie, tiny with a cap of short auburn hair, soft sea green eyes and lips that begged to be kissed. He'd fallen in love with her on sight, and didn't discover until after they were married that having babies and sharing a home with him was way down at the bottom of her list of priorities.

He waded through an assortment of squawking chickens as he headed toward the barn. Apparently he was a glutton for punishment because now he'd done it again. He'd mistaken Brittany Castle's sweet smile, fresh scrubbed beauty and charming personality as proof of a wholesome, well-adjusted young woman, when they were merely the outer trappings of a self-centered gypsy destined to drift through life with never a thought to such things as responsibility or commitment.

Surely somewhere between those two extremes there was a special woman who wanted the same simple kind of life that he did. During the years he'd worked in Omaha he'd seen more than he'd ever wanted to see of the underbelly of a big city. He was determined that his children were going to be raised with the knowledge that they would always be loved and cared for, even if he had to do it all by himself.

He pulled open the barn door and went inside, where he was greeted with the familiar pungent odor of fresh manure mixed with the sweet smell of alfalfa and hay. As he gathered up the tools he'd need for repairing the fences damaged by the storm his disappointment and frustration began to subside, and he could see that he'd overreacted.

What business was it of his how Ms. Castle lived her life? More important, why was he so upset about it? She was nothing to him. He'd known her less than twenty-four hours and hadn't spent more than four of those at the most in her company.

Hell, he was getting himself all worked up over a woman he'd never see again after tomorrow!

Come to think of it, why was he even seeing her tomorrow? He'd had no intention of asking her to stay over another day, and was as surprised as she'd been when he'd suggested it.

The last thing he wanted right now was to get married again, and becoming involved in an intimate relationship with a woman was out of the question. He had his children to consider, and he wasn't going to expose them to one, or a series of, short-term "companions" who'd share their daddy's bed but not their lives.

Jake shuddered with distaste. He had no illusions about remaining celibate for the rest of his life. He was an adult with a grown man's passions, but those could be satisfied without involving his deeper emotions.

So why did he find it so painful to think of Brittany walking out of his life tomorrow? Why did he keep thinking of her as his? His foundling? His waif? His salvation?

Salvation! Jake muttered an oath and tossed the last bale of wire into the bed of his scruffy old pickup. It's true he'd found Brittany on his doorstep, but she wasn't *his* anything, certainly not his salvation. He didn't need a woman to save him.

He got in the cab and started the engine. It purred like a contented kitten, thanks to Emmett's tender care.

Jake had better things to do than moon over his sexy houseguest. As soon as he caught up with Emmett he was going to send him out to have a look at Brittany's car, since he'd promised her he would. Once they had a list of damages and an estimated cost of repair Jake was going to call the rental agency himself and tell them to send a tow truck and another car out first thing tomorrow morning.

Then it would just be a matter of telling her goodbye, good luck and have a good life. She'd leave and he'd forget about her.

With a string of curses he'd learned in the Marine Corps, he stomped his foot on the gas pedal and sent chickens scattering in all directions as the car shot across the barnyard toward the two-lane gravel road.

After Jake's abrupt departure from the house, Brittany finally managed to catch her breath. Emmett rose and, with an embarrassed "Excuse me," followed after Jake.

She blinked and looked at Dagmar. "What did I say? Or was it something I did? Dagmar, why is Jake angry with me?"

Jake's mother was crouched over the kitchen chair, having stopped midway in her effort to rise. Abruptly she sat back down and sighed.

"It's not your fault. He's just taking his rage at Tina out on you. He did that earlier, too, if you'll remember. When you were talking about being raised by your grandparents."

Brittany did remember, very well. "But I don't understand. Who's Tina?"

Dagmar picked up her coffee cup and sipped. "Tina is Jakob's ex-wife. Kurt and Heidi's mother. He feels that she's deserted their children, and he doesn't understand how any woman could do that."

Brittany blinked. "But I haven't deserted my children. I don't even have children, so why is he mad at me?" Her hurt was turning to indignation.

"It's a long story," Dagmar said with a sigh, "and I won't bore you with the details, but Tina was never an enthusiastic mother. She turned the care of her babies over to Jake and a nanny as soon as they were born and put all of her energy into advancing her career. Jakob was very good with them, but he worked long hours, too.

"When Tina filed for divorce two years ago she voluntarily gave him full custody, and the little ones are lucky if they see her for a few hours once a month. She seldom takes them to her condominium and never keeps them overnight."

Brittany knew only too well the pain of being abandoned by a parent, and her heart bled for Jake's small son and daughter. Almost certainly they felt as unlovable as she had, although they were fortunate to have a loving father.

She looked at Dagmar and shook her head sorrowfully. "Why do people have children if they don't want to raise them?"

It was a question she'd asked herself hundreds of times over the past twelve years, but she'd learned not to expect an answer. She did have a theory, however. She'd observed that the couples in question had many excuses, but they seldom voiced the most obvious one because society wouldn't accept the fact that some people were not emotionally equipped to be parents.

That didn't make them any less worthy as members of society, but they still felt guilty. They caved in to their spouse, or parents, or friends who told them they were being selfish if they didn't have heirs or give their parents grandchildren. So they had babies, but they rarely learned to cope.

Dagmar reached out and put her hand over Brittany's. "I'm sorry, my dear. This conversation must bring painful memories for you, but please don't think too badly of either Jakob or Tina. They were young and impetuous when they married, and they'd only known each other a few weeks. I understand they'd never even discussed what they wanted from their marriage. He just assumed they'd have a family and Tina would be happy to be a mother, while she never doubted that he'd be supportive of her ambition to climb the corporate ladder. Unfortunately they were both wrong, but they didn't discover that until it was too late."

"So you're yet another grandparent forced to raise her grandchildren," Brittany observed ruefully.

Dagmar reared back and lifted her hand from Brittany's. "That's not what I said, and most certainly not what I meant," she said angrily. "Jakob raises his own kids, and I won't stand for anyone implying differently. He and I have managed the farm jointly since my husband died, and we split the work. I look after the house and garden, and he does the farming."

She took a deep breath and lowered her voice. "Oh, sure, I take care of Kurt and Heidi when he's out in the fields and can't be here, but he makes all the decisions and enforces the discipline. Actually, he probably spends more time with them than the average father, because they work right along beside him part of the time that they're not in school."

Brittany was almost in tears. My God, she couldn't even open her mouth today without putting her foot in it! Obviously she'd overstayed her welcome.

She pushed back her chair. "I'm sorry," she said, and stood up. "I didn't mean to offend you or to criticize Jake. I... I'll call the car rental agency and tell them to send a tow truck out right away. I mustn't intrude on your hospitality any longer."

As she rushed across the kitchen and into the dining room on her way to the staircase she heard Dagmar call after her.

"Brittany, no, I'm sorry. I didn't mean..."

Brittany didn't respond but ran up the steps, needing to get away before the other woman saw the tears in her eyes. Besides, her rental agreement with the agency's address and phone number was in her purse.

She reached the room and hurried inside, closing the door behind her. She'd just picked up her purse, when someone knocked. "Brittany, please, may I come in?"

Brittany snatched a tissue from the box on the dresser and blew her nose. "I... I'll just be a minute," she called back. "I have to get the agency's number. I'll use the phone in the hallway up here."

The door opened and an obviously stricken Dagmar walked in. She took one look at Brittany and crossed the room to where she was standing. "Please, don't take what I said so personally. It's not you I'm upset with, it's..."

She wrung her hands and her voice broke. "I guess you could say it's fate I'm railing against. When my husband died four years ago I was determined to keep the farm in the family, but it's Jakob who's had to make all the sacrifices so I could. It was taking the disability retirement and moving

out here that broke up his marriage, and I feel so guilty!''
Her voice wavered.

Brittany's curiosity was peaked. Disability retirement?
From where? She'd just assumed he'd always been a farmer.
And what disability? He seemed strong and healthy to her.
Before she could ask her questions Dagmar spoke again.

''I . . . I realize that you didn't mean to criticize him. I'm
just an interfering, overprotective mother, but he's had so
much sorrow in the past few years. He feels his children's
pain at their mother's indifference as well as his own. That's
why he tends to lash out when the subject is mentioned.''

She sighed. ''I guess I do, too. None of this was your
fault. Can you ever forgive us for being so snappish?''

Brittany's own anguish disappeared in the face of this
woman's even greater burden of guilt and remorse.

She reached out and put her arms around Dagmar.
''There's nothing to forgive,'' she said gently. ''I'm more to
blame than either of you. I don't know what's the matter
with me. I'm not usually so thin-skinned. That bump on the
head must have unsettled me more than I thought.''

Dagmar hugged Brittany, then moved away. ''Then you'll
forget about leaving this afternoon?

''If you're sure it's okay with Jake, I'll be happy to stay
until tomorrow,'' Brittany assured her. ''Besides, I'd really
like to see the kids again before I leave.''

Brittany insisted on helping the other woman wash the
dishes and clean up the kitchen, and as they worked Brittany learned a little more about the Luther family.

''Is Jake your only child?'' she asked Dagmar as she dried
a plate and put it in the cupboard.

''Oh, no, he's the middle one. I have an older son, Wilhelm—'' Dagmar pronounced the *W* as a *V* ''—who owns
the neighboring farm. He has a wife and two teenage boys.
I also have a younger daughter, Gisela, who's married and

lives in Green Bay, Wisconsin. She has two small daughters and is expecting another baby in late August."

Brittany felt a stab of envy. "So you have a big family. That's wonderful. I always wished I had brothers and sisters."

Dagmar beamed. "Yes, Arno and I were truly blessed."

Her smile faded as she added, "I only wish he could have lived to see the grandchildren grow up."

Brittany wasn't sure how to express her condolences. Instead, she hoped her sympathy was evident in her expression and her tone. "It's always sad to lose a loved one. Was he born in Germany, too?"

Dagmar washed the last pan and put it in the drainer. "No, his family has been in this country for four generations. His grandfather acquired this property during the Depression in the thirties, and it's been farmed by Luthers ever since. That's why I was so desperate to keep it after Arno died—"

The sound of the back door opening and slamming shut interrupted the conversation, and a high-pitched little-girl voice called from the utility room, "Hey, Grandma, I'm home. Is the lady still here?"

Heidi came bursting into the kitchen and skidded to a stop when she saw Brittany with her grandmother. She was a pretty child, five or six years old, with blue eyes, a sprinkling of brown freckles across her turnup nose and thick, wheat-colored braids that hung down her back. Brittany could see that she'd been stricken with surprise and a sudden attack of shyness that left her mute.

"Hello, Heidi," Brittany said as she smiled and adopted a relaxed stance to put the little girl at ease. "I'm afraid my car is too badly smashed up to drive, so your daddy's invited me to stay over until tomorrow, when I can get another one."

Heidi blinked but otherwise didn't move. "You look different," she said soberly.

Again Brittany smiled. "Better, I hope. I cleaned up and put on dry clothes. You look different, too. I like your dress."

The youngster looked down at herself, then back up at Brittany. "I like it, too," she said candidly. "Grandma made it. I got to pick out the material."

"It's a very pretty plaid," Brittany said. "Red's my favorite color."

Slowly Jake's daughter relaxed and smiled, revealing a lopsided gap where one front tooth was missing. "Mine, too. Do you have any little girls?"

Brittany shook her head. "No, but I hope to someday, after I get married."

"Do you have a boyfriend? Mommy's got a boyfriend." She wrinkled her nose in distaste. "He pulls my braids."

The specter of Ronny momentarily dimmed Brittany's smile, but she was more interested in "mommy's boyfriend." Did Jake know his ex-wife was involved with another man? Did Jake have a "girlfriend"?

Dagmar spoke from behind, apparently convinced that the conversation was getting too personal. "Heidi, run on up and change your clothes, then come back down and I'll give you your cookies and milk."

"Can *she* have some, too?"

"My name is 'Brittany.' May I call you 'Heidi'?"

The little girl giggled. "Sure. Don't go away. I'll be right back." She dashed off toward the stairway.

Brittany turned to look at Dagmar and chuckled. "She's a very bright and beautiful child. You must be proud of her."

Dagmar nodded. "We all are, but she can also be a handful. She's stubborn like her daddy and determined like her mother. She's going to lead Jakob a merry chase through the teenage years, I'm afraid."

Brittany laughed. "Probably so. How old is she?"

"Six going on fifteen," Dagmar said with a grimace, but Brittany could hear the strong thread of pride in her voice. "She's just finishing first grade."

"And Kurt?"

"He's ten and in the fifth grade. He doesn't get out until later in the afternoon. Usually the bus brings him home, but he has a Cub Scout meeting after school today, so I'll have to pick him up. You can come with me, if you like."

Brittany did like the idea. "I'd love to. It will give me a chance to get my bearings. I couldn't tell where I was in the middle of that storm last night, and I'm not at all familiar with this part of the state."

An hour later Heidi was outside playing with the black Lab, Dakota, Dagmar was in her room sewing and Brittany, left at loose ends, pulled on a pair of overshoes and a heavy sweater she'd found in the utility room and walked out into the backyard. It was large and roomy, but confined at the back by a tall embankment with a road at the top. The road she'd been on at the time of the accident.

Good heavens, a few more feet and she'd have ended up crashing into the house!

She'd spotted her car smashed into the tree from her second-floor bedroom window earlier, and now she headed west across the lawn and the barnyard. As she neared the site she followed the sound of male voices until she spotted the car, which was still attached to the tractor that had pulled it apart from the tree. Jake and Emmett were bent over the mangled front, inspecting the motor.

Jake was closest to her, and he raised up and turned when he heard her coming. "Brittany!" he exclaimed, and his expression was no longer cold but welcoming. "I'm afraid we have bad news."

Emmett also looked up. "Yes, ma'am," he said sorrowfully. "Looks like your car's totaled. The radiator's shoved clear back into the engine, among other things, and the body's sprung."

Brittany stood beside Jake. "I'm not surprised," she said. "I wasn't driving fast, but the car picked up speed as it careered down the steep embankment. And it hit that tree with an awful jolt. I guess I'm lucky that I wasn't badly hurt."

She was standing close enough to feel Jake shudder. "That's an understatement," he said emphatically. "It's a wonder you weren't killed."

He reached out and caught her hand in his. It wasn't until then that she realized she was trembling. She wasn't sure whether it was from the awareness of her brush with death or from the nearness of this man, who affected her as no other man ever had.

What had happened to the anger he'd displayed just a couple of hours ago? It confused her, because she couldn't tell if he was warm and caring or an opinionated bigot who expected everyone to live up to his unrealistic standards.

Brittany knew that later the answer would matter to her. Right now, however, all she wanted was to stand here with her hand in his, their bodies close but not quite touching.

"How are you?" he asked as he twined his fingers with hers. "Does your head still hurt?"

"A little," she admitted, "but the muscles in my back and shoulders are loosening up a bit. I'd better call the rental agency and report the accident. Hopefully they can still send a tow truck, another car and an insurance adjuster out here this afternoon so we can get all the paperwork taken care of. Then I can be on my way first thing in the m-m-morning."

Her voice wavered and she took a deep breath. "I don't want to wear out my welcome."

Jake didn't answer but looked at the other man. "Emmett, there's nothing more we can do about the car. Why don't you get started patching the leak in the chicken-house roof? We can't be sure we won't have more rain tonight."

The hired man started gathering up his tools. "Ya got that right," he said as he dumped the equipment into a large toolbox and shut the lid. "This Nebraska weather has a mind of its own."

He put two fingers to his forehead in an informal salute to Brittany. "Sorry about your car, miss. Don't let them rental people give you any trouble. T'wern't your fault that storm turned out to be such a ripsnorter."

Jake and Brittany watched his uneven rolling gait as he hurried back to the barnyard. When Emmett was out of hearing range Jake turned to her and searched her face with his heated gaze. "We need to talk," he said huskily.

Chapter Four

Jake's tone made Brittany's heart miss a beat, and she had to catch her breath before she could answer. "What about?"

He had this strong compulsion to make things right with her, and it wouldn't be denied. "I owe you an apology," he said. "I behaved like a jerk this afternoon. It's not even you I was upset with, and I had no right to jump to unwarranted conclusions."

She saw remorse in his expression and looked away. "It's all right, Jake," she said quickly. "Your mother explained a little about your... your ex-wife's somewhat casual attitude toward your children. It's not surprising that you misunderstood what I said."

Misunderstood? God, he hoped so. "How did I misunderstand?"

Brittany didn't want to admit that she'd deliberately misled him about why she'd left Independence, but neither could she bring herself to tell him that she was being stalked by a madman. It was such a bizarre story that he probably wouldn't believe it, and even if he did, he'd think she was a real flake for getting involved with such a twisted personality in the first place.

Was it so wrong for her to want him to think well of her even though she wouldn't ever see him again after tomorrow?

"I apparently gave you the impression that I enjoy being independent and with no ties, but that's not true. I'd give anything to have a big, caring family like the one you come from. I'm all alone in the world, and that's pretty scary when you stop to think of it. There's no one I can turn to if I need help. No one who needs me. That's why I can pick up and relocate whenever I want to, but that sort of freedom can be awfully lonely...."

She looked up at him and saw that his remorse had turned to compassion. Or was it pity? Good heavens, she'd become so absorbed in trying to undo his mistaken impression of her that she'd gone overboard in the other direction. Everything she'd said had been the truth, but now she sounded like poor, pitiful Pearl!

Jake felt as if a weight had been lifted from his heart. She wasn't irresponsible, after all, just alone and lonely. But she also had a head injury that worried him.

"Brittany, I don't want you to leave just yet" he heard himself say in a low, forceful tone.

She was momentarily startled speechless, something that should have happened to her more often today. Now she'd made him feel sorry for her, and also responsible for her well-being.

"Jake, please, I didn't mean to play on your sympathy." Her voice shook and she cleared her throat. "I'm perfectly capable of taking care of myself. I'll be fine, really—"

"I'm sure you can and will," he interrupted, "but that's not what I'm talking about. You were injured in that accident. A blow to the head is not something to take lightly, and it will be another day or so before your stiff muscles stop aching. I don't think it's safe for you to drive all the way to Raindance by yourself yet. Certainly not unless you see a doctor first."

Stay here longer in the protective care of Jake and his wonderful family? It was tempting. Lord, but it was tempting. It had been so long since she'd had anyone to worry about her. Take care of her.

It took all her strength not to cry "Yes! Yes! Yes! I'll stay until my welcome runs out," but she managed to maintain enough sanity not to give in to her overeagerness.

Everything was happening too fast. The only sensible thing to do was get away from here as soon as possible. She was much too attracted to Jake, and she was reasonably sure that he was attracted to her, too. But they barely knew each other. Her experience with Ronny had convinced her that she couldn't trust her judgment where men were concerned, and Jake didn't seem to have a very high opinion of women since his divorce.

Still, idiot that she was, she found it almost impossible to refuse his invitation.

She looked away from him. "I don't know, Jake," she answered. "I'd love to spend more time here with you and Dagmar and the children, but the truth is I ... Well, I don't want to get involved with a man at this time."

He looked startled, and she wished she could sink into the ground and disappear. Why had she made such a stupid comment? He hadn't said anything about getting involved with her. All he wanted was to make sure she was well enough to travel before she started on the trip.

"I-I'm sorry," she stammered. "I'm reading more into this than you intended, but I've had a frightening experience, and I'm especially vulnerable right now. You . . . that is, you and your family have been so nice to me and it would be easy for me to become, uh, dependent on you . . . and your family, of course, and I don't want that to happen."

The hot flush of embarrassment at her rambling, disconnected speech nearly suffocated her. Damn! Why hadn't she just said no and let it go at that? She hadn't meant to let him know how strongly he appealed to her, and here she was practically throwing herself at him.

Reluctantly she raised her head and looked at him, but she couldn't tell what he was thinking. "I'm sorry," she said anxiously. "I'm not doing this at all well. Do you understand what I'm saying?"

Jake's relief was monumental. So Brittany felt the attraction between them, too, and wanted to stay for a while, but she was as leery of a relationship as he was. With both of them aware of the enticement and determined to fight against it, they should be able to spend a couple of days together in the midst of his family with no problem.

He smiled and squeezed her hand. "Of course I understand. I don't want to get involved with a woman now, either. My marriage was a mistake, one I don't want to repeat. And a relationship without the vows is not an option. I have two young children to consider, but surely that doesn't mean we can't spend a few days together until you're in better shape to travel. I promise not to try to seduce you, although you are a very appealing woman and I have to tell you the temptation will be hard to resist. You've already admitted that you're in no hurry to get to Raindance, so spend the weekend with us."

She wanted to. Oh, how she wanted to. Yet she knew it would be not only unwise but dangerous.

She opened her mouth to tell him that spending two more days here was out of the question, but his fingers were gently

massaging her hand, and she heard herself saying, instead,
"Do you think that's wise?"

His gaze centered on her moistened lips. They were full,
with a slight natural pout that was sexy as hell. The urge to
lower his head and kiss them was almost overpowering.

Instead, he shrugged and answered her question. "Wise?
Of course not. The wisest thing I could have done last night
would have been to call the police and let them handle the
situation. That's what I'd intended to do as soon as I could
get you calmed down and able to deal with it yourself, but
you were so distraught that I couldn't bear to send you
away."

"I'm glad," she admitted softly. "I knew I was clinging
to you and behaving like a baby, but I was totally freaked
out and desperately needed the strength and concern you so
generously supplied. I don't know how I would have coped
if you'd just handed me over to strangers."

He smiled. He'd never met a woman who was such a mass
of contradictions. She was mature enough to have lived on
her own for years and still trusting enough to reach out and
accept help and comfort when she needed it. A combination that was both dangerous and appealing.

Unable to resist the need to hold her, he let go of her hand
and put his arm around her waist, careful to keep the embrace light and friendly. "Aren't you forgetting that I was
a stranger?"

Brittany's first reaction when he released her hand was to
resist, but she caught herself in time not to. Then his arm
encircled her waist and she melted against his side. She felt
warm and safe, just as she had last night when he'd held her,
and her heart sped up, even though his touch was devoid of
passion.

"But you weren't a stranger," she assured him. "From
the minute you caught me in your arms you were my salvation."

Jake flinched as the word hit him with the force of a blow. Salvation! He'd used the same overly dramatic term only a couple of hours ago to describe her effect on him. It was spooky that she would use it now to express how he affected her!

He hadn't been able to deny the strong magnetism between them, but this went deeper than that. You didn't bandy around words like *salvation* if the attraction was just infatuation or lust. *Salvation* had a spiritual connotation and was never uttered facetiously. It certainly wasn't a word he'd ever used to describe a romantic relationship. Not even with his wife.

So why did it spring to mind so effortlessly when he analyzed his feelings for this beautiful young woman who'd been blown into his life on a raging storm? And why did he find it so difficult to think of saying goodbye to her and sending her on her way?

"Jake?" The sound of Brittany's voice tore through the veil of his introspection, and he realized he'd taken too long to reply.

"I'm sorry," he said, being careful not to gather her closer as he wanted to do. "Just daydreaming, I guess.

"Look, I've got to get back to work, but first, tell me you'll spend a few more days with us. I promise to be good."

It sounded fine, but Brittany wasn't immune to temptation, either. And besides, there was the specter of Ronny to worry about....

She looked away, hoping Jake wouldn't see how difficult this was for her. "I really think I should leave tomorrow as planned, Jake. I'd love to stay longer, but I'm sure the pain in my head will be gone by morning. I appreciate the invitation, though."

She felt the muscles in his arm tighten, and he released her. "You're probably right," he said, and all emotion was

gone from his voice, "but the offer stays open. If you're not
feeling better by tomorrow you're welcome to stay until you
do."

He stepped away from her and turned. "I'll see you at
supper," he said, and strode off in the opposite direction
from the house.

As she watched him, aching with regret for what might-
have-been at a different point in their lives, she noticed for
the first time that he walked with a very slight limp. Was that
the disability Dagmar had spoken of? If so, what had happened to him?

Brittany returned to the house with the intention of calling the car agency to report her accident, but the line was
busy and Dagmar and Heidi were ready to pick up Kurt at
school, so she decided to try again later and went with them,
instead.

As they drove down the two-lane blacktop road in Dagmar's old blue car toward the town of Blair, Brittany was
surprised to see how hilly and green this rural terrain was.
Apparently they'd had a lot of moisture during the winter
and spring. Fields of corn, soybeans and grain had suffered
some damage from last night's storm, but the crops looked
healthy enough to survive and grow tall.

Blair proved to be a charming little town, with tree-shaded
residential streets, flower gardens and neat, well-kept
homes. Dagmar took Brittany on a short tour of Main
Street, with businesses lining both sides, then drove past the
post office, the library and the hospital before heading for
the elementary school.

"When Jakob and Wilhelm were Cub Scouts they used to
meet in the homes," she said as she parked in front of the
building, "but now, with so many mothers working, it's
more convenient for them to meet at school. They should be
coming out soon."

neck and shoulders tightened up again, reminding her that she hadn't gotten off as easy from her injuries as she'd thought. She asked Dagmar for aspirin, and Jake's mother gave her two, then insisted that she lie down for a while.

"Jakob was right," Dagmar told her. "Head injuries are unpredictable. It's just as well that you can't leave tomorrow. You haven't been taking proper care of yourself."

Brittany wandered into the living room and stretched out on the long comfortable sofa, one of the soft decorative pillows under her head. The cushions seemed to shape to her aching muscles, and she fell asleep almost immediately.

Sometime later she was aware of the stirrings of wakefulness, although her eyes were still closed and she was unaware of her surroundings. It was a familiar prickle at the back of her neck that disturbed her. A feeling that someone was watching her.

Ronny!

Her eyes flew open as terror gripped her, and she tried to [get] up, but the figure of a man with two big hands on her [sho]ulders bent over her and pushed her back down. She was [too] disoriented to focus clearly, and still too nearly asleep to [kno]w where she was.

[She] screamed. A shriek that split the air as she hit and [kicked] in an effort to get away from her tormenter.

[She] was vaguely aware of a dog barking and the sound of [step]s pounding on the floor in a dead run. Then she [heard a] familiar voice, raised in alarm but gentle.

["Brit]tany, wake up. It's me, Jake. I'm not going to hurt [you."]

[It was]n't Ronny—it was Jake! Her terror gave way to a [relief so s]trong that she shook with deep wrenching sobs.

[Dagmar] and the two children followed the barking black [dog in]to the room as Jake gathered Brittany into his [arms. She b]urrowed closer against him and buried her face [in his shoul]der, letting the tears flow. "It's all right, honey.

She'd hardly finished speaking, when several boys dressed in the familiar blue uniforms came tumbling out the door, laughing, shouting and pushing one another playfully. One of them, obviously Kurt, broke away from the others and came running toward the car. Brittany wouldn't have recognized the shadowy child in pajamas that she'd seen last night in the dim illumination, but now in the sunlight she could see that this was definitely Jake's son. The family resemblance was strong, from the black hair and brown eyes to the full face and the shape of the nose and mouth.

She glanced at Heidi, sitting in the back seat. Was she, then, a miniature replica of her mother? If so, Tina must be a beauty. That thought was not a welcome one, but Brittany was loath to admit it was jealousy.

Kurt pulled the car door open and slid into the back with his sister. Dagmar turned in her seat. "Kurt, you remember Miss Castle from last night."

Brittany also turned and extended her hand. "Hi, Kurt. Call me 'Brittany.'"

The boy stared at her, still too young to hide his surprise. "Hi. You look different."

Brittany laughed. "That's exactly what your sister said when she saw me. It's a change for the better, I hope. I was a pretty sorry mess last night."

"Yeah, you were," he said with the candor of a ten-year-old, "but you look good now. You got pretty hair."

She felt herself blush at his unselfconscious admiration. "Thank you. You look different, too. Much more grown-up. Do you like Scouting?"

He shrugged. "It's okay. I'm a Webelo, and Dad and I are goin' to camp this summer."

"You are! That'll be fun. I went to Girl Scout camp one summer."

"Honest? You were a Scout, too?"

"Only for one year," she said sadly. "Then my dad, who was in the army, was transferred, and I never joined another troop."

"My dad was an MP in the marines," Kurt announced proudly.

"He was!" Brittany was surprised. Jake hadn't mentioned anything to her about being in the marines. Come to think of it, he'd told her very little about himself. Everything she'd learned of him had been told to her by others.

"Yeah," his son confirmed. "He was on riot control one time and got stabbed in the chest with a big knife this long." He held his hands apart to nearly the length of a bayonet.

Brittany's blood ran cold. Dear Lord, he could have been killed! Is that why he was getting a disability pension?

Dagmar broke the shocked silence. "Kurt Luther, how many times do I have to tell you not to exaggerate?"

She turned to Brittany, who was still too stunned to voice her dismay. "It happened in San Diego in the mid-seventies. Jakob was trying to break up a fight between another marine and a drug-crazed war protester," she said calmly. "Jakob was stabbed in the chest with a hunting knife, but except for a small thin scar, it did little damage. No vital organs were hit."

Brittany let the air out of her oxygen-starved lungs and realized that she'd been holding her breath. A hunting knife might not do as much damage as a bayonet or a sword, but it was still a mighty wicked weapon. "Is he...is he all right? Does he have any lasting effects?"

Dagmar shook her head. "No, thanks be to God. He was very fortunate." She started the engine and it sprang to life. "We'd better get home. I have to bake a cake before I begin supper."

As soon as they got back to the house Brittany phoned the car-rental agency and reported the accident. "The car isn't

drivable, so you'll need to send a tow truck, as well as another vehicle for me."

"Sorry, ma'am, but you should have reported this earlier," said the man on the other end of the line. "We're backed up with damages because of the storm, and our tow trucks are all tied up for the rest of the day and most of tomorrow. We're also out of available cars in your size range."

"But I'd planned to leave for the northwestern part of the state in the morning," Brittany wailed. "I've imposed on these nice people who took me in last night long enough."

"I understand your problem, Ms. Castle, but all the folks ahead of you are in similar situations," the man said patiently. "I'll put you on our list and get to you as soon as w[e] can, but with the weekend and all it may not be until M[on]day."

She knew it was useless to argue. Now that sh[e] [was] stranded she'd have to take Jake up on his invitation[.] He'd said it would remain open.

After she'd concluded her conversation with [the] agency she explained the situation to Dagmar. "[I] don't want to wear out my welcome," she conc[luded.] Jake told me earlier that he thought I shoul[d put off the] long drive to Raindance for a few more days [because of my] head injury. I didn't want to impose on y[ou, but] now... I mean, I can go to a motel if it[']s [not conve]nient to have me here."

"I won't hear of it, and neither will J[ake]," [she as]sured her. "You're welcome to stay her[e as long as you want] to."

Brittany felt lighthearted and happ[y for the first time since] Ronny had begun harassing her. S[he was relieved that she] didn't have to leave here tomorr[ow, and she'd enjoy being] part of the family for a little wh[ile.]

A couple of hours later the [dull ache in Brittany's] forehead became a pounding [headache.]

[right margin torn fragments:]
sit
sho
too
kno
Sh
kicke
She
footste
heard a
"Bri
you!"
It was
relief so s
Dagma
retriever i
arms. She
in his shoul

You're safe here with us," he murmured, his mouth against her ear. "You were having a bad dream. Don't you know that I wouldn't let anything happen to you?"

He caressed her back gently and rubbed his cheek in her hair. He was so big and strong and still so tender that her terror began to fade. Her shaking stopped and the tears dried up as she gradually regained control of herself. She became aware of the dog panting with excitement as he sat on the floor beside them, and of Dagmar and the children hovering uncertainly in the background.

A wave of self-disgust splashed over her. She'd done it again, behaved like a scared child and upset the whole family. They'd think she was demented for sure. And how could she protest that she wasn't unless she told them about the man who was stalking her? But that was such a wild story that they'd really think she was crazy.

"When I came in to get ready for supper Mother told me you weren't feeling well and that she'd insisted you lie down," Jake said, and his warm breath blew softly on her skin making her shiver.

"I walked in here to check and see if you were all right, and must have disturbed your sleep. I'm sorry. I didn't mean to frighten you, but Mom said your headache was worse and you'd asked for aspirin."

"Yes, but—"

"No 'buts.' I'm taking you to a doctor—something I should have done last night."

He held her away from him and looked at her as she opened her mouth to argue. "Don't even think of refusing."

His tone was firm, and he looked past her to his mother. "You and the kids go ahead and eat, Mom. Just stick our food in the oven and keep it warm until we get back."

Brittany knew she'd never convince him that medical attention wasn't necessary. It would be easier to go along with his wishes. Besides, since he seemed to feel responsible for her she owed it to him to give him the peace of mind that an examination and a few tests would provide.

How could she refuse when he was obviously so concerned?

Their faces were only scant inches apart, and she leaned over and rubbed her cheek against his. It was rough, with a late-afternoon beard that sent prickles down her spine.

"Okay," she agreed in little more than a whisper, "but I have to freshen up first."

He chuckled. "You look just fine to me, but I need a shower and a change of clothes." He released her and stood, then glanced at his watch. "I'll meet you back here in twenty minutes."

Brittany felt suddenly bereft without his arms around her, holding her close against his broad muscular chest. Her smile faltered, but she shored it up as best she could and nodded. "I'll be ready."

Half an hour later they were in Jake's truck and driving south. Brittany had changed into black slacks and a black-and-white diamond patterned sweatshirt, and Jake wore clean jeans and a Western-style blue plaid shirt with a denim jacket.

"There's a hospital in Blair that's closer," he said apologetically, "but I know the staff at this clinic in North Omaha, so I'd rather take you there."

She glanced over at him and wondered how it happened that he was on personal terms with the staff of an emergency medical clinic. Did they have many injuries on the farm? She knew that was possible with all the heavy machinery and the big animals. If a horse threw you or a cow kicked you it could do a lot of damage. The thought made her shudder.

is important, Brittany, you were very lucky this time. It could easily have been much worse, so don't ever treat a head injury lightly. Jake was right to insist that you seek medical attention. Continue to take aspirin as needed, and see that you get lots of rest."

Brittany wasn't sure whether she'd been vindicated or reprimanded, but she suspected it was both.

"Do you have any questions?" Dr. Maitland asked.

She shook her head. "None that I can think of."

"Well, call me if the pain gets worse or if you have any dizziness."

Brittany nodded. "I will. Thank you, doctor."

She was about to rise, but the doctor turned his attention back to Jake. "So, Jake, how are the kids? And your mom? Is she still living with you?"

"The kids are healthy and growing up fast," Jake replied, "and you'd better believe that Mom's still with us. I couldn't work the farm and raise two kids without her. She puts in as many hours as I do."

The doctor nodded. "I'm sure she does. Do you ever miss the force?"

Force? Brittany thought. What force?

Jake scrunched up his face as he mulled over the question. "Yeah, I do sometimes," he admitted, "I gotta tell ya, it's easier to subdue an enemy you can see than one as nebulous as the weather, but I've never regretted leaving OPD for the farm. Guess the love of the land is in my blood, same as with my dad and granddad."

OPD? What on earth was he talking about, Brittany wondered. Could that be his old marine company? It must be. Where else would he have to 'subdue an enemy'?

Dr. Maitland's voice broke into her musing. "And your knee? Does it still give you trouble?"

Jake shrugged. "Oh, you know," he said slowly. "It hurts if I'm on my feet too much, and I can always predict a storm. But it's as good as it's ever going to get, and I really can't complain. It doesn't slow me down much."

So that was his disability? A bad knee? But what happened to it? Is that why he was no longer in the marines? Brittany vowed to find out. Jake didn't seem to mind talking about these things in front of her, so they must be common knowledge to everyone who knew him well. In that case it shouldn't be rude to question him.

Fifteen minutes later Jake had said goodbye to Dr. Maitland and Arlene, and he and Brittany were on their way home. Brittany leaned back and closed her eyes as the country music from the stereo system wafted through the air. She was glad now that she'd let Jake talk her into being examined. She'd been sure she wasn't badly injured, but even so it was nice to have it confirmed by a doctor.

Jake reached over and took her hand. "Does your head still hurt?"

She squeezed his fingers. "A little, but nothing a couple of aspirin won't help. I guess I'm not quite as indestructible as I thought I was."

"As soon as we get home you can get into bed and I'll ask Mom to take your supper up on a tray," he said.

"I'll do no such thing," she retorted. "I'm not an invalid and I don't expect to be treated like one."

They rode without speaking for a few minutes while the voice of Reba McEntire offered a soothing counterpoint to Brittany's disorganized thoughts. Finally she took a deep breath and turned to look at Jake. "Jake, what's OPD?"

He blinked. "Omaha Police Department, why?"

She gasped and straightened up. "You were a policeman? But Kurt said you used to be a marine."

Jake chuckled. "I was both. I enlisted in the marines after my second year of college, and when my hitch was up I was accepted at the Omaha police academy. I was a cop until three years ago when my dad died and I took over the farm.''

Now she was more puzzled than before. "Then you didn't retire on a disability? You quit to farm. But Dagmar said..."

He shook his head. "I did take a disability retirement. It was either that or accept a desk job, and that's the last thing I wanted. I retired and came back to farming.''

He didn't seem to mind talking about it, so she pushed further. "Was it your knee? I mean, the reason you couldn't work as a policeman?''

Jake nodded but said nothing.

She could see that she was getting into a subject that he did mind talking about, but she'd gone too far now. She had to know how he'd been injured.

The truck swerved, catching her off guard, and she grabbed the door handle to steady herself, then realized that they'd turned into the driveway.

Jake looked at her, and she could tell by his expression that their conversation had just drawn to a close. "I'll tell you about it some other time, Brittany, but we're home now, and Mom's been keeping our supper warm. I'm hungry, and I'll bet you are, too. Let's go in and eat.''

Chapter Five

Brittany overslept again the following morning, but she woke feeling much better. As she rummaged in her suitcase, looking for clean clothes, she made such a clutter that she decided it would be easier to unpack and put her things away in a drawer and the closet. She could repack her things on Monday morning before she left.

Fortunately, since she'd intended to stay several days in Omaha—although for a much different reason—she'd packed one bag full of essentials, so she didn't have to hunt through all her luggage when she needed something.

After gathering up her underwear, she opened the top drawer of the dresser. She'd expected it to be empty, but found, instead, that it contained several lace bikini panties in delicate pastel colors and an equal number of wispy bras to match.

She picked one of the bras up and looked at the size—32B. No way would that fit Dagmar! So who did it belong to?

She closed the drawer and dropped her own things into the second one, which was empty. When she opened the closet door to hang up her dress and robe she found a mauve chiffon nightgown and peignoir set draped on a satin hanger. Did these things belong to Jake's ex-wife? Or did he have a lover? Surely he wouldn't carry on such an affair here, not with his mother and two children in the house. He'd even said as much to her yesterday.

She noted that whomever the nightgown fit wore a size five petite and could afford to pay a lot for intimate garments that only the man in her life would see. Was Jake that man? The idea disturbed Brittany more than it should, considering that it was none of her business.

By the time she appeared downstairs Jake was long gone and Dagmar had finished half a day's work.

"I'm so sorry," Brittany apologized. She was both embarrassed and ashamed to have slept so late. "I don't know what's the matter with me. It must be the sweet fresh air. I always get up at six o'clock when I'm working."

Dagmar handed her a cup of coffee and put a thick slice of homemade bread in the toaster. "No need to be sorry," she insisted. "Don't forget, you got a nasty bump on the head in that accident. You need the rest. Now, sit down and I'll fix your breakfast. How do you like your eggs?"

Brittany poured cream in her coffee. "Just toast, please, and I can butter it myself." A thought occurred to her. "This is Saturday. Does Jake work seven days a week?"

Dagmar chuckled. "Actually, yes, although he slows up on Sundays." Her smile disappeared. "The only holidays a farmer takes in the spring, summer and fall are the days when it pours rain, but even then there are chores that have to be done morning and evening. You never really catch up on the work. And then there's always the threat that likely as not something will happen to ruin the crop and you'll lose everything and have to start all over.''

Her expression grew more serious. "Farming's a hard, demanding way of life. One that can break the spirit of all but the most rugged and dedicated individuals. I was born to it, but Jake's wife didn't last a year out here, and she had nothing to do with farming the place. She worked in town and was only here nights. Except when she was traveling, which was often. Then she wasn't here at all.''

Dagmar looked down at the faded jeans and sweatshirt she wore. When she spoke again, her tone was bitter. "There's nothing glamorous about being a farm wife. Just remember that, Brittany, if you're ever tempted to try it.''

Before an astonished Brittany could reply, Jake's mother turned and walked out of the room, putting an end to the conversation.

Jake was solicitous and friendly toward Brittany when he and Emmett came in at noon for dinner. He asked if she'd slept well and how she was feeling, but the conversation around the table consisted mostly of what had been, or still needed to be, done around the farm to repair the storm damage.

After the meal, Brittany cleaned up the kitchen while Dagmar made up her shopping list. When they finished they took Heidi and drove to a warehouse-type supermarket/ discount store on the outskirts of Omaha. Kurt had gone with his dad to the cow pasture.

The sun shone brightly, although the breeze was chilly. Together they had dried up the ground enough so that it was no longer necessary to slosh around in mud to get anywhere.

The shopping expedition was an adventure for Brittany. The discount store had a huge inventory of dry goods, and Dagmar bought jeans, T-shirts, underwear and socks for the whole family. Brittany was delighted to find a pair of beige pumps to replace the ones she'd ruined during the storm, in her mad dash from the car to the house.

In the supermarket section Dagmar filled two more carts with groceries. "Good heavens!" Brittany exclaimed as they waited in line to check out. "You have enough food here to feed an army, Dagmar. It will take you forever to use it all up."

The older woman laughed. "Farmers work hard and they eat hearty. This won't last more than a couple of weeks, and I don't like to be runnin' to the store all the time. We have our own dairy products and meat, and we raise all the fresh vegetables we can eat and preserve, so I just stock up on staples a couple of times a month."

Although Brittany had lived in a small town, she'd never been on a farm for more than an hour or two before, and she found the Luthers' way of life fascinating.

Supper that evening was a fun meal. Brittany fixed hamburgers while Dagmar peeled potatoes and put them through a cutter that sliced them into long curlicue strips that she cooked in the deep fryer. Brittany had never eaten french fries that way before, and she found them delicious. Crispy on the outside and soft on the inside. The kids loved them, and with the addition of home-canned peach halves and large squares of warm carrot cake dripping with cream cheese and pineapple topping, they didn't have to be told to clean up their plates.

Emmett didn't eat with them this time, and Jake explained that the hired man didn't live on the farm but had a room in his sister's home in Blair. He took breakfast and supper there. He also had Sundays off.

After they'd finished their meal Jake and Kurt did the evening chores, then Jake suggested they all take in a movie. The latest Disney release was playing in Blair, so they piled into Jake's late-model red American car—"My one extravagance," as he called it—and drove to the theater.

It was a small building as movie houses went, and after they'd bought their tickets and stocked up on popcorn and soft drinks they were unable to find five seats together.

"There are three seats over there," Dagmar said pointing to a place several rows down on their right. "The kids and I will take those. You and Brittany shouldn't have any trouble finding two together."

Jake readily agreed, and he chuckled as he and Brittany settled into seats several rows back and to the left of the aisle. "This couldn't have worked out better if I'd planned it," he said with relish.

She laughed. "Shame on you. Are you saying that you're happy we can't sit with your children?"

"Damn right. Even a father needs time off for courting once in a while."

"Are you courting me, Jake?" She meant it to be a lighthearted remark, but it came out sounding hopeful.

His grin faded. "Couldn't we just pretend for a while that I am?" His tone had lost its teasing lilt. "We have so little time left together. What would it hurt?"

It could hurt us both very deeply, Brittany thought, but immediately banished the idea. What could they possibly do that would compromise either of them in a movie surrounded by people?

"Why not?" she said. "I'm game if you are. We'll pretend we're teenagers on our first date together."

Jake's grin was back. "Okay, but we'll have to hold hands. Teenagers always hold hands."

"But ours are full," she protested halfheartedly.

"We'll find a way." He shifted his bags so the popcorn was propped in his lap and he gripped the cola in his right hand.

She followed suit, but her cola was in her left. The dim lights went out just as he reached for her empty hand, brought it to his mouth for a lingering kiss that sent shivers all the way to her shoulder, then rested it, still clasped, on the seat arm between them.

Brittany enjoyed the movie. It was a nice clean comedy with no violence or explicit sex. There were a couple of love scenes, however, that made her achingly aware of the big man with the tender touch sitting beside her, clasping her hand in his. He squeezed it when the tension between the hero and heroine heated up, and when they finally kissed Jake moved their entwined hands to his thigh with her palm downward.

The movie was over a few minutes later, much to Brittany's regret. Holding hands with Jake in a dark movie house was a wonderfully pleasing experience. One that could become addictive.

Dagmar and the children joined them outside the theater, and after stopping for sundaes at the quaint little ice-cream parlor on Main Street, they all went home. Too soon the evening was over. Bedtime came early in the Luther household. As Dagmar pointed out, "A farmer's workday starts at dawn and seldom ends before dark." They all went to bed in their separate rooms, but Brittany was a long time falling asleep, knowing that Jake was right next door.

Brittany was wakened at eight o'clock the following morning by a knock at her door. "You have a phone call," Dagmar said. "A lady from the rental agency."

Brittany rolled out of bed and fumbled for her robe, pulling it on as she groggily followed the other woman down the stairs. She'd been sleeping heavily again and was having trouble awakening fully. Apparently her body was still working at healing itself after the shock and injury of the accident.

She hadn't fully comprehended what Dagmar had told her, other than she was wanted on the phone.

"I took the call in the kitchen," Dagmar said when they reached the bottom of the stairway, "but you can pick it up in Jake's office, if you'd rather."

"Kitchen's fine," Brittany mumbled.

When they reached their destination she picked up the phone and said hello.

"Ms. Castle? This is Leslie O'Neil at the car-rental agency," said the voice at the other end of the line. "We're clearing up our backlog more quickly than we'd anticipated, and we can send a tow truck and a replacement car out to you this morning if that would be convenient."

Brittany was still struggling to wake up. "What? Oh...oh, yes, of course. That is... this morning would be fine. Can you tell me what time I might expect them?"

"Not exactly, but it should be sometime around ten."

Brittany glanced at her watch and was jolted fully awake. Ten o'clock! That was less than two hours away. She could probably be on her way to Raindance by eleven!

But she didn't want to go to Raindance. She wanted to stay right here.

The voice in her ear finally got her attention. "Ms. Castle? Is ten o'clock too early? I can schedule you later if—"

"No," Brittany interrupted as she finally pulled herself together. "No, ten o'clock is fine. This is a rural area. Do you need directions?"

"No, we've already pinpointed your address on the map. I'll call again if it looks like there will be a delay."

Brittany thanked the woman and hung up, but her thinking process was still short-circuited. She'd expected to spend today and tonight here with Jake, Dagmar and the children, but now her plans were suddenly changed. Her replacement car would be here in less than two hours, and after that she'd have no excuse not to leave for Raindance.

She'd looked forward to today because it was Sunday, and Jake spent more time with his family on Sundays. Last night Dagmar had invited her to go to church with them this morning, and afterward her other son, Wilhelm, and his family were coming for dinner. She'd been eager to meet Jake's brother.

Brittany was so lost in her disappointment that she jumped when a voice behind her spoke. "Brittany, is something wrong?"

She whirled around and almost bumped into Jake. He must have been sitting at the table across the room, but she'd had her back turned to it while she'd spoken into the phone.

A glance around revealed Dagmar standing at the stove, but no sign of the children.

"Oh, Jake, you startled me," she said, and combed her fingers through her tangled hair. Dear heaven, she must look a mess with her hair wild and untamed and her face still swollen with sleep. Jake would think she always looked like a street urchin. He'd never seen her at her best, and now he never would.

She made an effort to sound nonchalant. "No, nothing's wrong. The rental agency found a free car and tow truck and they're sending them over this morning. I should be out of your hair before noon."

Jake frowned and a feeling of dread stole over him. He must have misunderstood. The car-rental people had been adamant about not being able to process her claim until Monday at the earliest. "What do you mean, 'out of my hair'? Surely you're not leaving!"

His tone was more strident than he'd intended it to be, but he couldn't seem to get a grip on his emotions. Why did she have to be so damn desirable? She looked so...so sexy in her long lilac robe with her disheveled golden hair tumbling past her shoulders, her eyes still heavy with sleep and her face scrubbed clean and flushed the delicate pink of a newly opened rosebud. Her parted lips were soft and full and ripe for kissing, and it was all he could do to keep his hands off her.

Brittany stared at Jake. He looked and sounded so fierce. Almost as if he didn't want her to leave. Maybe she could delay her departure until tomorrow, after all. She could go to church with them and meet Wilhelm and his family....

But that would be foolish. It was going to be hard enough for her to say goodbye to these people as it was. It would be even worse if she got more intimately involved with them.

These past two days were just a respite between leaving Independence and relocating somewhere else. She was going through a very traumatic time in her life, and Jake and Dagmar had reached out to her, had eased her fear and uncertainty by taking her in and providing care and shelter.

That's all it was, a pleasant interlude, and to make more of it would just set her up for deeper anguish later after she'd grown to care too much for them. It was better to leave now, while she was relatively unscathed.

"Brittany, you're not thinking of leaving, are you?" Jake repeated, jolting her out of her contemplation.

"Yes, I am Jake," she answered, trying to keep her voice from quivering. "If I leave here around eleven o'clock I can be in Raindance by late afternoon. I'm going to be staying with a friend whom I haven't seen in several years, and this way we can have a long visit tonight before she has to go to work tomorrow."

Brittany tried for a smile that was vague at best. "You know women. We love to talk."

He wiped his hand over his face, leaving it unreadable. "I see." She couldn't tell if his flat tone contained disappointment or indifference. "Well, as I said before, if you should change your mind you're welcome to stay."

He turned and walked away, and Brittany's gaze met Dagmar's. "I'm sorry you feel you must leave, *Liebchen,* but since you do we'll skip going to church this morning."

Brittany felt a leap of joy that they would change their plans in order to spend more time with her, but then her conscience pricked her and she couldn't let them do it. "Oh, Dagmar, that's sweet of you, but I'll probably be leaving about the same time you would so please don't change your schedule because of me."

Dagmar looked doubtful. "Well, if you're sure...."

Brittany knew she'd better get out of there before she lost her composure. "I'm sure, really, and now if you'll excuse me, I'll go upstairs and dress."

The people from the car-rental agency arrived shortly before ten. There was one man driving a tow truck and two more men each driving a car. The middle-aged one in the white luxury car introduced himself as Paul, and the young one in the gray compact car, almost identical to the one she'd wrecked, as Jerry.

Jerry whistled when he saw Brittany's auto. "Jeez, lady, you really did a number on that car!"

She saw Paul scowl at the younger man as Jake came striding up behind Jerry. "She didn't do a 'number' on anything," Jake said in a rumbling voice. "The car was blown off the road in the storm."

Startled, Jerry jumped and turned around to confront a fierce scowl on the face of a man he obviously hadn't known was there. "Hey, sorry, it was just a comment. No offense."

Paul glared at his companion. "Get in my car and wait for me there," he said angrily, then looked from Jake to Brittany. "Is there someplace we can sit down? I have a report to fill out, and Ms. Castle will have to sign some papers."

The man with the truck began hooking up the damaged car as Jake led the other adults into the house. Kurt and Heidi, who had come running at the sight of the fascinating tow truck, were sent to their rooms to get dressed for Sunday school.

Jake sat down at the table with Brittany and Paul, while Dagmar followed the children upstairs.

"Now, then," Paul said as he produced a small tape recorder and set it on the table in front of Brittany, "tell me exactly what happened."

She gave him a step-by-step account of everything from the time she drove away from the rental agency that fateful night until she stumbled, frightened, injured and hysterical into the Luther home and disrupted the whole family.

Paul jotted down a few notes and asked a question now and then, while Jake listened intently but said nothing. When they were finished Paul turned off the recorder and asked Brittany to accompany him outside again, where he had her inspect the new car he'd brought for her, then handed her the keys.

"Okay, I guess that's it," he said. "When you're finished with the car just turn it in at our agency in either Norfolk or North Platte, depending on which direction you're headed."

She thanked him and he waved goodbye as he got into the white car with Jerry and drove off.

Jake put his arm around her waist as they stood watching the luxury vehicle speed down the road. "Where are you going when you leave Raindance?" he asked quietly.

Again she relaxed in his embrace, and her heart sank as she realized that it was probably for the last time.

"I really don't have any idea," she admitted, and knew she was only strengthening his suspicion that she was a wanderer. "I've thought of Cheyenne or Laramie, but the veterinarians in Wyoming handle mainly large ranch animals, and my experience is with pets.

"I might try Denver. We lived there for a time when I was a child, and I liked it. Or I may stay in Raindance if the vet could use an assistant. I have a lot of friends there, so I wouldn't be all alone...."

Her voice trailed off, and Jake's arm tightened. "Why don't you stay in Omaha or Blair?"

The suggestion was a tempting one, but a picture of Ronny Ralston at the airport flashed through her mind and she shivered. She'd had only a shocked glimpse of the man, not enough to swear that it was her stalker, but could she afford to take the chance that it wasn't?

Ronny was dangerous. He'd proven that when he'd beaten her up so badly that she'd been hospitalized. She still shuddered at the memory of his fists pummeling her. It would be natural for her to see him in every quick glimpse of a man of the same height and coloring, and that's very probably what had happened at the airport.

She wished now that she'd managed to get a better look at him, but she'd been so shocked that her only thought had been to get out of there before he saw her.

"I... I don't know, Jake." Her tone betrayed her uncertainty. "Maybe I will, but I'm not going to decide one way or the other until I've spent some time in Raindance. I guess I'm homesick, but I feel a deep-seated need to go back, renew friendships and relive happy memories. Do you know what I mean?"

He sighed and released her. "Yeah, I know," he said somewhat gruffly. "You need to come to terms with the past before you can get on with your future. I guess we all reach that point at some time in our lives."

Just then Dagmar and the two children came out the front door, dressed in their best Sunday clothes. "Golly, don't you look nice," Brittany said as they walked toward her.

Heidi ran ahead of the others to show off her pink ruffled dress and black patent leather shoes. She had matching pink bows tied at the ends of each of her braids, and she looked adorable.

"This is my Easter outfit," she said primly.

"You look beautiful," Brittany said, then turned her attention to Kurt, who stood back and seemed uncomfortable. "Kurt, you look great, too, in your slacks and shirt." She wanted to acknowledge his good looks but not embarrass him further. "And I like your sweater. That's a Native-American design, isn't it?"

The boy nodded. "Yeah, Grandma knitted it for me."

Brittany looked up at Dagmar and smiled. "You're a talented lady, and a pretty one, too. You look so nice in that dress."

It was true. Her only makeup was a light shade of lipstick, but she was wearing a gray-and-rose print dress with a white lace collar that had a slimming effect and made her look years younger than the baggy jeans and sweatshirts that were her everyday costumes around the farm.

Dagmar blushed but looked pleased. "Thanks. It's nothing special. Is everything settled with the car?"

Brittany nodded. "Yes, I'll be leaving as soon as I get my suitcase."

She looked down at her own somewhat scruffy outfit of stone-washed jeans and a cotton pullover sweater. She felt a twinge of regret that her need for comfort on the six-hour drive over less than top-quality two-lane roads had taken preference over her desire to look fashionable.

Saying goodbye to the Luther family was one of the hardest leave-takings Brittany had ever attempted, and she'd had more than her share of difficult ones. First the abandonment she'd felt when her battling parents had left her with her grandparents and gone their separate ways. Then the heartbreak of keeping a stiff upper lip when her grandparents had died only a few days apart, and, less than a week ago, the rage at having to sneak out of town and leave her friends and others dear to her in Independence because of a demented psychopath who wouldn't take no for an answer.

Now she was again being uprooted from a safe harbor. Jake and Dagmar had literally taken her in out of the storm and sheltered her, and she didn't want to leave. She wanted the warmth and security of being a part of this close, loving family.

If only...

Ah, but her life was a series of "if only's," and maudlin self-pity wasn't going to get her anywhere. She'd been given the gifts of intelligence and good health, and the strength and ability to take care of herself, which was far more than a lot of people had in these days of recession and homelessness. She could have anything she wanted badly enough to go after.

Except Jake. And if she'd use that intelligence she prided herself on having she'd admit that it was impossible to fall in love with a man she'd known less than three days.

Jake was physically appealing, a real hunk, and she had a lively libido, but she suspected that the real attraction was the security he represented.

As Jake stowed her suitcase in the trunk of the car Brittany turned to Dagmar and the children, who were waiting until she left before going on to church. Jake had spent so much time helping her deal with Paul and the accident report that now he didn't have time to clean up and go with them.

Another transgression on her conscience.

"Well, I guess it's time to say goodbye," she said tremulously, and reached for Heidi. "Goodbye, honey." She leaned down and folded the child in her arms.

The little girl snuggled into the embrace without hesitation. "I wish you didn't have to leave," she said sadly.

"Oh, so do I," Brittany answered, "but I have friends in Raindance who are expecting me, and I mustn't keep them waiting."

She released Heidi and turned to Kurt. "Goodbye, Kurt," she said as she extended her hand to the boy. She was sure he'd be embarrassed if she hugged him. "I'm so glad I met you, even though I had to wreck the car to do it."

She was trying to lighten the mood a little, but her voice had trouble squeezing around the lump in her throat.

Kurt shook her hand and nodded. "Yes, ma'am, me, too."

Then Brittany faced Dagmar, and this time she didn't hesitate, but threw her arms around Jake's mother and hugged her hard. She was soft and cushiony, a lot like Brittany's grandmother had been, and she hugged Brittany back.

"Oh, Dagmar..." Brittany's voice broke. "How... how can I ever thank you...?"

"No thanks necessary," Dagmar replied brusquely. "We've enjoyed having you with us. Just promise that you'll take care of yourself. If you get too tired or your head starts to hurt before you get to Raindance, stop at a motel and spend the night. You want to get there all in one piece."

Dagmar sounded like Grandma, too, and Brittany loved having someone fuss over her. "I will, and I promise to see a doctor for a checkup in a few days—"

The shrill ring of the telephone in the house interrupted her, and Dagmar broke out of the embrace. "Oh, dear, who can that be?" she said impatiently. "I'll just be a minute. Don't leave till I get back."

Turning, she hurried into the house, the children following at her heels.

Jake had hoped for a few minutes alone with Brittany, but now that he did he didn't know what to say or do. If he gave in to his desire he'd take her in his arms and kiss her, long and deep and lingering, then plead with her to stay.

But "desire" was a hell of a lot different from "responsible," and there was nothing responsible about getting involved with a much younger woman whom he'd known less than seventy-two hours. Especially one who seemed content to wander from town to town and job to job when the mood stuck her.

He shifted restlessly. Dear God, what had come over him? He'd had his fling with a beautiful face and a sexy body and what had it gotten him? Two kids to raise by himself and enough pain and disillusion to last a lifetime.

Sure, the coupling had been great, but a hot sex drive was all he and Tina had in common. In every other way they were totally incompatible, and he had no reason to think things would be different with Brittany.

If he could just get through the next few minutes without doing something stupid she'd be gone, and so would the temptation. Where in hell was his mother, anyway? Was she going to stay on that phone all morning?

Brittany's mind seemed to have gone blank. She'd wanted a chance to say goodbye to Jake privately, but now that they were alone she couldn't think of any way to fill the awkward silence.

She wanted to tell him how grateful she was to him for taking her in, how special he was to her, how much she regretted having to leave, but she couldn't. Not without revealing her unwise infatuation for him, and she didn't want to burden him with that. He already felt too much responsibility for her.

Well, this was her leave-taking, and she'd better get on with it. She took a deep breath. "Jake."

"Brittany."

Oh, great. First neither of them had spoken, then they'd both spoken at the same time.

"I'm sorry," she said. "You go ahead."

"Oh, no. Ladies first, please."

It was pointless to stand there arguing over who was going to start the conversation, so Brittany proceeded. "I just wanted to thank you for taking me in and…and taking care of me. I… I can't tell you how grateful I am—"

Damn! She sounded as though she was thanking him for some small favor, instead of practically saving her life.

"That's not necessary," he interrupted. "It was no more than we'd have done for anybody under the circumstances—"

Oh, hell. Why was his usually glib tongue tied up in knots just when he needed it most? He was telling her that she was no more special than any stranger who might wander by, and that's not what he meant at all.

"Brittany…"

"Jake…"

Again they'd both spoken at the same time, but now Jake muttered an exasperated oath and held out his arms to her.

"Come here and let's do this right," he said softly, and then she was wrapped in his warm embrace.

For a moment they just stood there holding each other, and for Brittany it was sheer magic. Jake was a big man, and he'd been working in the barnyard since dawn. His body was hard and muscular against the softness of hers, his lips rough as they caressed her temple, and he smelled of alfalfa and hay and the musky scent of the hardworking male. Far more potent than any cologne.

"You didn't really think I was going to let you get away without giving me at least as enthusiastic a hug as you gave Mom and Heidi, did you?" Jake's voice was husky, and muffled against her hair.

"I hoped you wouldn't," she answered truthfully into his chest, "but I wasn't sure whether or not you'd want me to."

"I'm a living, breathing man, aren't I? How could I not want you to?"

How, indeed? he thought. And how in hell was he going to let her go now that he knew how she felt in his arms, her soft cuddly body pressed against his and her smooth talented hands caressing the back of his neck.

A shiver ran down his spine and he barely managed to stifle a moan as the embarrassing hardness in his groin became a throbbing torment. Damn, he'd been too long without a woman. That was the only explanation for the powerful need this one ignited in him. It had to be purely physical; he hadn't known her long enough to fall in love even if he wanted to, which he most certainly didn't.

A combination of sounds—the front screen door opening behind them and Dagmar's voice calling his name—snapped Jake out of his erotic stupor and back to the real world.

"Jakob, that was Gisela's husband, Nicholas," Dagmar said as Brittany and Jake sprang apart.

Brittany knew immediately that something was wrong. Dagmar's tone was shrill and her face white and drawn.

Jake noticed, too, and he rushed toward her. "Mother!" he cried anxiously as he bounded up the steps "What's wrong? Is something the matter with Gisela?"

Brittany remembered that Gisela was the name of Dagmar's daughter, Jake's younger sister, who lived in Wisconsin with her husband and two small children.

"She . . . she fell down the stairs," Dagmar said.

Brittany gasped and walked toward the porch.

"Oh, Lord," Jake groaned. "The baby?"

"The baby seems to be all right, at least for now, but Gisela broke her leg." Jake's mother was making a valiant effort to keep her composure. "It's a compound fracture, and she's in the hospital in traction. Nicholas needs help with the children. He asked if I could get away to come to Green Bay.''

Jake didn't hesitate. "Of course you must go. I'll get you booked on the first flight out."

"But what about Kurt and Heidi?" Dagmar wailed. "School will be out for the summer on Thursday, so they'll be home all day, and you can't handle all the work of farming and watch them, too."

Brittany climbed the steps to the porch and joined Dagmar and Jake.

Jake blanched, but his voice was firm. "That's my problem, Mom, not yours. Right now your place is with Gisela and Nick. He can't take much time away from his fledgling business, and their little girls are preschoolers and need constant supervision. Don't worry about me and my kids. We'll manage."

How? Brittany wanted to ask, but knew that Jake didn't know the answer, either. He was just trying to make Dagmar feel better about leaving.

"Is there anything I can do to help?" she asked, instead.

Brittany could almost feel Dagmar's mind casting around in search of a solution to this dilemma, and almost oblivious to anything going on around her.

"Thank you, dear, but I don't think so," she said vaguely, her attention still focused on Jake. "I can't leave until I know the children will be properly looked after," she told him. "Surely Nicholas can manage for a day or two—"

"Mom, I told you not to worry," Jake said. "I'll see to it that my kids are well cared for...."

Brittany stopped listening as an idea began taking shape in her mind. At first she resisted it for the same reasons she'd resisted Jake's invitation earlier to stay with them for a few more days, but this was an emergency. She could put aside her personal concerns now that Jake and Dagmar needed her help. In fact, she owed it to them to make the offer.

"Jake, Dagmar," she said, breaking into their escalating argument over whether or not Dagmar should leave immediately for Green Bay.

Apparently Brittany had spoken more stridently than she'd intended, because they immediately stopped talking and turned to her.

"There's no pressing reason for me to leave for Raindance today, or even this week," she said. "I'll be happy to stay on and look after the children until Jake can find a temporary housekeeper. That is . . . if you'll let me."

She held her breath as she waited for an answer, hoping they'd say yes, but knowing she was putting her emotional well-being, maybe even her life, in jeopardy if they did.

Could she keep her growing attraction for Jake from blossoming into an unrequited love? And was her determined stalker really in Omaha and still looking for her?

Chapter Six

Both Jake and Dagmar stared at Brittany in stunned surprise. It was the obvious answer to the problem, and Jake's spirits rose.

Why not? This was a real emergency, and she'd offered. She'd even admitted that there was no reason for her to rush off to Raindance. It was almost three weeks before her class reunion, and her offer to stay here was a godsend.

Surely he could find a housekeeper within the next few days so she wouldn't be delayed long, and his mom really needed to go to Green Bay as soon as possible. Gisela was her youngest child and only daughter, and the two were very close. Gisela depended on her mother more than she should, but now was no time to try to change that.

His thoughts were interrupted when his mother spoke.

"That's awfully sweet of you, Brittany, but you mustn't feel that you are indebted to us. Are you sure it wouldn't interrupt your vacation? You said—"

"I'm not on vacation, Dagmar, remember?" Brittany replied. "I'm between jobs, and never did intend to look for another one until after my class reunion. I only came to Nebraska early because..." Oh, dear. Now she'd talked herself into a corner. "Because the new owners took over the animal hospital sooner than expected," she hurriedly said, improvising.

"I was leaving today mainly because I didn't want to overstay my welcome with you, but now that you need me here I can stay with a clear conscience and in some small way repay the kindness you showered on me."

It occurred to her that Jake hadn't said anything yet. How did he feel about her suggestion? Maybe he'd rather make other arrangements.

Jake was appalled at how overjoyed he was at the possibility of Brittany living in his house and taking care of his children, even though it was for only a few days. But, damn it, how could he ask her to live with him as an employee, chaperoned only by children who went to bed early every night, when he couldn't keep his hands off her?

On the other hand, if Brittany was willing he had no choice. His sister was seven months pregnant and had two little daughters, two and four years old, and a husband who didn't know diddly about keeping house.

Nick was a macho good old boy who loved Gisela but made it plain that a wife's place was in the kitchen, barefoot and pregnant, while he performed his role of husband by supporting her and the children. She didn't work and he didn't change diapers!

No, his mother had to go to Green Bay, today if possible, and the only way she could leave here without worrying about him and his family was if Brittany would fill in until he could hire someone else.

His gaze captured Brittany's and held it. "If you're sure you want to do this I'll be forever grateful," he said, then before he could stop himself added, "please stay, I need you."

And not just to cook and baby-sit, he amended silently.

I need you. Obviously he didn't mean it the way Brittany had heard it, but the three magic words melted her bones.

"I'll be happy to" she heard herself promise, and knew she'd made the right decision. The only one she could have made under the circumstances.

In spite of her fear of becoming too involved with Jake, the idea of staying here appealed to her. She felt reasonably safe in this rural area between the city of Omaha and the small town of Blair.

If Ronny had followed her, and that seemed more far-fetched every day, this was the perfect place to hide. And if he hadn't, he'd never find her here.

"Oh, what a relief," Dagmar said fervently. "I don't know how we can ever thank you."

"No thanks are necessary," Brittany assured her. "Now, why don't we go upstairs and start packing your things while Jake calls the airport and gets you on the earliest flight out?"

Jake touched her cheek and murmured, "Bless you," then turned and walked into the house.

Dagmar and Brittany followed, and were halfway up the stairway, when Dagmar stopped abruptly. "Oh, dear, I forgot. I have to finish cooking dinner. Wilhelm and his family will be here in—" she looked at her watch "—about an hour and a half."

"You go ahead and start packing and I'll put the vegetables in the pot with the roast," Brittany said. "It'll give me a chance to find my way around your cupboards while you're still here to direct me."

A voice coming from the living room distracted them. "Hey, Grandma, we're gonna be late for church."

It was Kurt, who appeared at the doorway with his little sister at his side.

"I'm sorry, *Liebling,*" Dagmar said as she turned her attention to the children. "We're not going to church, after all. That phone call was from your uncle Nicholas."

She explained the situation to them, and Heidi's expressive blue eyes grew round with apprehension. "Is Aunt Gisela going to die?"

"Oh, no, *Kindlein,*" Dagmar hurriedly assured her, "but she'll be in the hospital for a while, and she needs me to come to her house and take care of your cousins."

"Then who will take care of us?" the child persisted.

"Brittany is going to stay here while I'm gone. Now, come upstairs with me and change your clothes. Uncle Wilhelm and his family will be arriving soon for dinner."

Now that she wouldn't be leaving, Brittany changed her clothes, too. She unpacked her suitcase again and put on a royal blue dress and a pair of white pumps.

Jake managed to get his mother a ticket on a flight due out of Omaha at five-twenty, then drove to the airport to pick it up so they wouldn't have to bother with it just before she left. He returned about fifteen minutes before Wilhelm drove his brown-and-beige minivan up the long driveway and parked at the side of the house. Brittany was in the dining room, putting the finishing touches on setting the table, when she heard them arrive and looked out the window.

Dagmar was upstairs packing, but Jake strode out of the house to meet them with Dakota, the dog, at his heels. Brittany watched as a big husky man wearing a cowboy hat, a tall slender redhaired woman, and two lanky teenage boys spilled out of the vehicle.

Dakota jumped happily on the boys and barked an invitation to play, while Wilhelm and his wife talked to Jake.

Brittany could see that he was telling them about Gisela's accident and Dagmar's imminent departure.

After a few minutes they all hurried toward the back door of the house. Wilhelm was the first one inside, calling, "Mom. Hey, Mom. Where are you?"

He walked into the kitchen and spotted Brittany just as Dagmar came in from the dining room. "I'm right here," she said as the rest of the family trooped in.

Wilhelm's gaze switched to his mother. He resembled Jake, except that he was even bigger and somewhat older looking. He'd removed his hat and she noticed that his dark hair was sprinkled with gray. There were also deep weather lines at the corners of his eyes and mouth.

He wore brown dress slacks, a tweed sport coat over an open-throated shirt and boots. "Jake says Gisela's in the hospital," he said to Dagmar. "Is she going to be all right? How can we help?"

The redhaired woman, obviously his wife, chimed in. "What about the baby?"

"So far the baby seems to be all right," Dagmar said, "but the fracture of Gisela's leg is a bad one, and she'll have to stay off it for quite a while. Jakob was able to get me on a flight to Green Bay that leaves later this afternoon".

She sighed. "Thank God for Brittany. She's agreed to stay on here until Jakob can hire someone to take over...." She paused. "Oh, dear, you haven't been introduced to her yet."

She sent Brittany an apologetic glance. "Brittany, this is my son Wilhelm, his wife, Elena, and their boys, Scott and Ian."

She shifted her gaze to her family. "Brittany Castle is the young woman who's car was blown off the road and into our tree during the storm Thursday night. I've told you about that. She was just getting ready to continue her journey this morning when we got the call from Nicholas. It was such a relief when she generously volunteered to stay on for a few days to look after Kurt and Heidi."

"That was awfully nice of you, Brittany," Elena said.

"Not at all," Brittany replied. "It was the least I could do after all Jake and Dagmar have done for me."

"I'm sorry I can't take care of the kids," Elena continued, "but I work, so I'm gone all day."

"Oh?" That surprised Brittany. She'd had the impression that all the Luther women were full-time wives and mothers. All except Jake's ex-wife, who hadn't lasted long on the farm or in the family.

Elena certainly didn't look like the stereotype of a farm wife. She looked more like a model in her fashionable dress, high-heeled pumps and gold jewelry. She'd just come from church, but even so—

"I'm a legal secretary at a law firm in Omaha," Elena said, "and it's almost impossible for me to get extended time off without making a lot of arrangements in advance. Where are you from?"

"Well, I'm...I'm sort of in limbo right now. That's why I'm free to help out here until Jake can make other arrangements."

To Brittany's relief Wilhelm entered the conversation before Elena could question her further about her background. "If you have any problems when Jake's not around be sure to call us, Brittany, hear? Our home number and Elena's work number are in the card file right there by the phone. If you can't get me during the day, Elena is always available at work."

Brittany smiled. Jake's brother and sister-in-law were nice friendly people. "I'll do that," she assured him, "but I doubt that there will be any problems. The kids can direct me to the school and the nearest shopping center, and I know your mother's routine pretty well by now, so I don't expect any difficulty."

The meal was a pleasant one. The children were boisterous but well mannered, and it was obvious that the adults were not only family but also best friends.

At first the conversation centered around their concern for Gisela, then branched out to the damage done by the recent storm and finally settled on the day-by-day successes and failures of farming their adjoining property.

Brittany noticed that Jake and Elena called Wilhelm 'Will.' Apparently their mother was the only one who referred to her sons by their full names.

By the time they'd finished eating and Elena had helped Brittany clean up the kitchen while Dagmar finished her packing, it was time to take her to the airport.

As the two families got in their cars Brittany held back, trying not to get in the way but waiting to say goodbye to Dagmar. When she and Kurt and Heidi were seated in Jake's car he looked around and saw Brittany still standing off to the side.

"What's the matter? Did you forget something?" he asked her.

"Forget something?" What was he talking about?

He looked equally perplexed. "You don't mind sitting in back with the kids, do you?"

A cold shiver ran down her back. "Did you think I was going with you?"

He frowned. "Of course. Don't you want to see Mom off?"

He sounded almost offended.

Actually, it hadn't even occurred to her to go. No one had specifically invited her, nor had she expected them to, but now that Jake made it known that he wanted her to go along, the idea was repugnant.

Go back to that airport where she'd been terrorized by the image of Ronny just three days ago? No way! She'd be crazy even to consider it!

She cast around in her mind for an excuse not to go, but then her reasoning powers returned. Did she really think that Ronny Ralston, or any other man, would hang around the airport for three days on the wild chance that she just might come back?

Even if it had been him she'd seen that day—and the more she thought of it the less likely it seemed that it was—he'd either be checking out hotels and veterinarians in the area or he'd have returned to Independence.

"Brittany." She jumped when Jake's voice shook her out of her trance. "Are you going with us?"

He was standing by the car, waiting for her to make up her mind. She had to reach a decision one way or the other right now. Dagmar had a plane to catch.

"Yes, I'd love to," she said before she could change her mind. She'd have plenty of time to worry about her decision on the drive to Eppley Field.

Brittany was wrong about that, because Dagmar talked nonstop. She instructed Jake and the children to 'mind Brittany,' totally ignoring the fact that Jake was thirteen years older than Brittany and the head of the family.

Then she ticked off her list of activities and appointments, which Brittany would now be responsible for carrying out. "I promised to take a molded salad to Kurt's class picnic on the last day of school. I'll call tomorrow and give you the recipe. It isn't written down. Heidi has an appointment with the dentist on Friday. The time is noted on the calendar. Oh, and don't forget to take care of the chickens and weed and water the garden...."

Chickens and garden? But Brittany didn't know anything about chicken care and gardens!

On and on it went, until her head was spinning and her memory was saturated. Jake chuckled and turned to wink at her, but neither of them argued with his mother, the *Beloved Matriarch*. She was indispensable, and she knew it.

At the airport Jake parked at the curb and checked Dagmar's luggage, while Brittany's apprehension returned full force.

What had she been thinking of? She should never have come back here. Ronny was so unpredictable that she couldn't be sure what he'd do. The average man might not haunt an airport for days after a passenger failed to show up, but there was nothing average about her stalker!

It was only her near certainty that the man she'd seen wasn't Ronny, after all, that saved her from total panic. There was just no way he could have known she was catching that flight from Independence to Omaha. She hadn't discussed it with anyone but the police officer who'd been assigned to her case, and then only in the privacy of an empty office at the police station.

She'd been warned not to talk about her plans in her apartment or on her telephone because it was possible that her apartment was bugged. They'd searched and hadn't found anything, but that didn't mean that, with the cunning of a madman, Ronny hadn't managed to get in and bug it at a later date.

While Brittany and the children waited in the car for Jake and Dagmar to finish checking in her luggage, Will and his family came walking toward them from the lot where they'd parked their van. Kurt and Heidi scrambled out of the car to join their older cousins, but Brittany remained inside, loath to expose herself to the view of the milling crowds.

A short while later Jake came back and stooped to speak to her through the open window. "I have to move the car and park it. The rest of the family is going up to the gate where Mom's plane will be loading. Wouldn't you like to go with them?

No, she wouldn't! She wanted to crouch on the floor where nobody could see her.

"Could I . . . could I ride with you to the parking lot?"

Jake looked perplexed. "Well, sure, if you want to, but it's hardly worth the trip. It's just across the street."

"That's all right," she assured him.

He straightened and signaled the others to go on without her, then opened the front door and climbed in behind the wheel.

It only took a few minutes to find a space on the second floor of what turned out to be a parking *building*. He turned off the engine and got out to open the door for her.

She didn't want to get out, but neither did she want to stay in the car alone. If Ronny was still here watching for her and he found her in this nearly deserted garage there'd be no one to protect her from him.

She should have stayed at the farm, but she hadn't. Now she owed it to the Luthers' not to add to their distress by behaving like a frightened child.

She reached out and took the hand Jake offered, then stepped out of the car. But when they arrived at the door of the terminal she had to force herself to go inside.

As they went upstairs on the escalator to the proper loading gate her gaze roamed constantly from side to side, watching for a handsome young man with curly blond hair and blue eyes who looked like a choirboy and had the evil cunning of Mephistopheles.

By the time they reached the rest of the family she'd seen several who fit the physical description, but none of them were Ronny. After carefully checking the other passengers in the loading area she was able to relax somewhat as they waited for the call to board.

When it came it was almost a replay of her aborted leave-taking that morning, only more characters had been added and she and Dagmar had changed places. Now it was Jake's mother who was going away, and Brittany who would be staying with him and the children.

The thought made her tingle with anticipation, even though she knew that playing house with him was like playing with fire. She could get badly burned.

After hugs and kisses all around and last-minute instructions from and to Dagmar, she disappeared down the ramp and into the plane. The four children lined up at the window to watch it take off, and Brittany began to feel uneasy again. She didn't like the idea of lingering in the terminal, but the kids were insistent and their parents didn't mind waiting.

The seating area was empty now except for her and the Luthers, and she had no crowds to screen her from the big open view. Damn Ronny for making her so paranoid! She hated being afraid even when she had no real reason to be, and she wasn't going to insist on leaving immediately and deprive Kurt and Heidi of the excitement of seeing the huge planes take off and land.

She wouldn't do that to them. She doubted that they'd spent much time in airports and therefore seldom had the chance to see the spectacle.

Turning her back on the interior, she joined the children looking out the window. They were still loading baggage into the bowels of the jet, which meant it would be a few more minutes before it backed away and taxied out of sight.

Brittany shook her head to dislodge her frightening thoughts. She was just spooked. She didn't believe for a moment that Ronny was still around, if he ever had been. If she hadn't been convinced of that she'd never have come to the airport again.

Out of the corner of her eye she saw Jake, Will and Elena standing a short distance away, talking. She'd just started to relax, when a premonition brushed unseen fingers across the back of her neck, sending her muscles into spasm.

It was the same eerie feeling she'd had yesterday just before she'd wakened from her nap, fighting and screaming.

Someone was watching her intently!

She stood still, hardly daring to breathe. She shifted her gaze from side to side, but there was no one on her right, only Jake, Will and Elena on her left and the children in front of her.

Whoever was watching must be doing it from behind.

She didn't dare turn around and look. If it was Ronny this was an old trick of his. Those last few weeks in Independence when the police were searching for him he'd stay out of her sight for several days until she thought he'd finally tired of his maddening game.

Then, without warning, she'd feel a concentrated gaze at her nape, like a physical touch, and she'd look up to see him at a distance, smiling that cold evil smile of his that said as plain as if he had spoken, "you should know you can't get away from me."

It was no wonder her nerves were shot.

She was afraid he'd abduct her if he ever got the chance, but not in public. That wasn't Ronny's way. He was known to the public at large as the golden boy, the charmer, the man every mother wanted her daughter to marry.

He'd already made one mistake. He'd lost his fabled control after she'd broken up with him and had started dating other men, and he'd beaten her badly enough to leave marks and do physical damage that could be evaluated. It was only then that the police really believed the reports she'd been filing against him.

No, Ronny Ralston wouldn't tarnish his exalted image again. He'd stalk her secretly until he could lure her to a secluded place, and then . . .

She shuddered so violently that she was afraid Will's elder son, Scott, who was standing next to her, would notice, but his whole attention was centered on the airplane his grandmother was in, which had finally started to move.

She took a deep breath and tried to restrain her runaway fears. Refusing to confront her suspicion wasn't going to get her anyplace. She had to know if Ronny had found her, and the only way to find out was to turn around and look. If it was him he wouldn't go away until she did.

She closed her eyes and breathed a little prayer, then slowly turned.

There was a man standing there looking at her, but it wasn't Ronny. He was short with dark hair and hazel eyes, and he flushed when she glared at him. "Excuse me, miss," he said. "I . . . I thought you were someone I knew."

He looked embarrassed and walked quickly away, leaving her speechless and weak with relief.

They all left the terminal shortly after that and separated at the parking building, with promises to stay closely in touch. Then each family returned to their own vehicle.

The atmosphere in the car seemed strained on the ride home. The children were more subdued than usual, and Brittany was exhausted from the tension that had permeated the whole day.

She wasn't nearly as sure now as she had been earlier that she'd made the right decision in deciding to stay on with Jake and his children. It was the most humane thing she could have done, but probably not the wisest.

The tension that vibrated between them told her that Jake was having the same reservations. They were both hot-blooded adults, and smart enough to know that the sexual magnetism that pulled at them could easily get out of hand.

Well, they'd just have to make sure it didn't.

Back at the farm Jake and Kurt did the evening chores while Brittany and Heidi fixed a light supper, but the uneasiness persisted. At the table even the kids' chatter was toned down, and Brittany and Jake were excessively polite, like strangers trying to make conversation.

It was no wonder everyone was inhibited now that the excitement was over and Dagmar was gone. Everything had happened so fast.

The whole family had been in an uproar for most of the day, and now that all the decisions had been made, the problems handled and the action taken, no one was sure how to fill in the awkward silences.

When they finished eating Jake offered to help Brittany clean up the kitchen. She declined, sweetly but firmly, insisting that it would only take her a few minutes, and besides, he had enough to do outside without taking over her duties inside, as well.

He'd noticed that she'd been uncharacteristically jumpy all day, and at the airport she'd seemed on the verge of panic, but she obviously didn't want to discuss it with him and he sure didn't want to intrude on her privacy.

Instead, he excused himself and went to his office. He had plenty of book work and correspondence to keep him busy there, but once he sat down at the desk he couldn't concentrate on anything except the dilemma that now faced him.

Hell, he was as skittish as she was now that he had to confront a few home truths. It was going to be damned awkward living in the house with Brittany without any other adults around. Not only would he have to keep his own wayward impulses under control, but it wouldn't take long for gossip to circulate. Once tongues started wagging, people wouldn't bother to check with him and see if they had the facts straight before passing the gossip on.

If only Brittany weren't so drop-dead gorgeous. If she were even just the average beauty he could probably quiet the rumors down without much damage done, but not this young woman.

Brittany was stunning.

He ran his hands through his hair in frustration. He'd never known a woman quite like her before. Taken feature by feature she wasn't perfect. Her face was more round than oval, her nose was too large to be considered dainty and her lips had that slightly swollen look of a woman who's just been kissed.

Jake shifted in the chair and cursed the uncomfortable stirring in his crotch, but his mind continued its tormenting evaluation.

Pictures of her body would never appear in a fashion magazine. She wasn't skinny enough. Her breasts and hips were too pronounced. There was nothing bony about her. She was softly padded and roundly curved, with thighs that were fully outlined by the tight-fitting jeans she sometimes wore.

Probably her most nearly perfect features were her large almond-shaped hazel eyes with their long thick lashes and the abundant golden curly hair that spilled down her back to below her shoulder blades.

No, she wasn't fashion-model faultless; she was a hundred times better. She was earthy, sexy as hell and absolutely breathtaking.

There wasn't a man or woman in the whole area who would believe that his relationship with her was platonic.

Hell, he couldn't even convince his own eager body!

Chapter Seven

The following day Jake put an ad in the *Omaha World Herald* for a temporary housekeeper to care for a home and two school-age children, but by the end of the week it had attracted little response. Of those who did apply, the women interested in housekeeping didn't want to baby-sit, and the baby-sitters didn't want to keep house, and none of them wanted to live in the country.

For the first three days Brittany saw less of Jake than she had before. Although she got up at five o'clock every morning he was up and out of the house before that.

He came in at seven to have breakfast with her and the children, then she didn't see him again until noon. After dinner he disappeared until supper, and once the evening chores were done he helped the children with their homework, then disappeared into his office, where he stayed closeted until after she went to bed.

Not that she really minded. Actually, she was too overwhelmed with all the duties of keeping house on a farm to socialize, anyway. She'd had no idea what she was getting herself into!

She spent most of her time cooking, then cleaning up the kitchen so she could start cooking again. While she struggled with that the clutter piled up in the rest of the house.

Then there were the chickens. Good heavens, she'd always assumed they were born neatly dismembered in a tray at the meat counter! No one told her about feathers and beaks and claws, or the fact that they resented having their eggs taken out from under them.

She got Jake to show her how and when to feed them and gather the eggs, but she still saw no way that she could fit the gardening into her hectic schedule.

Dagmar had made it all look so easy! The woman must have the stamina of an Amazon.

Brittany began to identify more with Jake's ex-wife. Especially if he hadn't spent any more time with her than he did with Brittany.

On the other hand, even if Jake had wanted to spend his evenings with her, she'd have fallen asleep by nine o'clock. She went to bed right after she got the children tucked in and didn't wake up until the alarm went off the following morning.

On Thursday Brittany took a break. It was the last day of school, and the parents who had flexible working hours were encouraged to join their students for the playday and school picnic.

Brittany wasn't a parent, but Kurt and Heidi were eager for her to come and she'd agreed to. They were all excited at breakfast, and kept reminding her not to be late.

"I'll be there—I'll be there," she assured them, laughing. "Do you want me to dress up or can I wear jeans?"

"Wear jeans," Kurt said. "You can't play baseball in a dress."

"Baseball!" Her tone was more of a shriek than a question and she raised her stricken glance to Jake.

He threw back his head and laughed as Kurt modified his statement. "Well, it's softball, but all the grown-ups play. Teachers versus parents. They do it every year."

Brittany hadn't played softball since she was in the sixth grade, and even then she hadn't been good at it.

"But I'm not a ball player," she protested.

Jake reached across the table and patted her hand. "Don't worry. Neither are the rest of them. They just do it for fun and to entertain the kids." Again he laughed. "I'll bet you'll be the snappiest little hitter there."

Brittany groaned. "Why don't I muck out the barn and you play ball?" she suggested, not altogether flippantly.

"Aw, come on, Brittany," Kurt grumbled, obviously taking her seriously. "You can't be any worse than Tod's mom. She can't even run, but she always plays."

Apparently he wasn't going to be embarrassed if she made a fool of herself, and she certainly wasn't going to disappoint him. "Okay," she agreed, "but you're gonna be sorry when you see me try to hit a ball."

Jake surprised Brittany by staying at the house until it was time for the kids to walk to the bus stop.

"Don't forget," Heidi said as they prepared to leave. "You're s'posed to be at the park at ten o'clock."

The students were to be transported from the school to a nearby park by school buses.

"I won't," Brittany promised as she and Jake walked out the door with them.

"And don't forget to bring the salad," Kurt reminded her as they started toward the road.

"Don't worry. I made it last night," she called.

Brittany and Jake stood watching his son and daughter as they cavorted around each other down the driveway. The bus arrived a few minutes later, and she and Jake continued to watch until the children had boarded and the vehicle had rumbled on.

Then Jake turned to look at her. "Brittany," he said softly, "I know I haven't been much help to you since Mom left, and I want to tell you how much I appreciate all you've done for the kids and me."

"Oh, that's—" She'd started to say 'That's all right,' but Jake reached out and put his finger across her lips.

"No, let me finish. I realize that you're grossly overworked, and I'm going to do something about that. I didn't expect it to be so difficult to find a temporary housekeeper or I'd never have—"

Now it was her turn to interrupt. "Please, Jake, I can handle it. I'm just not as well organized as Dagmar—"

Again he pressed his finger to her lips. "You'll never be as organized as Mom. No newcomer could be. She's been keeping house for farmers since she started helping her own mother when she was about six years old. She's had fifty-seven more years of it than you have. The long hours and hard work are her way of life, and she refuses to let me hire someone to help her, but you can't keep up that pace. Even if you could I wouldn't allow it."

Brittany reached up and gently removed his hand from her mouth and held it between both of hers. It was big and strong and callused, but she knew from experience that it could also be gentle. "I appreciate your concern," she said breathlessly, "but there's a lot of work, and it has to be done. I don't see that we have any choice."

He clasped his fingers over one of her hands. "You've always had a choice, *Liebling*. This is my problem, not yours. You can walk away any time you want to. None of us would think any the less of you if you did, but if you're willing to stay on, then together we're going to find a way to make the tasks easier.''

A stab of uncertainty caught in the vicinity of her heart. He said it wasn't her problem, as if he didn't want to share his troubles with her. Was he really trying to tell her she was too inexperienced and he'd prefer to make other arrangements?

She cleared her throat and looked away, not wanting him to see how hurt and embarrassed she was.

"Do...do you want me to stay, Jake?"

Did he hesitate, or was she just overly conscious of a natural pause?

"Yes, I want you to stay," he murmured softly. "I want that more than I'm prepared to admit, but I won't try to keep you if you feel you've made a bad bargain."

A bad bargain? A foolish one, maybe, but being with Jake, knowing that he wanted her with him, even for just a few extra days, could never be bad.

Her hurt was replaced with gratitude that he was aware of how hard she worked and wanted to share the burden.

"But how can we make things easier?" she asked, seeing no way to cut down on the work load.

"I don't know, but I'm going to spend the day thinking about it. We'll start with the cooking. I know there's spaghetti in the fridge left over from yesterday. The kids and I will warm it up for supper."

"Oh, but—" She worked hard, but he labored even harder, and he had insisted on paying her for her services. She didn't like for him to have to fix his own meal, too.

"No 'buts,'" he warned with a frown. "You give some thought to other things Kurt, Heidi and I can do for ourselves, and we'll talk about it tonight. Okay?"

She knew it wouldn't do any good to argue with him, and he was right, she was on the verge of exhaustion.

"Okay," she agreed, "and Jake, thanks for caring."

His expression softened, and his mouth turned up at the corners in a tenuous smile. "Oh, I care, Brittany," he said just above a whisper. "I care very much."

Brittany had no trouble finding the small forest of huge old oak trees mixed with cottonwood and hackberry that housed the park. Jake had drawn her a map and she drove Dagmar's car, which he had put at her disposal after insisting she return her rental, right to it.

The buses had already arrived and discharged their passengers, who were now busy unloading the food and play equipment. Heidi spotted Brittany as she walked across the lawn and came running to meet her.

"Brittany, we're over here. You can put the cooler under the tree with the others." She was referring to the ice chest in which Brittany had brought her molded vegetable salad.

The little girl took Brittany's free hand and skipped happily along beside her, stopping every few feet to latch onto another friend and announce, "This is Brittany. She's living with us."

As they neared the row of tables where the covered potluck dishes of food were being set out, Heidi spied a middle-aged woman dressed in brown slacks and an orange plaid blouse, who was talking to a little boy. "There's my teacher!" she exclaimed. "Come and meet her."

She tugged on Brittany's hand and pulled her along as she called, "Mrs. Young! Mrs. Young!"

The woman looked up and the boy took off in the other direction. "Hello, Heidi," she said, then shifted her glance to Brittany.

"Look, Brittany's here," Heidi said. "She takes care of me and Kurt. And Daddy, too," she added.

Mrs. Young's eyes widened with surprise. "*You're* the new housekeeper?"

Brittany wondered why she looked so shocked. "Well, not exactly," she explained. "I'm just a . . . a friend of the family helping out until Jake, uh, Heidi's father can find someone."

Darn. The woman's pointed stare had made her stammer with nervousness, but she didn't have anything to be nervous about.

"Oh. Well, I shouldn't think it would take long to find a qualified person. There's a lot of unemployment around here," Mrs. Young observed.

Heidi's teacher's words were innocent enough, but her tone sounded almost...disapproving. Brittany wondered if she'd missed something in this conversation.

"He hasn't had any luck so far," she said. "If you hear of anyone who's interested in a temporary housekeeping position Jake would appreciate it if you'd refer them to him."

"I'll just bet he would," Mrs. Young muttered, then quickly changed the subject. "We at the school were so sorry to hear about Mrs. Luther's daughter's accident. Mrs. Luther is such a dear. How is Gisela?"

"She's still in traction in the hospital, but they expect her to be able to go home in a few days."

The teacher nodded. "That's good. Then Mrs. Luther will probably be coming home shortly afterward."

It was a statement rather than a question, and Brittany decided not to deny it, although it would be weeks before Gisela would be able to get around well enough to care for her children.

When Jake came home that evening for supper he was greeted by his exuberant son and daughter as a weary Brittany watched from the open kitchen window.

"Daddy! Daddy! Guess what!" Kurt called.

Heidi beat him to the punch. "Brittany hit a house run!"

Kurt stuck out his tongue at her, but Brittany couldn't stifle a giggle at the little girl's mispronunciation.

"That's *home* run, dummy," Kurt grumbled, mad about having his thunder stolen but determined to be first to tell the rest of the story. "She batted the ball clear into the forest, then ran three bases and slid into home on her butt."

She winced and rubbed said throbbing posterior as Jake frowned and looked toward the house. He saw her standing at the window and called, "Did you hurt yourself?"

She grinned. "Let me put it this way," she called back. "I'll be eating my meals standing up for the next few days."

He laughed and reached the back porch in three long leaps as the children took off in opposite directions, then he bounded through the laundry room door and into the kitchen, where he stopped and stared. "My God, what happened to your arm?" he demanded as his disbelieving gaze centered on the heavily bandaged lower part of her left limb.

Oh, dear. All she ever seemed able to do was upset him. "It's not nearly as bad as it looks. We were having three-legged races. Heidi and I did just fine, but then Kurt wanted me to be a partner with him. We started out doing great, but then I twisted my foot, veered off course and we fell. I hit my arm against a low tree limb. It...it bled quite a bit, but the cut was really not very deep."

Jake groaned and struck his forehead with the heel of his hand. "Good God, woman, you're a walking disaster. How many stitches did you need?"

"Oh, I didn't go to a doctor," she admitted. "I'm up to date on my tetanus shots, and the school nurse was there, so she disinfected and medicated the wound. She only put all this gauze around it so I wouldn't get dirt in it in case I..."

Laughter bubbled from her throat. "I'm afraid they think I'm pretty much of a klutz, what with the fading bruises on my face, my black-and-blue...um...derriere and the scratch on my arm."

"They're more likely to think I'm beating you," Jake growled, but then his expression lightened. "And tell me, Ms. Castle, how does the whole school know you're derriere is black and blue?"

She assumed an impish grin. "Well-l-l, if they don't they're sadly deficient in imagination. I tripped and fell on it and slid most of the way from third base to home."

Jake surprised her by walking over and taking her in his arms. "Brittany, what am I going to do with you?" he murmured tenderly, and pulled her close. "You keep me in a constant state of anxiety. You'll make an old man of me if this keeps up."

She put her arms around his waist and snuggled into his embrace. "I'm sorry. I know I'm more bother than help to you."

"I didn't say that," he protested. "I don't know how I'd have coped without you these past few days, but you can't keep up this pace. Now, go in the living room and sit down—"

Brittany winced. "Please, don't even mention 'sit.'"

Jake stroked his hands lightly over her sore buttocks. It was a tender caress with no hint of impropriety. "Poor baby," he said, his tone vibrating with sympathy, then he raised his hands to position them again at her waist. "Okay, then, *lie* down while I warm up the spaghetti and make a salad."

"That won't be necessary," she assured him. "The spaghetti and French bread are in the oven, and the salad's in the refrigerator. We can eat as soon as you get washed up."

He held her away from him and scowled. "Why did you do that? I told you I'd fix supper."

She put her palms on his chest and looked up at him. "I know," she said apologetically, "but you work so hard all day long, and besides, cooking is my job."

Again he folded her into his arms, and this time he rubbed his face in her hair. "Honey, that's a pretty chauvinistic thing to say. What's this nonsense about women's work and men's work?"

She raised her head to glare at him. "I didn't say that—"

"Maybe not in so many words, but you were implying that women work in the house and men toil in the fields."

She pulled out of his embrace. "Well, that's pretty much the way it is on this farm," she said huffily. "I notice you haven't asked me to slop the hogs."

She saw the wicked grin that Jake quickly banished. "Sweetheart, you're more than welcome to slop the hogs if you want to. I wouldn't dream of denying you the pleasure just because it isn't generally considered 'women's work.'"

Darn him, he was baiting her, but she couldn't keep from rising to it. "Ohh, you know what I mean," she snapped, barely able to stop herself from stamping her foot in exasperation. "You're paying me to keep house and baby-sit, and that's what I'm trying to do. If you could do it yourself and still work the farm then you wouldn't need me."

An odd expression crossed his face, and without a word he scooped her up in his arms and carried her into the living room, where he laid her carefully on the sofa.

"Stay there," he ordered when she tried to roll over. "Don't move. I'll be right back."

He walked out of the room and up the stairs, returning a couple of minutes later with three large bed pillows. Brittany had been too astounded to do anything but obey him, and now he issued another order. "Raise your hips."

She dug her heels into the cushion and bowed her body. He slid one of the pillows under her bruised buttocks, then settled her down onto the feathery softness.

Before she could protest he put his arm around her shoulders and lifted her to prop the other two pillows under her back and head. She sank gratefully into the cloud-like comfort and sighed.

"Let's get one thing straight." His tone was strictly no-nonsense. "You're right, I am paying you to work for me, and that entitles me to choose the tasks you'll perform, so listen up.

"You do not have to keep house the way my mother does. She still does things the way her mother did them, but there are a lot of shortcuts you can take. For one thing, the kids and I can clean our own rooms. Also, now that school's out there's no longer any need for you to get up until you wake up naturally. The kids and I can also get our own breakfast."

Brittany opened her mouth to say something, but Jake held up his hand. "No, don't talk, just listen. A lot of time and effort can be saved on cooking, but we'll discuss that after we eat."

He picked up her hand and rubbed it against his bristly cheek. "Just remember what you said. I can't handle all the work around here by myself. Even if I could I'd still need you, and that's why I'm not going to let you work yourself to death. Now relax and doze if you can until I bring your supper on a tray."

He put her hand back down on her stomach and left.

Brittany snuggled into the pillows, still stunned by his unexpected outburst. She could get used to this kind of treatment awfully fast. It was powerfully tempting just to relax and enjoy it, but that would be selfish. Jake must be just as tired as she was. After supper she'd insist on cleaning up the kitchen.

She broached the subject after they'd finished eating, but Jake wouldn't hear of it. Instead he removed her tray of dirty dishes, and a few minutes later she heard him stacking the dishwasher. When he completed that task he called to Kurt to come and help him with the evening chores. They took off with Heidi following closely on their heels, afraid of being left out of something exciting.

When Brittany was sure they were safely away from the house she rolled stiffly off the sofa and moaned as her tortured muscles clenched. She hadn't known the human body had so many, and every single one of them hurt.

She stumbled toward the utility room. It was sweet of Jake to want to make things easier for her, but she hadn't had time to do the laundry today, and it piled up at an amazing rate if she didn't keep on top of it.

After she'd loaded the washer and turned it on she set up the ironing board in a corner of the living room where she could be out of the way but could still watch television while she ironed. This was one chore she really hated and seldom did. Most of her clothes were wash-and-wear, and those that weren't needed to be dry-cleaned, but Dagmar ironed everything.

The basket Brittany brought from the utility room was filled to overflowing, and she put it on the floor beside her with a sigh. Oh, well, since she couldn't sit she might as well stand and iron.

As Jake and Kurt finished up the usual chores in the barn Jake decided it was time to introduce the talk he'd planned to have with his son. He pulled off his work gloves and tossed them onto a barrel, then pushed his Stetson back off his forehead.

"Kurt," he called to the boy, who was putting away some hand tools. "You almost finished with that?"

"Yeah, Dad. Where does this electric drill go?"

"Put it back in the case, then put the case on a shelf of the wall cabinet. After you've done that, come over here. I want to talk to you."

"Okay," the boy said, and Jake watched as Kurt did as he'd been told.

He was a good kid. Took directions well, and didn't object too strenuously to the chores he was assigned. He seemed to like living on the farm, for which Jake was immensely grateful.

Jake sat down on a bale of hay, and when Kurt came over he motioned for the boy to sit beside him.

"Hey, Dad, you ain't gonna make me go to summer school, after all, are you?" he asked as he settled himself beside his father.

"'Aren't,'" Jake corrected absently, then chuckled. "No son, but you may wish I would after you hear what I am going to do."

Kurt eyed him warily. "Yeah?"

"Yeah," Jake said, and ruffled the boy's black hair, which was so like his own. "You know that Grandma's going to have to stay at Aunt Gisela's for quite a while, don't you?"

Kurt looked down at the floor "I 'spect so. Is Aunt Gisela ever gonna get well?"

Jake felt a twinge of guilt. He hadn't realized that Kurt had doubts about that. He reached out and put his arm around his son's shoulders. "Sure she is, but it will take time for her leg to heal enough for her to take care of her two little girls. She needs Grandma to help her, and we don't want Grandma to worry about us, too, do we." It was a statement, not a question.

"No, sir," Kurt said solemnly.

"Then can I count on you to help Brittany with some of the work she has to do. She's a city girl and isn't used to such long hours and hard work. We don't want her to get sick from trying to do too much."

Kurt looked up at Jake. "Oh, Brittany won't get sick. She's strong." Jake saw the admiration beaming from his young son's face. "You shoulda seen her hit that home run. Boy, she socked that ol' ball so far into the brush we never did find it. And then you shoulda seen her run around them bases—"

"'Those,'" Jake corrected.

"Yeah, those," Kurt amended without missing a beat. "Gee, can that lady move!"

Jake had a hard time keeping a straight face. "I'm sure she's very athletic," he said patiently, "but she's not used to farm work, and putting in such long hours. If we don't make things easier for her she's apt to leave, and we don't want that, do we?"

Kurt's expression sobered. "You mean like Mom?"

Jake winced, and wished he'd phrased that last sentence differently. He knew the hurt of Tina's desertion was never far below the surface with his children.

"No, son," he said carefully, not wanting to criticize Kurt's mother but still unwilling to compare Brittany with her. "Brittany isn't a relative, or even a long-time friend, so she has no obligation or duty to stay here and take care of you and Heidi and me while Grandma is away. She's only doing it because she's a nice person and wants to help us out. In return we don't want to make her work so hard that she decides to quit and get on with her own life."

Jake paused and looked at the boy, unsure whether he was getting through to him. "Do you understand what I'm saying, Kurt?"

"Yeah, I guess so," Kurt said, "but what are we going to do to help her?"

Jake took a deep breath and plunged ahead. "Well, for starters we can all clean our own bedrooms, make our own beds, put our dirty clothes in the hamper and keep our things picked up. Even Heidi can do that.

"I'll start cooking breakfast and doing the heavier housecleaning, and I'd like for you to take over the care of the chickens and the garden. Do you think you can do that?''

Kurt's face clouded. "Ah, gee, Dad . . ." he moaned, but then paused. "Yeah, I guess I can," he admitted reluctantly, "but shucks, I can't tell the weeds from the vegetables."

Jake's chest swelled with pride in his son. He'd expected more of an argument.

"That's okay," he said, and put out his hand. "I'll teach you. You're a smart kid. You'll learn with no trouble at all.

Kurt flushed and took his father's hand in a hard grip. "I like Brittany," he said. "I want her to stay."

"So do I," Jake answered.

God help me, so do I.

Chapter Eight

The hunt for a housekeeper dragged on with no success, but after Jake had clearly defined Brittany's duties the work was much easier for her.

She still did all the cooking, but now she did it her way instead of Dagmar's. Using cake mixes, frozen pies, delicatessen lasagna and an occasional Chinese carryout from a restaurant in Blair, her food preparation time was cut in half.

With Kurt taking over the care of the chickens and garden, Brittany had time to keep the big old house neat and the laundry current. Especially after Jake had declared ironing a no-no when he'd caught her doing it last Thursday after he'd told her to lie on the couch and do nothing more strenuous than watch television.

"No one irons bedding anymore," he'd insisted when he'd seen her pressing pillow cases.

"Your mother does," she'd reminded him.

"My mother's stuck in the Middle Ages and not about to change, but you can bet I'd never find another housekeeper to do it. And that goes for everything else we use or wear. If anyone in this family wants something ironed they can do it themselves."

That was the night he'd spelled out exactly what her duties as an employee were and were not. He'd even typed them into the computer so he could make copies and give them to the women he interviewed.

So far he hadn't had any applicants to try them out on.

On Sunday, just a week after Dagmar had left, they again made plans to go to church. This time Brittany was going with them, and they'd all been invited to Will and Elena's house for dinner afterward.

Brittany couldn't have been more excited if she'd had a date with Randy Travis to have lunch at the Four Seasons, but she wasn't sure why. Certainly the prospect of going to church had never been all that thrilling before. Her grandparents had insisted that she accompany them every Sunday when she'd lived in Raindance, but since then her attendance had been spotty at best.

And while she looked forward to eating a dinner she didn't have to cook, she was sure it would be the same plain fare that Jake and his family enjoyed. Hardworking farmers seldom hungered for poached hummingbird under glass.

She applied makeup sparingly but with an expertise that hid any imperfections and highlighted her good points. The dress she chose was not new but one of her favorites. It was a peach linen coat style that buttoned off center on the right side. At mid-knee, it was long enough to be dignified.

She brushed her hair back on the sides and fastened it high with a bow so that it was off her face and shoulders but still spilled down her back in a mass of curls. Would Jake like the way she looked? Would his friends think she was pretty but not flashy?

A glance at her watch told her it was almost time to leave. She picked up her purse, and, with a last look in the full-length mirror, hurried downstairs.

Brittany found Heidi and Kurt in the living room, watching a cartoon on television. They were dressed in the same clothes they'd had on last Sunday morning.

Heidi apparently had heard Brittany's high heels on the wooden stairs and looked up as she came into the room. "Oh, you look beautiful," the little girl said.

"Yes, she certainly does," confirmed Jake from behind her.

A flush of pleasure swept through Brittany as she turned and nearly bumped into him. There was admiration in his dark eyes as he cupped her shoulders in his hands and held her away from him.

"She looks beautiful, indeed," he murmured as his gaze roamed over her. "Desirable enough to make a man forget all his good intentions," he continued softly, for her ears only, and his hands tightened on her shoulders.

She felt her flush deepen. She'd like nothing more than to have him forget his good intentions and kiss her, right here and now, in front of the children and anybody else who happened by.

So much for her lofty resolve.

Jake was darn near irresistible, too, in a navy-blue suit, white shirt and paisley tie. A lock of black hair had fallen across his forehead, and she reached out and stroked it back. His hands tightened again on her shoulders.

For a moment they just stood there looking at each other, the magnetism between them too strong to break. She wasn't conscious of moving, but their bodies were no longer several inches apart. They were almost touching as she raised her head and he lowered his.

She could feel his breath on her mouth, and she parted her lips and closed her eyes, unaware of anything but the seductive force that pulled them ever closer.

"Hey, Dad, it's almost eleven. Are we goin' or what?"

It was Kurt who broke the spell, and the trauma of it shook Brittany all the way to her toes.

Jake seemed equally affected as they wrested themselves apart, but he was the first one to find his voice. "Yeah, we're going." His tone was sharper than he'd probably intended. "Everyone get in the car. Now!"

Brittany was too shaken from the intensity of their encounter to pay attention to where they were going as they sped along the road. She'd assumed they were headed for either Blair or Omaha, and was surprised when they parked in the lot adjacent to a quaint old white wooden church, complete with a steeple, to see that they were still in the country.

It was a picture-postcard setting, with green rolling hills dotted with chokecherry and wild plum shrubs and stands of cottonwood, elm and ash trees. The ancient building had been well kept up, and was protected by several large silver maples.

The yard in front was deserted and strains of organ music accompanying the congregation in the singing of a hymn wafted through the air as Jake, Brittany, Kurt and Heidi got out of the car.

"You two go on to your Sunday-school classes," Jake directed the kids, who went scooting off toward the back of the structure.

"I'm afraid we're late," he said as he took Brittany's hand and put it in the crook of his elbow. "You're going to create a sensation, you know. I hope you don't mind."

No, she didn't know. She had no idea what he was talking about, but once they opened the door and started walking down the center aisle she found out.

The singing ended as Jake pulled the door open, and the sound of their footsteps on the uncarpeted floor caused all heads to turn. Self-consciously Brittany withdrew her hand from his arm. She wished she could sink through the floor as the congregation watched them walk toward the front.

Jake didn't seem at all perturbed as he smiled and nodded from one side to the other until they came to the third row. Then he stood back so she could precede him and they sat down together.

She clasped her hands in her lap as the minister announced the scripture reading.

Once more she had that cold tingle at the back of her neck, but this time she knew she was being watched. Good heavens, was it so unusual for Jake to bring a woman other than his mother or his daughter to church? And if so, why was it of such interest to everyone present?

Surely in a congregation as small as this one the word had gotten around about Gisela's accident and Dagmar's hurried departure to care for her daughter's family. They would also know that Jake had a temporary housekeeper, so why were they all so... so... The only word that seemed appropriate was *shocked*.

Brittany's attention was brought back to the service when she realized that the choir was singing an anthem that was familiar to her. There were a small group—six men and seven woman—but they were well trained and the music was soothing to the spirit, as well as the nerves.

Next the minister, fiftyish with glasses and a receding hairline, reported on the calendar of activities at the church for the coming week and any news of the members.

"I spoke with Jake Luther yesterday," he said at one point, "and he says Gisela is out of the hospital now, but won't be able to walk for a few more weeks, so Dagmar won't be returning for a while."

He looked at Jake. "Jake, wouldn't you like to introduce your guest?"

Brittany wanted to curl up in a ball under the pew, but Jake smiled and stood, then stepped into the aisle and turned to face the people. "Thanks, Pastor Gunner," he said, then turned to Brittany and held out his hand.

Oh, no! He wanted her to stand.

That was the last thing she wanted to do, but she couldn't leave him there all alone. She stood and joined him in the aisle.

"I'd like to introduce Brittany Castle, a friend of our family who is helping out in this crisis by taking care of the children and the house until I can find a housekeeper."

While he talked Brittany scanned the audience, which she took to be mostly farmers and their families, and spotted Will and Elena sitting among them, beaming.

The congregation clapped, surprising Brittany—her own church was seldom that spontaneous. But the applause created a warm feeling of welcome, and she smiled and nodded before taking her seat again.

As the service continued Brittany looked around her. It was a lovely little sanctuary, plain with no frills except for a large stunningly beautiful stained-glass window on one side wall. It didn't depict the usual biblical scene, but was a riot of colorful flowers and vines that brightened the room with the impression of perpetual sunshine. A sparkling reminder that nature blooms anew every spring.

She wondered if Jake had been married here. Probably not if his wife was a "city girl," as Dagmar had described her. They'd likely taken their vows in one of the big churches in Omaha.

Will and Elena's wedding may have taken place here, and almost certainly Gisela's had. Maybe Dagmar's, too, since she'd indicated that she'd lived in the area ever since coming to this country when she was a child.

A wave of envy swept over Brittany. It must be comforting to know that your kinsmen had been a part of the same community for generations. A family whose roots were planted deep in the earth, and whose history was also the history of their neighbors.

It was shortly after noon when the last hymn had been sung and the benediction delivered, and the congregation began to file out. The minister stood at the door to shake hands and chat for a moment with the people as they passed by.

He smiled as Brittany and Jake approached, and put out his hand to her. "Welcome, Miss Castle," he said pleasantly. "We hope to see you often while you're here."

She shook his hand. "Thank you, Pastor, but I'll be leaving as soon as Jake finds more permanent help."

It seemed to her that the pastor looked momentarily relieved, but the expression changed so quickly that she decided she was wrong.

He released her hand and took Jake's. "If you'd like I'll make some inquiries in the area. I may be able to find someone who's looking for a temporary position."

Brittany wasn't sure whether Jake hesitated or just took a breath before answering.

"Thanks, Gunner, I'd appreciate it. Brittany just stopped by on her way through Omaha to visit friends in the West and got caught in our family emergency. I don't want to detain her any longer than necessary."

Brittany blinked and opened her mouth to deny that she was in a hurry to leave, but he gave her a stern look and prodded her gently but firmly along.

During the time they'd been inside the sky had clouded over and a light breeze had sprung up. It hadn't rained again since the night Brittany had landed in Omaha and had been dumped so unceremoniously on the Luther family. She shivered and rubbed her arms, although the air was still warm.

"Are you chilly?" Jake inquired as they descended the stairs from the porch to the sidewalk.

"No, not chilly," she answered. "Just apprehensive. I hope if this turns into a storm it's not as vicious as the last one."

He put his hand at the back of her waist. "It's not likely to be," he assured her. "Our storms are usually nowhere near that bad."

Brittany noticed that the worshipers didn't go immediately to their cars, but strolled around the vast lawn surrounding the church and formed clusters as they stopped to visit with one another. She and Jake had barely reached the bottom of the steps before they, too, were surrounded.

Jake introduced her to several couples and a sprinkling of singles. At first the questions and comments revolved around Gisela and how she was getting along, but then they turned their attention to Brittany and became more personal.

"Where are you from?" "How long will you be here?" "What do you do for a living?" "Have you known the Luther's long?"

The questions were thrown at her so fast that she didn't have a chance to answer any of them, but it occurred to her, belatedly to be sure, that she didn't want all this attention. After her momentary relapse into terror at the airport, Brittany had all but put Ronny, her stalker, out of her mind.

She was absolutely certain that she'd been mistaken when she'd thought she's seen him, but still there was no point in giving out information that could help him to find her if he ever did manage to trace her to Omaha.

The confusion of several people speaking at once gave her the few minutes she needed to get her thoughts in order. Then she spoke to the group as a whole.

"I'm sort of in transition right now," she began. "My former employer sold his business, and the new owner had his own staff, so I decided to take this opportunity to visit relatives in California. That's where I'll be headed when I leave here."

A man whom Jake had introduced as his insurance agent spoke up. "What kind of job are you looking for? I may be able to help. If you're interested in staying here I need a secretary."

Brittany groaned inwardly. She'd worded her little speech so that she wouldn't give away her vocation. A veterinary technician was just unusual enough to be memorable.

"Well, I... um..."

At that moment she spotted Will and Elena walking toward them. Thank God, a distraction.

She waved and said, "Oh, there's Will and Elena. We're having dinner with them, and I guess they're ready to leave."

She put her arm through Jake's and tugged—unobtrusively, she hoped. "We'd better go, too." Looking around the group, she gave them an all-inclusive smile. "It was awfully nice to meet you," she said, and walked away, practically pulling Jake along with her.

"Brittany, you look lovely," Elena said as the two couples came together. "No wonder Jake's been keeping you under wraps. He'll probably have to beat the young men off with a stick now that he's introduced you to the community."

"He hasn't been keeping me under wraps," she protested. "We've been too busy to go anywhere. I'm not the most efficient housekeeper in the world."

She noticed that Jake gave Elena a quelling look, which Will intercepted just before Jake snapped, "Brittany's here to look after the kids, not to entertain a pack of lusty jocks."

Brittany bristled. Lusty jocks, indeed. Where did he get off thinking she made a habit of—

"Hit a nerve, did I, brother-in-law?" Elena's eyes had narrowed and her tone was sardonic. "Well, sorry, I was only kidding. So what happened to your sense of humor?"

It was then that Will stepped in. "Hey, lighten up, you two." He put his hand on his wife's arm. "Honey, you'd better go round up the boys so we can get on home. It looks like it's going to rain, and we left all the windows open."

Elena smiled and turned to Brittany. "See you a little later," she said, and walked away.

Jake didn't linger, either. "I think we'd better go back home and close things up, too, before we come to your house," he said to his brother. "We won't be long."

Again he put his hand on Brittany's back. "Come on, we'll have to find the kids. They're probably still having cookies and juice in their classrooms."

On the way home Jake seemed moody, withdrawn. He spoke only when spoken to, and Brittany tried to fill the silences with chatter so the children wouldn't notice. She didn't know what was wrong with him, but assumed it had something to do with that verbal skirmish with Elena. But why would something as harmless as a little teasing upset him?

Back at the house they all changed out of their good clothes, then Brittany shut the windows while Kurt took care of the chickens and Jake secured the barn. When it bothered to rain in the Midwest it usually came down pretty hard.

While she waited for them to finish their chores she folded the clean clothes and took them upstairs to put away. She entered Jake's room last. It was the master-bedroom suite, large with a private bathroom, a fireplace and windows that looked out on both the front and side yards.

He must have redecorated after his wife had left, because the decor was strictly masculine. Heavy solid wood furniture, neutral colors and no knickknacks. The only decorations were a framed photograph of Will and Jake holding a string of large fish between them, on the dresser, and an oil painting of a sunset on the prairie, hanging on the wall over the bed.

Brittany was putting his clothes in the dresser drawers, when he suddenly appeared in the doorway. "I told you I'd take care of my own room, didn't I?" He didn't sound angry, just amused.

"Well I... I was just putting your clothes away. I folded them in the utility room, and it was just as easy to bring them up and put them in the drawers as on the bed."

"Don't apologize." He grinned and leaned against the doorjamb. "If you enjoy handling my underwear I'm not going to stop you."

She dropped the stack of briefs she was holding. "Jake! I'm not *handling* your underwear." She felt the hot blush that stained her cheeks, but there was also a melting heat in the most intimate parts of her body.

He chuckled, then walked over and stooped to pick up the garments. "Then what do you call it?" he asked, and handed them to her.

Without thinking she reached out and took them, then dropped them again when he laughed and took her in his arms. He hugged her close and she put her arms around his neck and snuggled against him.

"Oh, sweetheart," he murmured, his lips against her cheek, "Elena was right. From now on I will have to beat the men who want to take you out off with a stick. And don't think I won't."

Brittany's heart pounded. "Is that what upset you so? But why? She was just teasing."

His hands roamed over her back and brushed the sides of her breasts in a tantalizing caress. "Because the thought of you going out with some of the studs around here is more than I can bear." His tone was rough. "Hell, the thought of you going out with *any* other man drives me crazy."

"I don't remember expressing a burning desire to go out with any other men," she said, and kneaded his nape tenderly.

He sighed and nuzzled her temple. "You didn't tell me you had relatives in California that you were going to visit, either, even when I specifically asked you where you were going after your stay in Raindance."

There was hurt in his tone, and she realized that he didn't know she'd been lying.

"I just said that because it was easier than trying to explain why I'm wandering around with no job and no home," she explained. "I don't have relatives in California, and I haven't made plans to go there. I was telling you the truth when I said I don't know what I'm going to do after the class reunion."

He didn't answer, just continued to hold her close, but she knew he was still troubled.

She raised her head to look at him. "Jake, tell me what's really the matter. I'm not in the habit of lying, if that's what's bothering you. I just... Well, I don't know those people, and I didn't want to go into a lot of long-winded explanations. But they were your friends and I didn't want to be rude, so I just improvised a little. Who knows, maybe I will go to California before I find a place to settle."

He lowered his face and kissed her square on the lips. She felt the tremor that shook them both, but when she tried to deepen the kiss he broke it off and settled her head against his chest once more, instead.

"Don't," he begged raggedly. "If we do that again we'll never make it to Will's for dinner or supper or even breakfast. I don't have much self-control where you're concerned, and what little I had is totally shot."

She loved hearing him talk like that, but it was scary, too. She knew this relationship had no future, but she also knew that in the short time she'd been here it had advanced way past friendship.

"What is it you want of me, Jake?" Her voice shook with emotion.

He groaned and rubbed his face in her hair. "I wish to God I knew. None of this is your fault, Brittany. I'm the one who's probably damaged beyond curing. My marriage was a disaster. Not that it was all Tina's fault. I've come to realize that we were equally to blame. We had absolutely nothing in common but a flaming lust for each other, and when that burned itself out all we had left were two innocent kids who were doomed to the torment of being raised in a broken family."

Brittany couldn't let that statement go unchallenged. She pulled back and looked at him. "Your family isn't dysfunctional! You and Dagmar are doing a great job of raising them."

He released her and turned away. "My children are entitled to a mother and a father. Mom has been wonderful. I don't know what I'd do without her, and I'm certainly not making light of her role in the kids' lives, but grandmothers are supposed to be the icing on the cake, not the cake itself."

He ran his fingers through his hair and began to pace. "My children have a mother who ignores them, and neither Mom nor I can fill that void or protect them from the pain of being abandoned. I have no intention of opening myself up for that kind of torment again, and I'm sure not going to set my children up with a stepmother who might take off when she got bored or fed up with me."

Brittany could understand his caution, but he was being awfully unfair to all the decent, loving women who took their commitment to marriage and family seriously.

"Jake, I can understand your disillusionment with your ex-wife, but you shouldn't blame all women for her shortcomings."

He turned and looked at her. "I know that," he said hoarsely, "but obviously I'm not a good judge of character. When I look back I can see that both Tina and I should have recognized the fact that we wanted different things from life, but we were too caught up by the heat of the sexual attraction between us to care. I can't take the chance of that happening again. I don't want another woman in my life. At least not until Kurt and Heidi are grown. I owe it to them to protect them from my mistakes."

How could she argue with him? He'd obviously given this a lot of thought and had his mind made up. She'd only lay herself open for a lot of anguish if this attraction between them went any further.

They left shortly after that and by the time they arrived at Will's it was pouring rain. His house was a one-story rambling type commonly known as ranch-style. It was newer and more modern than Jake's, but without the charm and old-fashioned grace of the family home.

Brittany's mood lightened as she worked in the kitchen beside Elena, mashing potatoes and creaming the peas while the other woman dished the fried chicken onto a platter and made gravy. The sound of rain pelting the roof added an extra dimension to the warm intimacy of the family gathering, and Brittany felt included.

The banter around the table during dinner was both interesting and informative to Brittany. She learned that Will and Elena's two teenage sons were involved in 4H and that Scott, the elder, was planning to major in agriculture when he started at the university next semester.

"Did you major in agriculture in college?" she asked Jake.

"I did the first two years," he said, "but then I joined the marines. By the time I went back to get my degree I was working as a police officer, so I switched to social science."

"Comes in real handy, too," Will said with a grin. "If his corn's slow about growing he just goes out and has a few counseling sessions with it and it pops right up."

Jake eyed his brother fondly and chuckled. "You nut. Tease if you want to, but you have to admit that my cows give more milk than yours do."

Will hooted. "Would you believe it, my little brother here actually pipes 'contented' music into his barn."

They all laughed, enjoying one another's company as well as the meal.

Afterward Elena and Brittany cleaned up the dishes while Jake and his brother went out to the holding pen to inspect the steers Will was raising for market. The rain had stopped by then, so they walked instead of driving the truck.

Later, as the two men walked back to the house, the conversation took an abrupt turn.

"Jake, you can tell me it's none of my business if you want to," Will said, "but there's something I'd like to talk to you about."

Oh-oh! Jake thought. When he starts out like that I know he's going to ask questions I don't want to answer.

"Then I'll tell you right now—it's none of your business," he said good-naturedly. "But go ahead. You will, anyway."

"Smart-ass," Will said, and slapped him on the shoulder. "This is important. What's going on between you and Brittany?"

Jake was taken aback by his brother's brashness, and he reacted angrily. "You're right, it is none of your damn business. What in hell do you think is going on?"

"I don't know. That's why I'm asking you. After this morning you two have tongues wagging all over the county."

Jake muttered an oath. "That's crazy. I need help looking after the kids and Brittany is supplying it. I'm not sleeping with her, if that's what you mean."

"I didn't think you were," Will assured him, "but don't try to make me believe you don't want to."

A hot flush of both rage and guilt swept through Jake. "Now, that damn sure is none of your business! Where do you get off prying into my private personal life?"

Will stopped walking and put his hand on Jake's arm to stop him, too. "For God's sake, Jake, quit spouting off and listen to me. When you started playing house with Brittany your right to privacy got trampled in the stampede."

Jake's hands knotted into fists. "I'm not playing house—"

"The hell you're not," Will roared. "When you moved that girl in with you and the kids—"

"She's not a girl," Jake objected. "She's a young woman—"

Will nodded grimly. "So the age difference bothers you, too. How old did mom say she is? Twenty-five? That's young, man, considering that you're thirty-eight. You know how people are around here. Everyone knows everyone else's business and there's no such thing as privacy."

Jake slumped and sat down on a stump, rubbing his knee. "Damn it to hell, haven't I got enough problems without a batch of gossiping busybodies complicating things? I need Brittany!"

"That's exactly what I'm afraid of," Will said sadly, then held up his hand in surrender when Jake raised his head and glowered at him.

"No offense meant, Jake. I just don't want to see you hurt again, and I'm afraid Brittany has the potential to do just that without even trying. If you could have seen yourselves walking down that aisle at church this morning you'd know why the congregation is jumping to conclusions. The two of you radiated enough emotion to form a glow around you."

Jake was too stunned by his brother's pronouncement to react immediately, and before he could Will continued.

"They're not gossiping busybodies. They're your neighbors and friends. They care about you and your children. You know that there isn't one of them who wouldn't come to your aid in a minute if you had a fire or were flooded out or were even in a financial crisis. They'd have seen to it that your kids were taken care of until you could find a housekeeper if you'd asked them, but you didn't. Instead you jumped at the excuse to keep Brittany with you—"

Jake's rising temper reached boiling. He wasn't going to sit here and listen to his pompous brother spouting half-truths, but when he jumped up from the tree stump to tell him so the throbbing in his bad knee became an agony of white lightning that shot through his leg in both directions, throwing him off-balance and back down on the stump.

He let out a string of curses and grabbed his knee as Will hovered over him. "Jake! What happened? Your knee…?"

Jake nodded, unable for the moment to speak until he could catch his breath. "I'll be okay," he panted as the pain began to subside. "Sorry, I should have known better than to straighten it so fast. It's been bothering me all morning. Always does when the humidity gets high."

"I'd noticed your limp was more pronounced than usual today," Will said anxiously. "I'd better go get the car—"

"No!" Jake insisted as Will turned to leave. "It's only a block to the house. I'll just sit here a few minutes until it calms down a little. Then I'll take my time about getting up and putting my weight on it, like I should have done in the first place."

"Damn, I'm sorry," Will said. "I didn't realize it still bothered you this much. Don't you have a cane you can use?"

"Yeah, I have a couple of them at home, but I never use them anymore. It only hurts when the weather acts up."

"What does the doctor say?"

Jake shrugged. "He says it's a miracle I can bend the knee at all, and I'll just have to live with the discomfort and limitations. It's really not that bad. Most of the time I don't even think about it."

He grinned, determined to get off the subject of his aching joint. "To get back to our conversation, I was about to cuss you out for something, but I don't remember what."

Will grinned, too, but he still looked anxious. "I think it was for sticking my nose in where it didn't belong and acting more like a father than an older brother."

"Yeah. Right," Jake said, but without his former belligerence. "So now that you've got my attention just what is it you're trying to tell me?"

Will sighed with exasperation. "You know what I'm trying to tell you. You just don't want to hear it. You're attracting a lot of unsavory speculation by living alone in your house with a woman as young, beautiful and sexy as Brittany Castle."

Jake winced. Will was right, but he didn't want to hear it. "We're not alone," he protested. "The kids are there."

Will muttered an obscenity. "Oh, get real! The kids being there just makes it worse. What do you think Tina's going to say when she hears about it?"

Jake was jolted. "Tina! What business is it of hers?"

"She's the kids' mother, for God's sake," Will pointed out.

"Try telling her that," Jake scoffed. "They haven't seen or heard from her since Mother's Day, and then only because I called and told her to get her tail over here because they had gifts for her they'd bought out of their allowances."

Will put his hand on Jake's shoulder. "I know. She's never been an enthusiastic parent, but don't count on her not to use the kids to get to you if she thinks you've got a live-in lover staying with you. You know she's still bitter because you took over the farm instead of taking a desk job with the OPD."

Jake slumped forward and dropped his head in his hands. Damn. Was he going to spend the rest of his life paying for the mistake of marrying unwisely?

"What do you suggest I do?" he asked. "I need someone to look after the children."

"Then why haven't you hired someone?" Will asked reasonably. "I know you've interviewed several applicants."

"Well, because they weren't suitable. One was too old, another didn't want to do housework—"

Will hunkered down beside his seated brother. "Jake, are you sure they weren't suitable because you didn't want to hire them?"

He spoke with no hint of accusation, and Jake took no offense. He couldn't. He knew that what Will said was true.

"I'm not judging you," Will continued. "You certainly have a right to fall in love again. If that's what you want then go for it. I'll be your most enthusiastic supporter, but if you're just lonely and in need of some temporary loving, then hire the next applicant for housekeeper and send Brittany on her way."

Will patted Jake on the thigh and stood up. "She's a nice girl, and you're a responsible guy. Don't break her heart as well as your own."

Chapter Nine

Brittany was standing at the front window, looking out over the colorful gardens of dahlias, snapdragons and pansies that were Elena's pride and joy, when she saw Will and Jake walking up the road.

That is, Will was walking. Jake was limping!

Brittany gasped. This wasn't the slightly off-center gait of his that was hardly noticeable, but a limp so bad that he was leaning on a heavy stick for support as he hobbled along, wincing with every step.

She rushed to the door, threw it open and hurried across the porch and down the wet gravel driveway. At the road she realized she was probably overreacting and forced herself to walk instead of run toward them.

"Jake," she called breathlessly as her pace accelerated in spite of her effort to hold back. "What happened? You've been hurt!"

Jake dropped his stick and put out his arms. Forgetting caution, she ran into them and they closed tightly around her. "I'm okay, honey," he said softly against the top of her head. "I just twisted my bad knee when I stood up too fast."

"I'll drive you to the doctor," she said, but couldn't force herself to move out of his embrace.

"That won't be necessary," he assured her, and cradled her closer. "When we get home I'll put some heat on it, and I have pills I can take if the pain gets worse."

She couldn't bear the thought of him suffering. "Then you stay here and I'll go get the kids and the car and pick you up so you don't have to walk any farther."

Jake would have endured twice the agony if it had given him the chance to hold her and have her hold him like this. He'd seen the "I told you so" look on Will's face when he'd clasped her to him, but he couldn't help himself. When she'd come rushing down the road, her lovely features twisted with concern for him, his eager arms had opened and beckoned to her without any planning.

And now that he had her, warm and soft and incredibly cuddly, in his embrace he wasn't sure he'd ever be able to let her go. Not out of his arms, not out of his life. And he didn't care if the whole world filed by and judged him foolish and irresponsible.

Will had gone on ahead, leaving them alone, and for several minutes they just stood there, lost in the swirl of emotions that buffeted them. Eventually it was Brittany who came to her senses and broke the spell. "I . . . I'd better go get the car." Her voice quavered as she pushed back and Jake loosened his hold on her.

"No," he said, his own voice unsteady. "I can walk. If you'll just hand me my stick . . ."

He motioned to the short sturdy tree branch that he'd dropped on the ground.

She stepped out of his embrace, then picked it up and handed it to him, but still protested. "You shouldn't put your weight on your knee, Jake."

He smiled. "I won't. I'll lean on you." He put his arm around her waist and pulled her against his side. "See, now I have a good excuse for holding you."

She managed a smile, too, and put her arm around him. "All right, but for heaven's sake don't stumble and fall."

This time he chuckled. "I won't. If I did I'd take you down with me, and I don't think the country folk around here are ready yet for a view of unbridled passion in the mud by the side of the road."

Brittany couldn't hold back the laughter that bubbled up from her throat. "I'm not sure I'm ready for that, either."

Jake winked at her but made no reply.

They left for home as soon as they could round up the kids and say goodbye to their host and hostess. When they arrived at the ranch Jake exchanged the tree limb for a cane, then filled the downstairs bathtub full of hot water and soaked in it, hoping to draw out the worst of the burning pain in his knee.

By the time the water had cooled his leg was more limber. He was toweling himself dry, when there was a knock on the door.

"Jake." It was Brittany. "I have your pajamas and robe."

Just the sound of her voice aroused him. Quickly he knotted the towel around his waist and opened the door a crack. She was standing on the other side of it with his nightclothes over her arm. He had a strong urge to invite her in to dry his back, but managed to resist it. "Honey, I have my clothes in here. I can't put on pajamas. It's still early, and I have the evening chores to do."

Brittany looked at him through the narrow opening of the door. All she could see was his head and one nude shoulder. She wondered if he was bare all over. The idea of him standing naked just a few inches from her made her blush, and being familiar with male anatomy, she shivered at the image her imagination imprinted on her mind.

If the raw masculinity that radiated from him in clothes was any indication, he must be magnificent in the buff!

"You don't have to do the chores," she told him. "I called Emmett and he's coming over to do them for you."

Jake looked startled. "Why did you do that? I'm not an invalid."

She'd been afraid he'd be angry, but she knew he'd never ask for help on his own.

"I know you're not," she said patiently, "but you will be if you don't stay off that knee until the inflammation goes down."

She took his nightclothes from her arm and handed them through the opening. "Here, put these on, then come to the living room. Kurt told me you use the heating pad sometimes, and showed me where it was. You can lie on the couch and be comfortable."

"Damn it all, Brittany, you're not my mother," Jake grumbled.

"That's true," she said sweetly, "but I happen to be substituting for her at this time, so indulge me."

She walked away and left him mumbling.

Emmett arrived a few minutes after Brittany got Jake settled on the sofa with pillows at his back and head and the hot pad wrapped around his knee. He grouched and complained that she was making too much of a fuss, but he looked pale and tired and she noticed that he stopped his protesting short of refusing to let her pamper him.

He even dozed while she fed the children a light supper and supervised their baths. Their bedtime had been delayed by an hour once school was out for the summer, so she let them put on their robes and slippers and watch television in their father's room.

When Brittany came back downstairs Jake had shifted around and was sitting up with his leg out in front of him, supported by the coffee table. He was watching a cable-news program on television, and looked more rested and comfortable than he had earlier.

"There you are," he said with a smile. "It was so quiet around here I thought you'd taken the kids and gone somewhere."

She laughed. "Obviously you were still asleep and didn't hear your little angels put up a fuss when I tried to send them to bed early."

Jake frowned. "Are they giving you any trouble?"

"Not at all," she assured him. "I told them they could watch television in your room until nine-thirty and they settled right down. You can bet they'll stay there and be quiet in the hope that we'll forget they're still up when the time comes to put them to bed."

"That's a safe wager," Jake observed, and patted the cushion beside him on the sofa. "Come and sit with me."

She'd intended to take the comfortable chair across from him. It didn't seem like a very smart idea for them to sit so close together, especially with him wearing that sexy matching pajama and robe set, but she decided not to make an issue of it.

She walked over and sat down beside him. "How's your knee? Does it still hurt?"

He rubbed his shin just below the heating pad. "I hate to admit it, but you knew what you were doing when you insisted I apply heat and stay off my feet. It feels a lot better."

"I'm so glad," she said. "Sometimes my veterinary training comes in handy with humans, too."

He chuckled. "How many dogs have you treated that got shot in the knee?"

A shudder went through her. "Is that what happened to you?"

He nodded. "Yeah. It was four years ago. I was working undercover out of narcotics at the time. My partner and I had set up a buy. Everything went just great until we tried to put the dealer under arrest. Before we could get the cuffs on him he pulled a Saturday night special and shot at us. I was hit in the leg. Close enough to the knee to do a lot of damage but not enough to put the joint totally out of commission."

Brittany clasped her hands together to keep from reaching out to him, and she wondered if his wife had been loving and supportive at that time.

"Oh, Jake, how awful. Did the man get away?"

Jake grunted. "Not a chance. My partner took care of that, but I was in the hospital for two months."

This time she could no longer resist touching him, and she put her hand on his arm. "I hope he was sentenced to a long term in prison. My God, he could have killed you."

He put his hand over hers and brought it to his mouth. "But he didn't," he said, and rubbed her thumb across his lips. "Did anyone ever tell you that you've got the softest, most comforting hands?"

She blinked at his sudden change of topic. "No, not that I remember. Does your knee bother you often?"

He turned her hand over and kissed her wrist, sending erogenous messages up her arm. "No, hardly ever. Only when I do something foolish like I did today. It'll be okay by tomorrow. See, I can even bend it now."

He raised his knee to a tent position, but Brittany saw him wince before he could control it.

She wrenched her hand from his and put it on his thigh to stop him. "Damn it, Jake, what's the matter with you? If you don't quit trying to prove what a macho man you are you're going to undo all the good the therapy has done.''

Again he put his hand over hers so she couldn't move it away, then slowly straightened his leg before he looked at her and grinned. ''I'd like nothing better than to prove my manhood to you, sweetheart,'' he said huskily.

Brittany felt her face flame. ''That's not what I said.''

She tried to pull her hand out from under his, but he applied more pressure and kept it palm-down against his thigh. Or rather against the silky material of his pajamas, since his robe had fallen open when he'd first moved his leg.

She could feel the heat of his bare flesh under the slippery fabric, and had an almost irresistible urge to caress him with her fingers.

''Don't take your hand away,'' he said. ''I'm sorry if I embarrassed you. I have no right talking to you that way.''

His apology caught her by surprise, and she spoke before she thought. ''Why not?''

Oh, heavens. She sounded as though she were coming on to him. On the other hand, would that be so bad?

''Because you're not that kind of girl.''

Who said? The question popped into her head so abruptly that she almost asked it, but this time she was more discreet.

''I'm not a girl, Jake. I'm a woman, and I don't need to be treated like a child.''

With his hand still over hers guiding it, he rubbed her palm against his thigh. ''I understand that,'' he told her, ''but if I treat you like the desirable woman you are I can't guarantee I can control the situation. It's easier when I think of you as a girl.''

''The age difference between us isn't all that great, if that's what's bothering you,'' she assured him.

He sighed. ''It's more than is prudent. You're twenty-five and probably still a virgin—''

"Jake!" It was a yelp of outrage.

He put back his head and laughed. "I'm sorry, that wasn't meant as an insult. So maybe you're not a virgin, but you're not very experienced, either. Whereas I'm thirty-eight, was married, divorced and have two kids...."

Brittany was only partially listening. His crack about her being a virgin still rankled. Even worse was the fact that he knew exactly how inexperienced she was.

Was she that transparent?

It wasn't that she hadn't had plenty of chances to gain experience. Actually, she'd always been proud of her high standards. But she didn't want Jake to think of her as too young and innocent to touch.

"Are you listening to me, Brittany?" The harshness of his tone rather than his words cut through her musing and brought her attention back to him.

"Ye-yes, of course I am," she blustered, but knew she hadn't been. "You accused me of being a virgin."

He laughed again, and she knew she'd said something stupid. She seemed to be entertaining him hugely tonight with her silly schoolgirl innocence.

"I was telling you why I have no business coming on to you," he said. "I would be taking advantage of your willingness to help out in a difficult situation, and that's a despicable thing for any man to do."

He picked up her hand, kissed it and put it in her lap. "I'm not in the market for a wife, and you don't want a short-term lover, so there's no point in getting all stirred up."

He was right, of course, but unfortunately she was already "stirred up" and had been ever since she'd stumbled into his house and into his arms ten days ago. And he was just as stirred up. He hadn't made any effort to hide that fact from her, but apparently he could turn his emotions on and off easier than she could.

She slid forward, preparing to stand up. "You're right, there isn't, so how about something to eat? Heidi and Kurt had supper while you were sleeping."

She stood, but Jake caught her hand and pulled her back down beside him again. "Don't run off. I'm not hungry. Are you?"

She landed almost on his lap. "Jake!" she cried, and squirmed against him in an effort to put a little space between them, but he put his arm around her and held her where she was.

She didn't really want to protest, so she gave in and stopped struggling. "No, I'm not hungry. We had lunch later than usual and I overate. Elena's a great cook. How does she handle all the housework and have a full-time career, too?"

Brittany felt safer talking about impersonal matters with this man who affected her so strongly.

"She doesn't," Jake said. "She stayed home when the boys were little, but once they were in school full-time she hired a housekeeper and went back to work. Now that the kids are teenagers she just has a cleaning woman who comes in once a week, but they rely a lot on take-out dinners and frozen food."

He shook his head. "Believe me, she doesn't try to compete with Mom."

Brittany sighed and put her head on his shoulder. "I guess Dagmar is one of a vanishing breed."

Jake cradled her to him and stroked his fingers through her hair. "I guess so," he murmured, and nuzzled her cheek.

The gentle roughness of his lips sent shivers down her spine, and she rubbed her other cheek in the sleek fabric of his robe.

"I like the feel of your robe against my skin," she said softly, and rubbed her palm over his chest. "It must be new. I'm sorry I had to take the pajamas out of the clear plastic sack they were sealed in, but I couldn't find any of your others.''

He chuckled and kissed the pulse at her temple. "I don't have any others. Gisela and Nick gave me this set for Christmas several years ago. I've worn the robe a couple of times, but the pajamas had never been opened because I don't wear pajamas."

The thought of Jake lying nude between the sheets of his king-size bed sent a buzz through her, and she raised her head to look at him. "Really?"

"Really. Why does that surprise you? A lot of men sleep raw or in their underwear."

He paused, and his eyes narrowed. "Brittany, tell me the truth. Have you ever...uh...*been* with a man?"

Her teeth worried her bottom lip. "Yes. One. My first year of college. He was a student, too. We had an...an intimate relationship for several months...." Her voice trailed off and she didn't know what else to say.

"What happened?" Jake asked. "What did he do to you? Was it so bad that you never wanted to get involved with anyone else?"

She shook her head, vigorously. "Oh, no, nothing like that. It wasn't bad, but it wasn't all that great, either. I mean...well, maybe I expected too much. Or, like you said a few minutes ago, maybe I'm just not the type to take a temporary lover."

She knew that wasn't altogether true. Or, at least it was true as far as it went, but what she didn't tell him was that he was the exception. That no other man had ever made her feel the total awakening that she experienced when she was with him. The delight when he came into the room, the thrill of his touch, the incredible joy of knowing he wanted her.

And then there was the indisputable fact that if he asked her to make love with him she would, eagerly, gladly, and he wouldn't have to promise marriage in return.

That unsolicited revelation embarrassed her so that she buried her face in his chest to keep him from reading it in her expression.

He obviously misunderstood, because he lowered his head and nuzzled the side of her throat. "I'm glad you're not," he said softly in her ear. "Promiscuous sex is not only dangerous, it's just a temporary hedge against loneliness. You deserve so much more than that."

She raised up and put her arms around his neck as their gazes meshed. "So do you," she whispered just before their lips met and clung.

It was a gentle kiss, almost chaste, but the emotions it stirred in Brittany were anything but. Her heartbeat sped up, and her breath seemed to catch in her throat as Jake's arms tightened around her, bringing their upper bodies in close contact.

She didn't need much experience to recognize that he was a strong, virile lover who knew how to pleasure a woman. His hands roamed slowly over her back, seeking out and relishing curves and hollows that sprang to life under his touch.

Tenderly his tongue outlined her lips and they opened like a rosebud to sunshine, but instead of taking immediate possession of her mouth, he continued to play with her lips, moistening them, nipping at them and sucking tenderly, while his hands found the sides of her breasts and brushed back and forth across them with his palms.

She wanted to give Jake the same incredible excitement that he was giving her, but he blocked her every time she tried to use her tongue or her hands to do so. She didn't understand. The only other man she'd ever gotten this intimate with had complained that she wasn't responsive enough.

He pulled her turquoise shirt out from beneath the waist of her matching slacks and put his hand on her bare flesh. His palm was warm and rough with calluses as it moved between them and cupped her lace-and-satin covered breast. He released it from her bra, and it spilled into his hand as she stiffened and her fingers dug into his shoulders.

"I won't hurt you," he whispered, then rimmed the inside of her ear with his tongue while her fingers dug deeper into his back.

She heard herself moan as he caressed her passion-swollen nipple, but it wasn't pain she was experiencing. It was a melting heat deep in her groin that throbbed and vibrated and made her squirm against him, panting for breath.

He put his hands on either side of her waist and lifted her onto his lap, and she felt his compelling hardness press into her buttocks. For a moment his whole body went rigid and his hand clutched her thigh.

"Jake. Oh, Jake, I..." Her voice broke and she could neither think nor speak as his hand moved slowly upward.

She was sure that every muscle from her waist to her knees went into spasm, and she gasped and tightened her arms around his neck.

"It's all right, sweetheart," he murmured raggedly. "Don't hold back. Relax and let it happen."

"Let what happen?" she sobbed as his hand moved to the inside of her thigh, then continued inching upward.

"This," he said, and reached his goal, cupping her intimately with his searching palm.

Brittany's whole body exploded. It was as if he'd pressed a button and set off enough energy to spiral her dizzingly upward, to the stars and beyond.

Her head spun and she heard herself softly moaning, but she was totally out of orbit. All she could do was clutch Jake and hold on until the wild ride was over.

He held her and caressed her and murmured endearments in her ear until she slowly drifted back to earth and a semblance of control.

She rubbed her face against his chest, too embarrassed to look at him. "Jake, that's never happened to me before. I'm sorry—"

"Don't ever be sorry, Brittany." His voice was unsteady. "Don't apologize for being so responsive. It's a gift, not a curse."

"But what about you? You didn't... That is, it..."

Brittany was completely out of her depth. How could she talk about such an overwhelming experience? There were no words...

"It didn't happen for you," she finally blurted out, then buried her face deeper into his unyielding chest, once again mute with embarrassment.

He kissed the top of her head. "Only because I wouldn't let it," he assured her. "I'm all right, honey."

She knew enough about men to know that he couldn't be "all right." It must have been incredibly difficult for him not to seek release.

She finally found the courage to raise her head and look at him. He smiled, but it was obvious that he was deeply shaken.

"Jake, please, let me...um...I mean I'm willing..." Oh, damn! Why couldn't she just come out and say what she wanted?

Before she could try again he covered her mouth briefly with his and sent sparks flying in all directions, then lifted his head. "No, Brittany. Much as I'd love what you're proposing, I'm not going to take advantage of you. I've done enough of that already, but I couldn't resist the temptation to show you how good it can be, should be, between a man and a woman. I didn't want you to ever settle for a lukewarm relationship simply because your first lover was young and clumsy."

While she was still trying to figure out just what he was telling her, he reached up and took her arms from around his neck. "Now," he said as he released her. "If you really want to help me you'll go upstairs and stay there until morning. I'll sleep down here on the couch."

"Oh, but—"

"Brittany," he interrupted. "Go. Now. Please."

She finally understood what he was asking and nodded. He didn't want the incredible intimacy of joining their bodies in the usual way, but he did want to be the one to teach her the wondrous feelings making love could unleash.

As she made her way up the stairs she pondered sadly over how illogical a smart man like Jake could be. He'd truly believed he was doing her a favor. That once he'd introduced her to the miracle of lovemaking she could experience it with any man who was reasonably skilled. But he was badly mistaken.

She knew with a certainty as old as time that no man but the one she was deeply, passionately in love with could bring her to the height she'd reached tonight. She had no doubt about who that man was, and it was obvious that her feelings were not reciprocated.

If Jake had loved her he'd have joined her on her first trip to the stars, instead of just sending her.

The atmosphere between Brittany and Jake became strained after that night. Jake seemed as uncomfortable as she was. His limp was more pronounced than usual, but she didn't comment on it when he put in his usual long hours of work. They avoided each other whenever possible, but were friendly and pleasant when they were together.

Brittany was still painfully embarrassed, but she felt cheated, as well, even though she knew she was as much to blame for what had happened as Jake. He'd been open and honest with her, had told her he was attracted to her but wasn't interested in anything permanent. Still, that hadn't stopped her from coming on to him.

She'd practically thrown herself into his arms a couple of times, and she had never rebuffed his tentative advances. She'd discussed sex with him, even knowing full well that kind of thing usually turned a man on, and when he'd started making love to her she not only encouraged him but was aggressive enough that he'd had to block some of her moves.

Every time she thought of how she'd behaved she felt a wave of humiliation. What must he think of her? It was all she could do to face him, and she began to think seriously about leaving.

On Friday morning she was on the phone with a sixteen-year-old girl who had seen Jake's ad in the paper and wanted more information.

"I believe Mr. Luther is looking for someone older," she told the girl, "but if you'll leave your name and a number where you can be reached I'll have him phone you between twelve and one this afternoon."

Ordinarily she wouldn't have encouraged the teenager, since she knew Jake didn't want anyone that young, but by now maybe he was eager to be rid of her and would make an exception.

She'd just hung up the phone, when the doorbell rang. Out of habit from living in a big city, Brittany kept the front door locked since it was seldom used. Family and friends used the back one that opened onto the driveway. Jake and the kids teased her about her compulsion, since there was very little crime in this sparsely settled area, and few people locked up even when they weren't home.

She hurried out of the kitchen, through the dining room and into the entryway, all the while wondering who it could be. The bell rang again and she quickly opened the door to confront a petite, auburn-haired woman with green eyes and a flawless complexion. She was dressed in impeccably tailored peach slacks with a matching jacket and color-coordinated blouse, and she carried an expensive leather weekender in her right hand.

She looked as surprised as Brittany felt.

The woman's lovely eyes narrowed. "Who are you?" she asked coldly, as if she had a right to question the residents of Jake's house. "And why is this door locked?"

Brittany bristled. Who was this woman to treat her like a trespasser? "I'm Brittany Castle," she answered crisply. "May I help you?"

"What are you doing here?" the other woman snapped ungraciously.

Brittany's hand tightened on the doorknob, but she fought to keep her temper. "Perhaps I should ask you that question," she said as calmly as possible. "Whom did you wish to see?"

The woman drew herself up to her full stature, which couldn't have been more than five feet but was formidable nevertheless. "I'm Tina Luther, Jake's wife, Heidi and Kurt's mother, and I want to see my family."

Her voice was tinged with ice as she pushed past Brittany and stormed into the house.

Chapter Ten

Brittany shut the door and made a massive effort to collect her shattered composure as Tina Luther headed up the stairs, calling for Dagmar and the children.

Jake's wife. She'd introduced herself as Jake's wife, not his ex-wife! And she was positively gorgeous. That is, she had been until her fragile features had twisted with anger when Brittany hadn't paid her the respect she apparently thought was due her. Then she'd looked older and hard.

Brittany shivered. Why hadn't Jake told her his wife was coming? Or did he even know? The children would almost certainly have said something if they'd been expecting a visit from their mother. Wouldn't they have?

Brittany could hear Tina wandering around upstairs as she headed back to the kitchen. Darn it all, what was that woman doing here? How long was she going to stay? She'd brought a suitcase, so she must be planning on days instead of hours.

So where was she going to sleep?

Brittany was putting large scrubbed potatoes in the oven to bake when Tina came storming into the kitchen. "Look, you," she said angrily, "I want some answers. What's going on here? Where are Dagmar and the kids? *Who are you?* And who's taken over my room?"

So those were Tina's clothes that had been left in the spare bedroom.

Brittany's first inclination was to throw something at the woman, but she was, after all, only an employee, whereas Tina was playing "lady of the house" to the hilt. Well, maybe she still was. Brittany had no way of knowing how her family treated her when she came visiting.

Brittany took a deep breath in an effort to control her temper, and told Tina about Gisela's accident and Dagmar's hurried departure to care for her daughter's family. "I'm a friend who is working as temporary housekeeper until Jake can find someone else," she said in conclusion. "I'm using the spare room."

Tina frowned. "A friend of whose? And why don't you go home at night?"

It occurred to Brittany that Jake's ex-wife was jealous. "A friend of the family, and I don't live in the area," she answered shortly.

"How come I've never heard of you before? Where do you live?"

This was turning into an interrogation, and Brittany had no intention of putting up with it. "I've no idea why you haven't heard about me before," she snapped, "and I live here for now. I'm sorry if my use of the extra bedroom has inconvenienced you, but if you're planning to spend the night I'm sure it would be all right for you to sleep in Dagmar's room."

Tina's eyes widened, but her voice deepened to a husky purr. "Oh, I don't spend nights here to sleep, Ms. Castle, and you're not inconveniencing me. I'll just bunk down in Jake's bed with him, since we always wind up there together, anyway. We're usually more discreet about it, but Dagmar's not here now and the children won't know or care. I guarantee you Jake won't mind.''

She strolled out the back door, and this time Brittany did throw something, but not until Tina was gone. Then she bounced a pan off the wall with such force that it chipped the plaster.

Brittany was shaken all the way to her toes. Jake had never indicated that he still had a sexual relationship with his ex-wife! In fact, he'd seemed quite bitter toward her. Was that just a facade to mislead Dagmar and the children so they wouldn't know that he and Tina were still making love?

But what was the point? They'd been married for a long time. If they still wanted each other whose business was it but theirs? But if Jake still loved his ex-wife, even had a sexual relationship with her, why was he coming on, albeit reluctantly, to Brittany?

She went through the motions of fixing dinner in a haze of anguish. Had she really been as big a fool as she suspected? No wonder Jake hadn't wanted to get intimately involved with her. He didn't need her; he had a willing wife.

Well, ex-wife, she conceded, but what difference did it make if they were still sleeping together?

Brittany somehow managed to country-fry the steak, fix a cheese sauce for the cauliflower and toss a salad by the time Jake came in at noon, bringing Tina and the kids with him. They were all smiling and joking and Kurt and Heidi seemed delighted to see their mother.

In the kitchen they turned their attention to Brittany. "Brittany, see, my mommy's here!" exclaimed Heidi, her pretty brown eyes shining.

"Yeah," Kurt confirmed. "She's gonna stay for a while this time."

"She and Daddy are going to take us to the movies to-night," Heidi announced, then added as an afterthought, "you can come, too."

Brittany couldn't look at Jake but kept her gaze downcast as she responded dully, "That's nice. Now, run along and wash up. Everything's ready."

The heat of the kitchen plus the press of so many people crowded into it made her dizzy. The room spun, and she dropped the empty pan in which she'd steamed the cauli-flower on the floor and clutched at the sink as she fought to regain her equilibrium.

Jake caught her by the shoulders from the back. "Brittany! Good Lord, you're white as a sheet. What's the matter?"

She took a deep breath and her head cleared, but she'd had all she could take. She had to get out of there so she could be alone.

She shrugged Jake's hands off her shoulders and straightened up. "I'm sorry. I don't feel very well. Probably a touch of flu. Go ahead and eat. I think I'll lie down for a while."

She started to leave, but Jake reached out and caught her. "I'll go with you," he said.

"No." She pulled away from him. "I'd rather you didn't, Jake. I'll be fine."

She still couldn't look at him as she left the room and made her way up the stairs.

What a fool she'd been. She was so sure he didn't have a woman in his life because he never went out by himself in the evening or invited a date home. She'd further assumed he didn't have a lover because he was too circumspect to take a woman to his bed while his mother and children were in the house.

How naive of her! When was she going to stop being such a blind romantic and grow up? There were no Prince

Charmings out there just waiting to fit her with a glass slipper. She was living the wrong fairy tale. Little Red Riding Hood and the wolf was a story more fitting to her life.

She went into her room and shut the door behind her. She wished she could lock it, but there were no locks on any of the inside doors except the ones to the bathrooms.

It was a long-standing custom in these parts never to lock anything up, not your house, your car, or barn. Everyone trusted everybody else and claimed that trust had never been misplaced.

Well, she'd trusted Jake, and he'd stolen her heart.

Kicking off her shoes, she lay down on the bed and curled up in a ball. She really didn't feel good. Her head hurt and her muscles ached. Not a result of the accident, but of the long hours of hard work she'd been doing since Dagmar had left. She was tired. Weary all the way through.

Also, she'd come to a long overdue decision. She was going to leave the farm, and Jake, tomorrow. At least then she could get some rest. No more getting up before the sun and working until she dropped into bed at night. No more nasty shocks like the one she'd had today. Let Tina look after her own children. Neither they nor Jake were Brittany's responsibility.

A wave of sadness washed over her. Why was she such a lousy judge of men? The student in college had looked like Tom Hanks and danced like Patrick Swayze, but that's all there was to him. Once away from the mirrors and off the dance floor she found that he was a boring companion and an indifferent lover.

On the other hand, Ronny had been the perfect escort, handsome, skilled in all the social graces, and well-off financially, but he was also violent and a sociopath.

And now Jake. Good-looking, kindhearted, and apparently still in love with his ex-wife.

Great track record, Brittany.

She must have dozed, because she was awakened by a knock on her door. Burrowing her face deeper into the pillow, she hoped it would go away, but instead it came again, along with a voice.

"Brittany, may I come in?"

It was Jake. What did he want? Why couldn't he just leave her alone?

She glanced at her watch and saw that she'd been sleeping for almost three hours.

The knock was repeated, only louder. "Brittany, are you all right?" He sounded worried. "If you don't answer I'm coming in."

She rolled over and sat up on the side of the bed. "I was asleep, Jake," she called. "Come on in."

The door opened and he walked in somewhat timidly. She knew that her hair was disheveled and her face probably swollen with sleep as she looked up at him. "I'm sorry I slept so long," she said anxiously. "The children...?" Good heavens, she was supposed to be watching them.

"Tina took them to the zoo in Omaha." He moved closer to the bed. "Don't get up. I'm sorry I woke you, but I was worried...."

She shook her head to dislodge the remnants of sleep. "I'm glad you did. I have no business sleeping in the middle of the day. If you'll just give me a couple of minutes I'll be right down to clean up the kitchen."

She started to get up, but he stopped her and sat down beside her. "The kitchen's already cleaned, but I saved a plate of food for you. It won't take but a minute to warm in the microwave."

"Did Tina wash the dishes?" That surprised her. She would have assumed that the woman who'd stormed into the house earlier would leave the dishes for the hired help to do.

Jake grinned, as if the idea was equally incredible to him. "No," he said emphatically. "I did them, right after I sent her and the kids off to the zoo so they wouldn't bother you."

His admission caused her more pain than gratitude. Darn it all, why did he have to be so nice? How could he be so thoughtful about most things and still not even mention...

"Jake, why didn't you tell me she was coming today?" Brittany blurted out. "I had no idea who she was or what she wanted when she appeared at the door. I'm afraid I was a little rude—"

"Honey, I didn't know she was coming. I was as surprised as everyone else when she appeared in the barnyard. She said she'd been out of town on business for a while and just got back...."

He paused and frowned. "Did she do or say something to upset you? Is that why you came up here and wouldn't eat with us?" His tone was harsh, but she didn't know whether he was exasperated with her or with Tina.

Brittany wasn't going to let him know that the fact that he was still sleeping with his ex-wife had shaken her so. If Jake didn't think their relationship, such as it was, was important enough for him to tell her he was still involved with Tina, then Brittany certainly wasn't going to admit her silly fantasies.

"She just surprised me is all," Brittany said, "and I was a surprise to her. We both sort of got our hackles up, but I really wasn't feeling well."

She might as well tell him what she was planning right now and get it over with. "Jake, I'm afraid I'm not up to the hard work and responsibility of this job I volunteered for. I...I'm sorry, but I'm exhausted and I... Well, now that Tina is here and...and can look after the kids I'd like to leave tomorrow."

It had been even harder than she'd expected, and she wasn't prepared for the look of desolation that crossed his face and settled in.

"Brittany, you can't mean that." There was pain as well as disbelief in his voice. "Look, take a few days off and go to a hotel in Omaha. I'll pay for it. God knows I owe it to you if I've been overworking you so badly. Tina can stay with the kids tomorrow, and I know Elena will take them Sunday. Just please don't leave. I promise that from now on I'll be more thoughtful. I'll cut down on your duties, and I'll make sure you have every weekend off...."

It took all her control not to put her arms around him and promise him anything he wanted. She didn't for a minute doubt his sincerity. He couldn't fake the anguish in his voice and his expression, but why did her being here matter so much to him? Or did he just hate to lose a good housekeeper?

She couldn't let him beg. "Jake, we both know that I only intended to stay a few days when I agreed to help out, but it's already been a week and a half. My class reunion is coming up at Raindance next weekend, and I promised to arrive early and visit friends...."

He abruptly stood and walked over to the window, keeping his back to her. His shoulders slumped, and for a minute or so he just stood there, looking out over the driveway and the barnyard.

Brittany was confused and heartbroken. Apparently she'd finally gotten through to him, but all she wanted to do was cry and plead with him to let her stay.

The silence stretched her nerves to near breaking before he spoke.

"I'm sorry, Brittany." His voice was now firm and impersonal. "I've been selfish and inconsiderate. Of course you must leave, if that's what you want. You're relieved of your duties as of right now, so you can either go back to sleep or start packing. I'll make out a check for this week's wages and have it waiting for you when you come downstairs."

Still with his back to her, he turned and walked out the door, shutting it carefully behind him.

Brittany collapsed on the bed in tears.

Jake felt as if he'd been kicked, and it served him right. What had he expected, for God's sake? He'd been wandering around in a constant state of turmoil ever since the night Brittany had pounded on his door to be let in, then taken up residence in his very soul.

The feelings she'd stirred in him had scared him so he'd strenuously denied them, and now that he'd lost her he'd learned in the most painful way possible that she was indispensable to him.

What a blind idiot he'd been!

He'd let his bitterness for Tina poison his attitude toward all pretty and successful females. And now he'd driven away the one woman who was as dear to him as his own children.

How had it happened? Brittany had seemed so happy here with him and the kids. He'd known she was working too hard, and had made every effort to lighten her load. She'd never complained, but for the past several days there'd been an awkwardness between them. Ever since that night...

Last Sunday. The day he'd hurt his knee. He'd really lost it that night. He never should have touched her. He'd known it then, but he couldn't stop himself.

The pain in his knee had been like a red-hot coal, and she'd been so sympathetic and loving. He'd told himself he could stop before they went too far.

Ha! Famous last words!

She'd gone up in flame in his arms, and afterward he'd compounded the mistake by trying to convince her, and himself, that he was just teaching her what sex was all about. Yeah. Sure. Some teacher.

She'd had him burning in hell ever since, and now she was going to leave.

Brittany was packing, when she heard a car drive into the driveway and stop. It was no doubt Tina and the kids. A car door opened and closed, and a few seconds later the front door opened and closed, but there were no boisterous voices or the scuffle of childish feet to be heard.

That was unusual. Kurt and Heidi were never still.

She looked out the window and saw Tina's car, but no sign of the children. Her uneasiness increased, but she wasn't going to give in to it and question their mother. It was no longer any of Brittany's business. She'd been relieved of her duties.

She continued to pack for several minutes until she heard Tina coming upstairs, then her anxiety won out and she stepped to the door and opened it. Tina had just reached the landing.

Brittany took a deep breath and even forced a smile. "Hi," she said in what she hoped was a casual tone. "Did the kids enjoy their trip to the zoo?"

Tina sighed and stepped out of her high-heeled pumps. "Oh, yes," she said wearily. "A whole lot more than I did. God, I'll bet we traipsed through a mile of high and low trails in that rain-forest recreation."

Brittany was surprised. "Oh? That must be something new since I was last there."

Tina nodded. "Yeah, it is, and you can get hoarse trying to make yourself heard over the roar of eight waterfalls, to say nothing of the animals."

It sounded interesting, but right now Brittany was more curious about the children, so she dropped all pretense and came right out and asked, "Where are the kids?"

Tina leaned against the wall and massaged first one stocking foot and then the other. "We ran into some former neighbors of ours, good friends we hadn't seen in quite a while, and they invited Kurt and Heidi to spend the night with them. You can pick them up in the morning." She picked up her shoes, limped past Brittany and went into Jake's room.

Brittany was dumbfounded. Tina had been out of town and hadn't seen her children in weeks, and when she finally makes time to visit them she sends them off to spend the night with friends! Why?

Then it hit her. Like a blow to the solar plexus. Since Tina and Jake were planning to spend the night making love, it would be nice not to have two inquisitive kids around.

And they were probably wishing they could get rid of her, as well!

The thought of spending the night in the room next to Jake's while he and his ex-wife indulged their sexual appetites was sickening.

No way was she going to stay around and let that happen.

She quickly returned to her packing. As a farewell gesture she'd fix supper, but then she'd ask either Jake or Tina to drive her to a hotel in Omaha. If Jake felt obliged to encourage her not to leave until morning she was sure Tina would be only too happy to take her.

When Jake came in for the evening meal he looked tired and upset. He and Brittany didn't greet each other, but he watched for a minute while she stirred the hash she'd made from yesterday's leftover roast beef and boiled potatoes.

"Brittany, I thought I made it clear that you're no longer expected to work around here," he said. "You didn't have to cook supper."

"I know," she answered, "but I wanted to. Also, I have a favor to ask of you after we eat."

She tried to smile and make a joke of it, but wasn't very successful.

A spark of something lightened his expression. "If you want to stay you have only to say so. . . ."

The sound of a woman's high heels bouncing down the stairs interrupted them, and they turned just as Tina came through the dining room door.

"Sorry if you've been waiting on me," she said breezily. "I lay down to rest and fell asleep."

"We weren't waiting," Jake said grumpily, then looked around the kitchen. "Where are the kids? Have they been called to come in? I didn't see them outside."

"Oh, we met the Fowlers and their kids at the zoo, and they invited Kurt and Heidi to spend the night at their house. I said you'd pick them up tomorrow."

Jake's head snapped up. "You mean you let my children go off with people I haven't seen in years without even consulting me?"

Tina glared back. "What do you mean, *your* children? They're mine, too, and I don't need *your* permission to make decisions—"

"The hell you don't," Jake roared, and Brittany turned and fled upstairs to her room.

She sat down on her bed and realized she was trembling. This was an impossible situation. She was glad she was all packed. As soon as they either calmed down or one of them left she'd call a taxi to take her into Omaha.

Jake was in no mood to put up with his ex-wife's sudden rush of maternal responsibility. Tina didn't care about the kids, she just wanted to get back at him. But why? What had he done to set her off. He hadn't even seen her for six weeks or so.

After they'd shouted at each other for several minutes Jake realized this was getting them nowhere. He sighed and ran his fingers through his dark hair.

"All right, Tina," he said when there was a lull in the bickering. "Tell me what it is you want."

She blinked. "I don't know what you mean."

He turned away in disgust. "Oh, come off it. We know each other too well for coyness. I've obviously done something to displease you, so tell me what it is so we can clear it up."

For a moment she didn't answer. When she did her voice had changed to a whine. "I want you to get rid of that underage sex kitten you've got living with you."

Jake felt the blood pound in his head as rage boiled up in him. He didn't need to ask whom she meant. He'd heard the acid in her tone before when she'd spoken of Brittany—

Brittany! He quickly looked around the kitchen. Where was she? She'd been right here a minute ago.

Without bothering to answer Tina, he strode out of the room, calling Brittany's name. He figured she was probably in her room, and took the stairs two at a time.

Her door was shut, and he forced himself to knock instead of busting right in. "Brittany, are you in there? Please let me in. I want to talk to you."

He waited a moment, but then the door opened and Brittany stood there, looking tense and shaken. She stepped back to allow him to enter, then pointed to several suitcases on the floor. "I'd appreciate it if you'd carry my luggage downstairs for me while I call a cab," she said politely.

Jake stared at her, stunned. "You're not leaving tonight!" It was more a cry of protest than a statement. "Look, honey, I'm sorry about that shouting match downstairs. It was a tacky way for Tina and me to behave, but I promise you it won't happen again. Since the kids aren't here there's no reason for her to stay. She'll be leaving right after supper."

Brittany's eyes widened. "Leaving? But she said..."

So he'd been right. Tina had said something to upset Brittany. "She said what?" he rasped, barely able to control his fury with Tina but knowing he had to or he'd scare Brittany off.

"Uh...oh, nothing...."

Her voice had trailed off, but he wasn't going to leave the matter at that. "Brittany," he said through clenched teeth. "I want to know what Tina said to make you so determined to run away from me. At least give me a chance to defend myself."

She looked so uncertain that he wanted to grab her and demand the truth, but he forced himself to wait quietly for her answer.

"You don't have to defend yourself to me," she finally said, but he noticed her chin quiver. "It's none of my business if you're still sleeping with your ex-wife, but you two certainly don't need me around. Especially since the children won't be here tonight."

Jake just stood there, struck mute for probably the first time in his life. His hands knotted into fists, and he had a fierce desire to hit something but managed to contain it and charged out into the hall instead.

"Tina," he roared down the stairwell. "Get up here. Right now!"

For the first time since he'd known her she didn't argue when he told her to do something instead of asking her. Instead she came running. "Jake, what's the matter?" she said as she hurried up the stairs.

"You damn well know what's the matter," he snapped as he took her by the arm and ushered her into Brittany's room.

He was amazed to notice that she cowered when he touched her, and he immediately let loose of her arm and fought to get his rage under control. He was a big man with bulging muscles from the heavy work of farming, but he wasn't a bully.

He knew he intimidated people with his size and quick, fierce temper, but even as a marine and later as a cop he'd never been violent, at least not until he was forced into it, which was seldom. Usually just the sight of him was enough to make an aggressor back down, but he'd never knowingly frightened a woman and he didn't intend to start now.

He took a deep breath and faced his ex-wife. "I'm sorry, Tina, I didn't mean to scare you, but I want you to tell me what you said to Brittany to make her think we're still lovers. That we were planning on sleeping together tonight."

Tina gasped, and her light green eyes grew wide with apprehension. "Well, I just assumed . . . I mean, we always do when I sleep over."

Jake bit back an obscenity and again fought to remain calm. Instead he raised one eyebrow. "Oh? Always?"

She flushed. "All . . . almost always."

She didn't sound nearly so sure of herself now.

"When was the last time you spent the night here?"

A look of annoyance flashed across her face. "You know when it was," she snapped.

"Dammed right I do, so you'd better tell the truth. When?"

"I prefer to talk to you in private," she said, her natural haughtiness returning. "I can't see where this is any of *her* business."

Jake smoldered inwardly, but managed to keep his tone cool. "It wasn't, until you made it her business by intimating that I was screwing you every chance I got."

He saw Brittany turn pink, and regretted his bluntness even before she spoke. "I . . . I think I'd better wait downstairs," she said, and started to walk away.

"No, Brittany, wait," he said, and stepped in front of her. "I'm sorry if I embarrassed you, but I want you to hear this."

He glared at his ex-wife. "When, Tina?"

"February. The weekend of Kurt's birthday." She almost spit the words at him.

"Did we sleep together then?"

"No." Her tone was icy.

"When was the last time we had sex?" He was going to get the truth out of her if he had to drag it out a word at a time.

She threw up her hands and turned away. "How on earth should I know?" she blustered. "I've got better things to do than keep track of unimportant details."

Jake couldn't help but smile at that. She'd always been the one to come to his bed. He hadn't approached her for sex since they'd separated, but he wasn't going to mention that.

"Fortunately my memory is better than yours," he said, instead. "It's been over a year. Ever since you told me that you were involved with another man. How is Ted, by the way? What would he think of you spending the night in my bed?"

Tina's delicate features twisted into an ugly mask. "You bastard," she grated. "Ted and I aren't seeing each other anymore."

Jake shook his head. "I'm truly sorry it didn't work out, Tina, but I'm not interested in taking up where we left off. I think we should both stop clinging to the past and get on with our lives. You're welcome to stay for supper, but since the kids aren't here there's no reason for you to stay the night."

"Oh, go to hell," Tina rasped, and stomped out of the room.

Jake and Brittany heard her slam things around in Jake's room for several minutes, then clomp down the hall, down the stairs and out of the house, slamming the door behind her. After more slamming of doors in the car she started the engine, backed out and roared off down the road.

It was only then that Jake turned to Brittany, his heart hammering with hope and his nerves screaming with anxiety.

Would she stay and be his, or was he going to lose her, after all?

He held out his arms and his stomach muscles clenched with uncertainty.

"Now, my darling," he said in a voice that trembled. "What about you? Will you come downstairs and let me explain my rather tangled former relationship with my children's mother? I can't promise you'll like what you hear, but I swear it will be the unvarnished truth."

Chapter Eleven

Brittany's mind was in turmoil. She couldn't even think, much less speak. If this was the way Jake and Tina had behaved as lovers it was no wonder they'd gotten divorced.

So Jake's ex-wife had lied to her, and Brittany hadn't even had the good sense to question the unlikely story she'd been told. Admittedly the two had been intimate on occasion since their marriage had broken up, but not since long before Brittany had come on the scene.

She saw the torment in Jake's expression as he beckoned to her, and she stumbled into his embrace, grateful that he still wanted to hold her, even knowing that she'd had a woeful lack of trust in his integrity.

"Oh, Jake, I'm so sorry—"

He lowered his head and covered her mouth with his, shutting off her words as well as her thoughts as he cradled her against him. She felt the stirring of his desire against her belly, but to her dismay he released her.

"You're too much woman for me, sweetheart," he admitted. "If we keep that up my mind will be mush within minutes, and I want to straighten out this nonsense Tina's been feeding you."

He put his arm around her and held her against his side as they walked downstairs to the kitchen.

"We'd better eat supper before it gets cold," he said. "I can talk and eat at the same time."

They dished up the meal, then sat down at the table.

After they'd filled their plates Jake spoke. "What Tina told you is partially true, Brittany. We did have a monogamous sexual relationship for a few years after our divorce. Even though our marriage was a stormy one, that part of it was always good. After we separated we found that we had the same strong...uh...appetites that we'd always had, but no one to appease them with."

He made a face and shook his head. "Damn, I'm botching this badly." He reached out and took her hand. "I hope I'm not offending you, honey. I've never talked about this with anyone before...."

She squeezed his hand. "You're doing just fine, but you really don't have to tell me about it if it makes you uncomfortable. As long as you weren't bedding her at the same time that you were...well...coming on to me, it's none of my business."

He squeezed her hand back, then let go of it. "It is your business, because Tina gave you an erroneous impression of what was going on.

"Maybe it would help if I start at the beginning. Tina and I met while I was at the police academy after I got out of the marines, and we were married shortly after I graduated and went to work with the Omaha Police Department. We thought we were in love, but I seriously doubt that now. We were for sure in lust, though, and wouldn't listen to our parents, who told us we should wait and get to know each other better."

It was like a stab in the heart every time he mentioned his earlier strong sexual feelings for his wife, even though she knew it was unreasonable. That had been a long time ago, and although he and Tina had continued to make love after they were divorced, Brittany knew it was unreasonable of her to expect a man in his thirties to have remained celibate while he waited for her to come along.

"We found out very soon that we were almost totally incompatible," he continued. "We had opposing goals for our lives. I wanted a family and she wanted a career. She finally gave me two children, but I was the one who raised them, with the help of the nanny she hired. Tina travels a lot in her job, and was so seldom home that the kids hardly knew her."

Brittany was incensed. "I don't know how she could not love Kurt and Heidi. They're such wonderful kids—"

"She does love them," Jake interrupted, "but they're way down on her list of priorities. She thinks that as long as they are well cared for it doesn't matter who does it. She's not a bad mother, just an absentee one."

Brittany disagreed, and a twinge of jealousy jarred her. "Why are you defending her, Jake?"

He shook his head sadly. "Because I've finally come to the realization that she can't change her personality any more than I can change mine. It's not her fault that she has no maternal instinct. She was born that way. I never should have talked her into having children, but I'm eternally grateful to her for letting me have custody of them."

Brittany's jealousy escalated. "So grateful that you continued making love with her long after you were divorced?"

Jake seemed to stifle a chuckle, but he couldn't hide the amusement that sparkled in his eyes.

"No, sweetheart, gratitude had nothing to do with that. It was strictly an arrangement of convenience. Since neither of us was involved with anyone else and we both had normal sex drives that needed an outlet, we reasoned that it was safer to be partners with each other than to take a chance with casual relationships."

His expression turned serious. "It was an accommodation that suited our needs, but it was never a love affair. When Tina met another man she wanted to have a relationship with that was fine with me. We haven't had sex since."

He took a long swig of his coffee. "Actually, I suppose you could be flattered. In spite of her high-powered career and her unencumbered life-style, she's jealous of you."

Brittany's eyebrows raised in disbelief, but he didn't give her a chance to comment. "Tina won't share my life or our children's, but she can't stand the thought that I might find another woman to love."

He shook his head. "So, you see, she has demons to fight, too. I'm sorry to hear that she and Ted are having problems. I hope they can work them out. She's my children's mother and I wish her happiness."

Brittany was humbled by Jake's understanding and compassion for the wife who had caused him so much pain. Few men would forgive so generously.

She looked up and saw that he was watching her. The amusement was gone from his eyes, replaced with... apprehension?

When he spoke again it was as though he were wending his way through a mine field of words, trying to find the right ones.

"Brittany, I don't want to lose you." His tone was low and uneven. "I want you to stay here with me."

She must have looked puzzled, because he rushed on, almost stumbling in his haste. "Oh, not because I need a housekeeper or a baby-sitter for my children. I'll hire someone for those duties if you prefer.

"I want you with me because I need you in my life. I need your warmth, your musical laughter, the touch of your smooth little hands caressing me. The magic of your arms around me and your mouth under mine, soft but firm and responsive."

He wasn't even touching Brittany and she was melting. Then he reached for her hand and she gave it up gladly. He tugged gently on it and she moved around the table and onto his lap.

Putting her arms around his neck, she cradled his head in the valley between her breasts and held it there as she stroked her fingers through his hair.

"I want you, too," she whispered. "I want your strength and your gentleness and your caring."

She could feel his heart pound and his chest rise and fall against her stomach as his trembling fingers sought and found the buttons down the front of her red-and-white striped cotton shirt and struggled to unbutton them.

"But most of all," she continued, a little stronger this time, "I want your passion and your heat and your urgency...."

She paused to catch her breath as the last button came undone and Jake raised his head to push the blouse off her shoulders and arms, leaving her exposed from the waist up in only her satin-and-lace bra.

His gaze roamed hungrily over her, then with a muffled moan he reached behind her back, unhooked the bra and cupped her unencumbered breast with one hand while disposing of the unwanted garment with the other.

Brittany was on fire, and the flames escalated when he took her nipple in his mouth and caressed it with his tongue. She squirmed against him and cried out, "Oh, Jake! I want to make love with you, but this time I want you with me all the way."

He moved his head to nuzzle her other breast. "I will be." His voice was raw with need. "Oh, God, Brittany, I will be. I couldn't stop if my life depended on it."

Quickly he pulled his knit shirt over his head and tossed it aside. His lips captured hers, and he took full possession of her mouth as his tongue plunged and retreated, plunged and retreated, in an erotic game of seduction.

His hands roamed over her bare back, then around to cup her breasts and roll her sensitive nipples tenderly between his thumb and finger, sending spasms to her very core. She could feel his arousal, hard and struggling against her hip, and every time she shifted in his lap Jake caught his breath and clutched her closer.

"Am I hurting you?" she asked as his fingers dug into the fleshy part of her derriere.

"Hurting me?" he rasped. "Sweetheart, what you're doing to me can't be described. We'd better go upstairs right now or I'm going to take you here on the floor."

The picture that brought to mind was anything but unpleasant. "Sounds interesting," she teased, and bit his earlobe.

"Don't say that," he begged, and moved her off his lap, then stood. "This time we're going to do it right, and that means upstairs in my room, in my bed and with the proper protection."

Brittany was shocked. She hadn't even thought of protection. How could she have been so careless? Thank heaven for Jake's good sense!

"Oh, darling, I forgot all about that."

He put his arm around her and hugged her as he walked her toward the stairway. "I'm flattered, and I'm also surprised that I managed to keep my wits about me long enough to remember."

"But I . . . I don't have anything. . . ."

His hand brushed the underside of her breast. "Don't worry about it. I do."

At the top of the stairs they turned and walked along the stairwell to Jake's bedroom. Once inside he shut the door, then strode over to the bed and threw back the spread and covers.

The interruption in their frenzied lovemaking had cooled Brittany down enough to think more coherently, and she was suddenly self-conscious about parading around the house half nude. She'd been with only one other man, and they'd usually undressed and made love in the dark.

Instinctively she crossed her arms over her bare breasts and huddled back against the wall, feeling both embarrassed and impatient with her foolishness. She'd had enough trouble convincing Jake she wasn't too young for him, and now she was behaving like a backward teenager.

Before she could convince herself to uncross her arms and stand straight he turned around and looked at her. She felt the warm rush of color that spread over her face and was even more disgusted with herself.

Jake didn't say anything, but his expression changed from eagerness to uncertainty.

Now she'd really messed up. He didn't want the shrinking virgin type for a bed partner. He wanted a woman like Tina, a strong sexy experienced woman who could sense what he needed and give it to him.

While she watched, unable to unlock her stupid tongue and speak up, he went to the closet and took out a blue plaid flannel shirt. Folding it over his arm, he walked across the room and stood in front of her, his expression still guarded.

"Here, Brittany," he said softly, and held out the garment. "Put this on."

However, instead of giving it to her, he proceeded to put it on her himself in the way he would dress Heidi. Patiently he uncrossed her right arm and put it in the long sleeve, then did the same with her left arm, all the while watching her with a question in his eyes.

She felt more comfortable covered, but when he reached out for the buttons she took his hand in both of his. "No, Jake, don't button it." Her voice was hoarse with strain.

He put his other arm around her and held her loosely against him. "We don't have to go any further if you're not ready for this," he murmured against the top of her head. "We don't ever have to go any further if you don't want to. You know that, don't you?"

A long shuddering sob shook her, and she buried her face in his hard, hairy chest. "Oh, Jake, I'm so ashamed."

She felt him tense. "Ashamed? Brittany, you have a beautiful body."

She shook her head. "Not of my body. I'm ashamed of the way I'm behaving. What must you think of me?"

She was still clutching his hand in both of hers, and he pulled it away and cupped her head to lift her face upward. "You want to know what I think of you?" he asked as his gaze locked with hers. "I'll tell you. I think you're a sweet and caring young woman who has the same old-fashioned values that I have. Your modesty is refreshing. Don't ever apologize for it.

"And I also think you were willing to let me 'have my way' with you because you knew how desperately I wanted you and you couldn't stand to see me frustrated, only you weren't experienced enough to carry it off—"

Brittany was horrified. "No! Oh, Jake, no. That's not it at all. I want you so much I think I'll die if you send me away, but I'm not used to... to exposing myself to a man, and... well, I'm afraid—"

"Afraid?" It was more of a yelp than a roar as he dropped his hands from her head. "Brittany, I know I'm big and strong, but I can control myself. I'd never hurt you. Never!''

This conversation was only confusing the issue more. How could he possibly think...? "Jake, that's not what I meant. I'm not afraid of you. I love you. I'm just afraid that if we make love you'll be disappointed in my...in my performance.''

Jake gasped, and her mind went into another tailspin. Damn! She sounded so clinical.

She rushed on before he could speak. "I mean I'm not experienced enough to...to know how to satisfy you.''

For a moment she thought he was going to laugh, but if so, he managed to stifle the impulse. Instead he put his fingers under her chin and lifted her face, then placed his forehead against hers.

"Brittany, my darling, I'm going to have a great time teaching you all the things you don't know about men. You don't have to worry about 'satisfying' me, although I'm not quite sure what you mean by that.''

He kissed the tip of her nose. "You satisfy me every time I look at you. You arouse me every time you get close to me. And when you touch me..." She felt the involuntary shiver that ran through him. "Well, let's just say that there's no way in hell I could hold back from being positively ecstatic once I get you in bed.''

Her relief was so great that she practically collapsed against him. He caught her in his arms and she was no longer embarrassed. "Then what are we waiting for?'' she murmured as her palms moved over his warm nude back.

"We're waiting for you to be sure this is what you want,'' he said against her temple.

"Oh, I'm sure. I'm very sure,'' she told him. "I'm so sure that I'll even take off this shirt.''

She started to pull the shirt open, but he stopped her. "Leave it on if it makes you feel more comfortable. Your shyness pleases me more than you can ever imagine."

He put his hand under the shirt and fondled one breast. "I'm glad your experience is limited." His voice was husky. "I want to be the man who teaches you all the delights of making love."

She snuggled against him and kissed the hollow at the base of his throat. "You already have," she said dreamily, remembering the explosiveness of her first encounter with his loving.

"That was only a preview." His hand moved down to unfasten the snap at the waistband of her jeans. "It happened too fast. This time we'll take it slow and make it last."

Brittany had serious reservations about that. "How do you propose we do that?" she asked as she brushed her lips across his chest and made his muscles twitch. "A game of cards, perhaps?"

He chuckled and swatted her bottom playfully. "You may have a point there. Are you going to let me take off your jeans?"

The very thought of his rough but gentle hands sliding her pants down her hips and legs sent fingers of fire down the same area. "Please do." Her voice shook.

"Come with me," he said, taking her hand.

He led her over to the side of the bed, then hunkered down in front of her and unzipped her jeans. The intimate placement of his fingers made her catch her breath. He pulled the slacks down but left the bikini underpanties in place, and in spite of her determination to be mature about this, she was grateful for his sensitivity.

"Now, sit down," he said, and she lowered herself to the side of the bed. When he'd disposed of her sandals and jeans he stood and began to unbuckle his own belt.

"Don't I get to undress you?" she asked, nervous but determined.

He hesitated a moment, then raised his hands. "I'm all yours," he said somewhat shakily.

Good, she thought, but now what was she going to do with him? She'd never taken off a man's pants before.

She stood and tackled the belt. It had a big Western-type buckle on it that fortunately he'd managed to unfasten before she'd stopped him. She slid the belt out of the loops and tossed it on a nearby chair, then reached for the snap on his jeans. It was only then that she realized his fly buttoned instead of zipped!

Her mouth flew open and she just stood there staring as he whooped with laughter. "Sweetheart," he said as he made an effort to contain his mirth, "there's no way I'm going to let you struggle with these buttons. The ball game would be over before it ever started if you did, so climb into bed and I'll be with you in a second."

She giggled as the humor of the situation finally got to her, and she did as he told her, but not before she removed the shirt he'd loaned her.

The sun had set, and twilight dimmed the room, giving it a soft ethereal quality. Brittany propped herself up on her elbow, holding the sheet across her breasts, and watched as Jake sat down on the side of the bed and pulled off his boots and socks.

A wave of heat washed over her, and she was shocked at how erotic such a mundane act could be in an intimate setting. She continued to stare as he stood and unfastened his jeans, then stepped out of them and his briefs both at the same time.

Her first impulse was to close her eyes, but they wouldn't obey. Instead they widened as he straightened up and turned to face her.

Her suddenly nerveless fingers dropped the sheet and her undisciplined gaze traveled over his nude body. *My God, the man was gorgeous!*

He was all muscle and sinew and *male*.

With his clothes on he looked husky, but naked he could have posed for one of those ancient Greek or Italian sculptors whose statues of powerful, symmetrical and overidealized men were national treasures.

There wasn't an ounce of spare flesh on him, and even standing still his muscles seemed to ripple. The only blotch on his otherwise flawless body was a wicked-looking scar in the area of his injured knee, and even that turned her on. It made him less perfect but more human, more vulnerable, more in need of her tender, loving care.

And on the subject of needs, there was another part of his anatomy that was most obviously and quite desperately in need of her attention.

Her gaze flew back up to his face, and she saw that he was smiling. "Do you approve?" he asked softly.

She swallowed and ran the tip of her tongue over her suddenly dry lips. "Oh, my goodness, yes." Her voice was thick with desire. "You're even more beautiful than David."

His smile was replaced by a frown. "David who?" he rasped.

She blinked. "You know. *David*. The famous statue by Michaelangelo."

A look of relief chased away the frown and he chuckled. "Thank you, I think, but I promise you, I'm a hell of a lot warmer than any statue."

She lay down and held out her arms. "Would you care to prove it?"

"Yes, ma'am," he answered as he threw back the sheet and climbed into bed beside her.

He leaned over her and she embraced him as he wrapped his arms around her waist and laid his head between her breasts. His day's growth of beard was just prickly enough to send an unscratchable itch to her already overpowered electrical system, and she trailed her nails lightly up and down his back.

He twitched and shifted so that his hard shaft pressed against her pelvis. "You make me feel so good," he said with a sigh, and nuzzled her nearest breast.

"You mean when I do this?" she asked, and ran one hand down his side, then thrust it between them to lie on his belly.

He shuddered and pressed harder against her, then took her nipple in his mouth and suckled as his hand caressed the outside of her thigh before turning inward and kneading gently upward.

She gasped and arched her body against his as her hand instinctively lowered to clasp his turgid manhood.

He stiffened and cried out, and a few seconds later he was inside her, filling her, rocking with her in the ancient rhythm of life. Her burning body was wracked with tremors as she locked her arms around his back, her legs around his hips and rocketed with him to ecstasy.

It was almost dark by the time Brittany stopped soaring and came slowly back to reality. Jake had rolled over, taking her with him, and she was now lying on top of him.

She could feel his long, hard body beneath her, his legs twined with hers and his arms holding her close. Her head was nestled on his shoulder with her face against his throat. His skin was slippery with sweat, but so was her own.

Forcing her eyes to open, she raised her head and looked down at him. His brown eyes were open but unfocused, and she knew he was as befuddled as she. His breathing was still heavy enough to move her up and down with each gasp.

She smiled contentedly and rested her head back on his shoulder. "You were right," she said, and her voice had a sexy languid sound. "The other time was just a preview."

She wished she could describe how wondrous it had been for her, but, as before, there were no words.

He moved his head and nuzzled her hair with his lips as his hands lazily caressed her bare back. "That never happened to me before, either," he murmured, and there was astonishment in his tone. "Not that powerful. Not that...that all-encompassing. Good Lord, Brittany, you didn't tell me you were a sorceress!"

She made little circles with her tongue on his skin. It tasted salty. "I wish I were." Her tone was wistful. "I'd like to bewitch you."

"You bewitched me that very first night when you clung to me so trustingly, and I haven't been able to free myself from your spell since."

It seemed to her that was a rather left-handed compliment. "Do you want to be free of my spell?"

As soon as the question was out she wished she'd kept her mouth shut and accepted his admission that she bewitched him, then ignored the rest. She was almost certain she didn't want to hear his answer.

Unfortunately it was too late. "I did," he said, confirming her suspicion, and her heart sank.

"It's pretty scary being so emotionally dependent on another person," he explained. "But I don't now."

She blinked, and dared to hope. "Oh? Why did you change your mind?" She tried to keep her voice from shaking.

His arms tightened around her. "Because I fell totally, hopelessly, irrevocably in love with you."

His words exploded in her, like a giant sparkler sending tingling sparks in all directions, but this time she thought before she questioned. "Are you sure?"

He raised his head and looked at her, puzzled. She hated doubting him, but she had a reason.

"I mean we just had some pretty spectacular sex," she explained, "but you told me yourself that lust isn't necessarily love."

He reached over and dragged her pillow on top of his own so that his head and shoulders were propped up. She slid down slightly so that she was straddling his lap and started to move off him, but he stopped her.

She felt a stirring in his groin that would have amazed her if she hadn't been getting a like reaction in her own. How was that possible? It had only been a few minutes since—

"Brittany, my love," he said as his hands encouraged her to relax against his chest. "What we had together wasn't only sex. That was making love. Love at its very best, but it had nothing to do with my falling *in love* with you."

He held her cheek against his breast, and she could feel his heart beating, strong and steady. "That probably happened the night you burst into my life, too, but I managed to deny it until last Sunday when I hurt my knee."

He sighed softly and stroked his fingers through her disheveled hair. "You were so concerned and so gentle, and I knew then that what I felt for you wasn't just a surface infatuation that would burn brightly for a while, then turn to ashes. My love for you is deep and abiding. A joy as well as a torment that caught me by surprise and blossomed fully in the deepest recesses of my being."

He sat her up and held her at arm's length, his gaze meshing with hers. "I love you, Brittany Castle, and I want you to be my wife. I promise to cherish you always and do my best to make you happy."

She was caught totally off guard, and tears of happiness welled in her eyes. Jake had asked her to stay with him earlier, but she'd never dreamed he meant marriage. He'd been so adamantly against it.

She could feel her love for him radiating from her face as she reached out and put her trembling hands on his shoulders. "Oh, Jake, I love you." Her voice quivered so that her words were slurred. "I told you that, didn't I?"

He nodded. "Yes, downstairs earlier, but I was afraid it just slipped out in the heat of the moment."

"Well, it did," she admitted sheepishly, "but it came from the heart. I was afraid you didn't want to hear it."

With a groan of protest he sat up and clasped her to him again. "I wanted to hear it so bad that I couldn't bring myself to ask you about it. I was afraid you'd say you didn't really mean it."

She wound her arms around his neck and touched her lips to his. "When do you want to get married?"

The stirring of his body quickened, and he recaptured her mouth and rimmed it with his tongue. "As soon as possible."

She opened for him, and the enchantment of the kiss made words unnecessary. When they finally came up for air his manhood was hard and pressing urgently against her.

"See what you do to me," he murmured. "This has got to be one of the quickest recovery times on record. I'll wear you out before the honeymoon's over."

She was wet and ready, too, as she moved sensuously against him. "So who's complaining?" she asked with a sigh of utter bliss.

Chapter Twelve

Jake pushed his cowboy hat back, rubbed his forearm over his eyes and glanced toward the sun. Like most farmers and others who worked outdoors he'd learned to tell the time by the position of the sun or moon. It was ten o'clock, maybe a little after. He'd been daydreaming while he worked, and now he was going to be late picking up the kids.

He grinned, and knew he probably looked lovestruck and silly. Well, that's exactly what he was. Thirty-eight years old and feeling like a teenager who'd made love for the first time.

What a night! Actually, he had good reason for feeling like a stupefied novice. Brittany was the first woman, other than his ex-wife, whom he'd made love with since he and Tina had started dating so many years ago.

But even then it had never been this good. He and Brittany seemed to light sparks off each other and go up in smoke every time they touched. It was spectacular.

He chuckled as a picture of her curled up in his bed, nude and disheveled, stuck in his mind. That's the way he'd left her early this morning after the last time they'd made love. She'd fallen asleep almost immediately after they'd climaxed, worn out by all their activity during that fantastic night, and he'd vowed to let her sleep as long as she could.

After putting aside his tools, he headed back to the house. There was no sign of Brittany when he got there, but he heard the shower running upstairs and assumed she was in it.

He washed up in the utility room, then went up to ask if she wanted to go into town with him. He entered the bedroom just as she was coming out of the bathroom clad only in two towels, one wrapped turban-style around her head, the other knotted sarong-style at her breast and just barely covering her...uh...modesty.

He knew he was staring, but the sight of her was almost his undoing. He bit back a curse as his body hardened and strained against his jeans. If this kept up she was going to think he was some kind of sex addict.

"Holy Moses!" he exclaimed. "How am I ever going to get any work done with a distraction like you waiting for me at home?"

A smile lighted her lovely face before she shoved her lower lip out in a pout. "Would you rather I didn't disturb you?" she teased.

He could no more resist her than he could stop loving her, and he crossed the room in two long strides to take her in his arms. "Honey, you disturb me just thinking about you," he said huskily, and ran his hand up her bare thigh to the bottom of the towel. "But it might help if you'd keep your clothes on in the middle of the day. If I start daydreaming of you up here in my bedroom wearing nothing but a scrap of terry cloth, I'll be running in every hour on the hour and we'll go bankrupt."

Her pouty lips beckoned, and he covered them with his own, hungry and urgent, as his hand traveled under the towel to caress her bare bottom.

She had skin like a baby, soft and warm and resilient, and he knew that if he didn't stop right now he wouldn't be able to. "Enough of that," he said raggedly as he dropped his hands to his sides and stepped away from her. "I'm leaving to pick up the kids. Do you want to come with me?"

He was selfishly happy to see that she looked almost as disappointed as he felt by his abrupt withdrawal, but then she sighed. "I'd love to, Jake, but I have to get dinner started."

"No, you don't," he assured her. "Emmett isn't here today so we can stop in the city and eat. I want you for my wife, not my slave."

He knew he had to get out of there before the throbbing heat of his desire for her got the better of his good sense. "Now, for God's sake, put some clothes on before you drive me clear around the bend," he said, more sternly than he'd intended, then turned and went downstairs to wait for her there.

It was a great outing for Brittany. On the way into the city they'd decided to wait and tell the kids about their marriage plan that evening when they would have the time to do it gracefully and in the privacy of their own home. Then they would call Dagmar and after that Will, to let the whole Luther family in on their exciting news.

After they picked up Kurt and Heidi, they stopped at a family-type restaurant for the noon meal. Jake and Brittany held hands under the table while Kurt and Heidi chattered about their trip to the zoo and their overnight stay with their friends.

On the way home they stopped at a shopping center for groceries and various other items. When Jake spotted a jewelry store he looked at Brittany. "When we talk to Will tonight I'll ask him if they'll take the kids home with them after church tomorrow so we can go shopping for rings," he promised.

After a light supper that night Brittany cleaned up the kitchen while Jake and Kurt did the evening chores. When they were finished Jake would tell the children of their coming marriage.

Brittany had been in such a euphoric haze all day that she hadn't thought to wonder how they'd take the news. They seemed to like her, but that didn't mean they wanted her to be their stepmother. They had all their daddy's attention now. Would they resent her as an intruder?

She tried to banish the thought, but it continued to niggle at her as she finished the dishes.

A short time later Jake and Brittany went into the living room, where the children were watching television. Jake turned the set off.

"Hey, Daddy, I was watching that," Heidi protested as the animated cartoon on the Disney channel faded from view.

"I know, *Liebchen*," Jake said, "but Brittany and I have something to tell you and Kurt."

"Aw, gee, you haven't changed your mind about summer school, have you?" Kurt groused.

Jake laughed. "No, son, how many times do I have to tell you that you don't have to go to summer school. This is good news."

Brittany prayed that they would agree.

She was standing with Jake in front of the fireplace, and he put his arm around her. If he had doubts about the children's reaction to their announcement he didn't betray them. He seemed totally at ease.

"Kurt, Heidi," he began, and his tone was confident and happy. "Brittany and I are going to be married."

"Married!" Heidi's face split into a big smile, and her brown eyes danced with joy. "You mean a wedding? Is she going to wear a beautiful white dress with lace and a long train and a crown with a veil?"

She jumped up and came running to throw her arms around Brittany. "Can I be a flower girl and wear a beautiful long dress and throw flowers in the aisle?"

Brittany hunkered down and hugged the excited little girl, who had no conception of the deeper meaning of marriage but was delighted with the pageantry of a wedding. "Of course you can, honey. I'd be honored to have you throw flowers at my wedding."

She heard Jake laugh, but it was Kurt who caught her attention. He was still sitting on the couch, looking serious. "Is she gonna be our mother?" he asked his dad.

Jake glanced at Brittany, apparently taken off guard by the starkness of his son's tone. "Well...uh—"

"No, Kurt," Brittany interrupted, anxious to get Jake off the hook. "You already have a mother. Legally I'll be your stepmother, but I hope you'll come to think of me as your good friend. You'll still call me 'Brittany,' and nothing will change much, except that I'll be your dad's wife and live here with you from now on."

"What about Grandma?" the boy asked. "Won't she live with us anymore?"

Again Jake looked at Brittany. These were questions they should have anticipated and talked about, but they'd been so besotted with each other that they hadn't thought ahead.

"Of course your grandma will live with us," Brittany assured him. It had never occurred to her to think otherwise. "This is her home, too. She'll come back as soon as your aunt Gisela is well enough to take care of your little cousins."

Jake's arm tightened around her, and he shot her a look of gratitude, but neither of them was prepared for the next question.

"Are you gonna sleep in Dad's room now?"

Brittany blinked with surprise, and she felt Jake tense. A quick glance warned her he didn't consider that information any of his son's business and was about to tell him so.

She pressed his hand at her waist and answered quickly before he could. "Yes, I will," she said as nonchalantly as she could manage. "Most married couples sleep in the same bed."

She was aware that he'd used the word "room" instead of "bed," but she also knew that he wanted to know if they'd be as intimate as his dad and mother had been when they were still living together. "That's part of the closeness a husband and wife enjoy," she continued. "Does it bother you, Kurt?"

He turned red and looked away. "Naw, I just wondered," he said with bravado, but Brittany knew he had reservations about his dad sleeping with a woman who wasn't his mother or he wouldn't have brought it up. It was probably something that all stepmothers and stepfathers had to deal with in the beginning.

"Can we have the wedding tomorrow?" Heidi chimed in, lightening the mood considerably.

Jake laughed, no doubt relieved at the change of subject. "I'm afraid not, honey. It takes time to plan a wedding. We haven't set a date yet, but we'll make it as soon as we can."

Heidi jabbered on, asking questions such as "What color will my flower-girl dress be?" and "Can I invite all the kids in my class to come?" but Kurt sat quietly, apparently sorting out his feelings about this new turn of events in his life.

Jake had just learned another facet of Brittany's delightful character. She was amazingly mature at fielding children's awkward questions. Maybe it was because it hadn't been all that long ago since she'd been a child herself, but he was deeply grateful that she and his kids got along so well. He'd never give them up, but a future without Brittany was unthinkable.

God help him if he ever had to make a choice between them.

He finally put a stop to Heidi's incessant chatter by telling them they could turn the television back on and watch whatever they wanted to until bedtime.

When the children were settled down Jake and Brittany went into his office to make their call to Dagmar. Jake shut the door, then sat down in the chair behind his desk and pulled her down on his lap.

"You'll need to be close by so you can talk to Mom, too," he explained, then kissed her.

She wrapped her arms around his neck and opened her mouth, blotting everything out of his mind but the fact that it had been fifteen hours since they'd made love and it seemed like fifteen days. She was so damned receptive when he stroked and fondled her that it was almost a physical pain when she suddenly pulled away and sat up.

"Jake, this isn't a good idea," she said shakily.

"I think it's a great idea," he murmured fuzzily, and tried to pull her back down into an embrace.

Again she pulled away. "No, Jake, please, listen to me. It'll just be unbearably frustrating if we get all steamed up. I can't sleep with you while the children are in the house until after we're married."

That caught his attention quick enough. "I guess you're right," he said reluctantly, "we can't spend the whole night together, but we can make love while they're sleeping."

Brittany shook her head. "I just don't think that would be wise. You heard Kurt. He's old enough and smart enough to know what's going on. I think he'd figure out pretty quick what we were doing, and it could make him resent me.''

Somewhere, way in the back of his mind, Jake knew she was right, but he wasn't ready to admit it. "Damn it, sweetheart, he's only ten years old. I haven't even had that all-important father-son talk with him yet. What does he know about it?''

Jake was casting around for any excuse. "Besides,'' he continued, "we're going to be married. It's not as if you were just a stranger passing through.''

"Going to be married just isn't the same, Jake. He—''

The sharp ring of the telephone on the desk made them both jump, and Jake picked it up and was astonished to hear Dagmar's voice.

"Jakob, this is mother.''

"Mom,'' he said, and motioned for Brittany's attention. "We were just going to call you. We have something to tell you.''

"I have something to tell you, too,'' Dagmar said.

This time he caught the strain in her voice. "What's the matter?'' A strong feeling of foreboding knotted the muscles in his stomach. "Is it Gisela?''

"Yes, son, it is. That fall not only broke her leg, but we've just learned that it's also endangered her pregnancy.''

Jake groaned, and Brittany put her arms around him. "Oh, no! Is she going to lose the baby?''

"We hope not, but she'll have to stay in bed for the next two months until it's born.'' His mom sounded distraught. "I...I know this will be difficult for you, but I'll have to stay here. Someone has to look after Gisela and her family, and there just isn't anybody else. Nicholas's mother is in a nursing home and needs full-time care herself.''

"Hold on just a minute,'' he said. "Let me tell Brittany what's happened.''

He put his hand over the receiver and gave Brittany a quick account of his conversation with Dagmar. When he finished Brittany took the phone from him and spoke into it. "Dagmar, I'm so sorry," she said. "Is there anything we can do here?"

She held the receiver between them so he could hear, too. "The one thing you could do that would help most would be to stay on there until Jakob finds a housekeeper." Dagmar's tone was almost a plea.

Brittany smiled at Jake. "Oh, you can count on that," she said to Dagmar. "Let me put Jake back on. He has something to tell you."

She handed the phone back to him. "Mom, you don't have to worry about us," he told her. "Brittany has agreed to marry me. We just finished telling the kids."

There was a pause at the other end of the line before Dagmar answered, "That...that's wonderful, but isn't it a little sudden? You've only known each other a couple of weeks or so." She didn't sound very enthusiastic.

"I'm in love with her, Mom, and she says she's in love with me. I don't know how I got so lucky, but I'm not taking any chances on her getting away. You'll come for the wedding?"

"I wouldn't miss it," his mother assured him, "but I'll be seeing you before then. That's another reason I'm calling. I'm flying into Omaha Monday afternoon. I need more clothes, and there are a lot of things I have to take care of back there if I'm going to be gone so long. Nicholas is taking the week off to care for his family."

Jake was doubtful about his brother-in-law's abilities as a nursemaid, but Dagmar chuckled. "It'll do him good," she said with a touch of asperity, as if reading Jake's thoughts. "Can someone meet my plane?"

Jake assured her she'd be met, then hung up and relayed the conversation to Brittany. "We'll have to tell Will and

Elena about this as well as announcing our engagement, so I think we'd better go do it in person," he said in conclusion. "If you'll round up the kids, I'll call and make sure they're home."

Brittany left the room and Jake dialed his brother's number. There was something else he wanted to ask Will, and he preferred not to have an audience when he did.

Will answered the ring and Jake got right to the point. "I have some things to discuss with you. Will it be okay if we bring the kids and come over for a while?"

"Sure thing," Will said. "Is something wrong?"

"Well, yes and no. We'll talk about it when we get there." He paused, not sure how to ask the next question. "Uh...look, Will, is there any chance that Heidi and Kurt could spend the night at your place?"

Jake could almost hear his perceptive brother's brain ticking away as it came up with the obvious conclusion. "Of course they can spend the night," he said, "but are you sure you know what you're doing?"

Jake smiled to himself. "Very sure," he said emphatically, "And even your Puritan conscience will approve when I tell you about it."

"Puritan conscience!" Will roared in mock outrage. "Listen up, boy, my conscience is just as sinful as yours is and don't you forget it. Puritan conscience, hell."

They both laughed. "Brag, brag, brag," Jake taunted. "I'll debate that with you some other time, big brother, but right now Brittany is reluctant to 'sin' with me while the kids are in the house. It's perfectly proper, I swear. We'll tell you all about it when we get there."

Will chuckled. "*All* about it?"

"In your dreams," Jake teased. "See you in a few minutes."

He hung up and bounded upstairs, where he gathered pajamas, robes and toothbrushes for the children and stuffed them in Kurt's school backpack.

Downstairs again, he found Brittany and the kids waiting for him in the living room. "Here," he said, and handed the bag to Kurt. "It's got yours and Heidi's pajamas in it. You're going to sleep over at Uncle Will's house."

"Hey, neat!" Kurt said, and Heidi joined in with enthusiastic comments of her own.

Brittany's eyes widened with surprise, then narrowed with suspicion as the implication became clear to her. Jake laughed and hugged her. "Will was happy to have them," he said, and winked.

Her complexion turned a rosy pink, but her smile was as wide as his.

Late on Monday afternoon Jake and Will met Dagmar at the airport and brought her back home, where they all had supper together. The talk around the table centered on Gisela's accident and rather precarious recovery, then switched to catching Dagmar up on what had been happening at home.

Afterward, over dessert and coffee in the living room, the conversation shifted to Jake and Brittany's marriage plans.

"Have you set a date yet?" Dagmar asked.

Brittany's thoughts flashed back to Saturday night when she and Jake had discussed that during a lull in what would probably be their last night of uninhibited lovemaking until they were husband and wife.

"Let's make it soon," Jake had said. "It's going to be just plain hell knowing you're right next door and not being able to come to you or have you come to me."

Brittany had been as aware of that as he, but she also didn't want to compromise her reputation in the eyes of his children. Maybe she was just being silly, but these youngsters had been raised with the same old-fashioned morals that had been part of her own upbringing and she didn't want to disillusion them.

Wrenching her thoughts back to the present, she looked at Dagmar and smiled. "We talked to Pastor Gunner this morning and reserved the church for the second Saturday in August, just two days short of six weeks from now."

Her gaze shifted to Elena and Will. "Elena has agreed to be my matron of honor, and Will will be Jake's best man."

Heidi piped up with "I'm going to be a flower girl."

"An' I'm gonna be an usher," Kurt announced, with a mixture of pride and reluctance.

"It sounds as if you've got a nice start on your plans," Dagmar said, "but what about your class reunion, Brittany? Isn't that coming up this weekend? Now that I'm here I'll be happy to take over again if you still want to go."

Brittany was caught off guard. She'd given up all thought of attending the reunion in Raindance. She'd even called Susan, the friend she'd planned to stay with, to cancel. There'd been no one to leave the children with. But now...

She really did want to go. She hadn't seen any of these people, who had been such close friends when she'd lived in Raindance, since she left to go to college in Independence seven years ago. Much as she hated to leave Jake, it would only be for four days—

"Honey?" She jumped as Jake's voice interrupted her musing. "Do you want to go?"

She looked at him sitting beside her on the couch. "Would you mind?" she asked.

He put his fingers under her chin and tipped her face up. "Hell, yes, I'd mind," he said, but he was smiling. "I don't know how I can survive for four days without seeing or talking to you, but I'll manage."

He leaned over and kissed the tip of her nose. "It's probably the last time I'll let you out of my sight, so you'd better take advantage of Mom's offer."

Before she could answer Will spoke up. "Why don't you both go? You need to get away together for a while."

He grinned and Brittany blushed, remembering that he and Elena had kept Jake's children Saturday night so she and Jake could have some privacy.

"Emmett won't mind working Saturday and Sunday," Will said, "and I'll send one of my boys over if he needs help."

Jake looked at Brittany. "Would you like for me to go with you?"

She was overjoyed. "Oh, yes," she breathed. "That would be just . . . just wonderful!"

Without thought of the roomful of people, she threw her arms around him and hugged him. "Oh, Jake, are you sure? I mean—"

He hugged her back, but his tone was serious. "I'm sure, but are you? I don't want to intrude on your reunion with your friends. I was only kidding when I said I'd mind if you went."

"Intrude? Don't be silly. I'd love to have you come with me. I want to introduce you to them. Show them what a handsome, smart, hardworking man I'm going to marry."

Jake actually blushed as the rest of the folks laughed at her enthusiasm, and Brittany was sure she'd never before been quite so happy.

Jake and Brittany left Omaha shortly after breakfast on Thursday morning, had lunch at a small town along the way and arrived in Raindance in the early afternoon. The area looked pretty much the same as it had when Brittany was living there, with wheat fields and cornfields along the highway and the big ancient water tower to the west that was visible for miles.

The road bisected the small town of approximately twenty-five hundred people, and as they drove through it on their way to the motel where they'd reserved a room, she noticed that the restaurant where she and her grandparents had come for dinner after church every Sunday was looking shabby. However, a brand-new church sat proudly on the corner just down the street.

The City Park, which took up a whole block, was neatly trimmed, as always, and in the center of it a new courthouse had replaced the disreputable old former one that the city fathers had been trying to have torn down for years. Apparently they finally succeeded. The "new" library that had been built in another section of the park shortly before Brittany left was still bright and inviting.

She sighed happily and gave herself over to the sweet reminiscence of coming home after a long absence.

"That must be our motel up ahead on the left," Jake said as they approached the western outskirts. A few seconds later he pulled into the parking lot of a two-story medium-priced motel chain.

It was new since Brittany had left, and had been enthusiastically recommended by her friend Susan when Brittany had called to tell her she'd be coming for the reunion, after all, and was bringing her fiancé with her.

They were given a room on the second floor with a peaceful view of green trees and half-grown fields. It wasn't luxurious, but it was clean and comfortable and *private*.

Brittany turned to Jake, and he took her in his arms and molded her body to his. "These past four nights have seemed like an eternity," he murmured in her hair.

"I know," she said against his chest. "They have been for me, too, but we'll have the next four nights together."

"And four mornings?" Jake supplied hopefully.

Brittany giggled. "And four afternoons?"

His arms tightened as he rubbed against her, sending tingles of excitement to her core. "But this afternoon is half gone," he reminded her. "We don't want to miss out on it, do we?"

"Oh, my, no," she said emphatically. "We certainly don't."

This time she wiggled against him and felt the shiver that rippled down his body. "Brittany!" It was a cry of rapture mixed with frustration. "Have a little mercy. At least until we get our clothes off."

He pulled her shirt out of her pants, put his hands under it, unfastened her bra and pulled them both over her head. Then he reached for the waistband of her jeans and unzipped them.

At the same time she ripped open the pearl-covered snaps down the front of his Western-style shirt and slid it off his shoulders and down his arms, where it stuck. With a grin he held up his hands to show her the three buttons at the cuffs.

"You have to undo these, too," he said, and pulled them open, then finished removing the shirt.

"Well, how was I supposed to know that men have more snaps and hooks and doodads on their clothes than women do," she asked petulantly.

He cupped her head with his hands and kissed her. "You aren't," he said, and nuzzled her jaw. "Don't you know how much it pleases me to be the one to teach you how to undress a man?"

She kneaded his bare shoulders gently with her fingers. "Are you saying that you don't mind that I'm so clumsy and awkward?"

He moved his hands down to her waist and held her close. "You're never clumsy and awkward. Naive and inexperienced is what you are, and that's the most endearing gift you could give me. Your shy little caresses are so erotic that I can barely control myself.''

Talk about erotic! Brittany had never realized before that just talking like this could be such a turn-on, but she was heating up to the boiling point.

''May-maybe we should finish getting undressed,'' she said. ''Are you going to let me take off your pants this time?'' She eyed the button-down fly that strained to cover the bulge underneath.

He took her hands in his and held them together against his bare chest. ''No way. It will probably be years before I can muster enough control to stand still and let you fumble with those fasteners.''

''Then I'll take a quick shower while you finish undressing,'' she said, and pulled away to sit down and unlace her shoes.

''*A shower.* You want to take a shower now?'' He didn't sound very pleased.

She looked up and blinked. ''Well, yes. I feel kind of grimy after traveling all day. Do you mind?''

She watched as his expression softened. ''Is it okay if I join you?''

The idea startled her. She'd never showered with a man before, but the more she thought of it the better it sounded. ''Fine,'' she said, and grinned as she pulled off her shoe. ''First one in gets dibs on the soap.''

In the scramble that followed she beat him by a few seconds because he had to pull off his boots. The water was warm, the washcloths were soft and the shower stall was snug and cozy.

They took turns washing each other, but when she started lathering him below the waist his patience snapped. With a smothered groan he caught her in his arms, braced himself against the wall and lifted her off the floor.

Instinctively she wrapped her arms around his neck and her legs around his hips as he gently lowered her to receive his hard pulsating thrusts.

The steamy cubicle and the cascading water spraying over them only heightened their urgency until the explosion that rocked them blotted out everything but the shuddering rapture that united them in body and soul for eternity.

On the following Monday morning, while Brittany was packing to return to Omaha, she thought back over the past four days and knew it had been the most enjoyable vacation she'd ever had. Seeing all her old friends again at the parties, barbecues, breakfasts and the reunion banquet and dance had stirred up all the happy memories of her years spent in Raindance.

Although nearly two-thirds of her classmates no longer lived in the area, most of them had shown up for the reunion, and, like Brittany, had brought along spouses or sweethearts. Jake had captivated everyone, and she'd been so proud of him.

As she folded the miniskirted, metallic blue taffeta halter dress that she'd bought in Independence especially for this occasion and put it in the suitcase, she reflected on the joy of spending days and evenings with old friends.

It had been wonderful, and she was truly grateful for the experience, but best of all had been those glorious nights spent right here in this room, in this bed, all alone with Jake. No mother or children or hired man to intrude. No family to worry about setting an example for, no relatives to justify their behavior to and no nosy friends to worry about offending.

They'd just been a man and a woman in love, doing what comes naturally. The sex had been awesome as always, but so had the quiet moments when they'd just held each other and talked about their dreams and their hopes for the future.

She'd confessed that she'd like to have children, and was surprised when he was so pleased. She'd been afraid he'd figure the two he already had were enough.

He'd expressed his very real concern that he was too old and set in his ways for her. That she'd eventually tire of being a farm wife and mother since she was bright and well enough educated to do anything she wanted to.

That fear was understandable after his experience with Tina, but she'd managed to convince him that what she wanted was exactly what he was offering—love, children and a stable home.

She shut the suitcase and locked it, then wandered over to the window. Jake had gone down to the office to check out while she finished packing. The small parking lot that had been crowded over the weekend was now rapidly thinning.

A sound at the doorway behind alerted her, and she turned, expecting Jake. Instead she froze with horror when she came face-to-face with the man who'd been terrorizing her for months.

Piercing blue eyes met her stunned gaze and blazed with triumph as a delighted smile lighted his handsome face. "Brittany, my darling, you've been leading me a merry chase," he said in a soft voice loaded with menace. "You should have known I wouldn't let you get away from me. Didn't I tell you that if I couldn't have you nobody could?"

It was Ronny. Ronny Ralston. The stalker who had made her life such a nightmare. The madman who was determined to have her!

Brittany screamed. A high-pitched, bloodcurdling sound that seemed to reverberate throughout the building.

Chapter Thirteen

In seconds the room and the hall outside it was a madhouse filled with people. Jake and the motel manager were the first to arrive. Their booted feet pounded up the stairs while Brittany was still screaming, and the maids and rudely awakened guests followed directly behind.

Jake grabbed her and held her close, demanding to know what was the matter as the others crowded around, but Ronny had disappeared as quickly as he'd appeared.

"It's Ronny! He's here!" she sobbed through chattering teeth as she huddled in Jake's protective embrace. "This time I know it was him. He did follow me. He did!"

She thought she was making perfect sense, but Jake and the manager didn't seem to understand. "Who's Ronny? What did he want of you?" Jake entreated. "Brittany, why are you so terrified?"

How could she not be terrified? How could Jake be so dense? "Don't you see?" she asked impatiently. "He's found me. He'll do something awful to me. He'll never let me alone.''

"Who is this Ronny?" Jake said. "What is he to you, and why won't he leave you alone?"

Why was everyone just standing around? Why was Jake asking all these questions? Why didn't he go after Ronny, find him before he got away again?

"I told you?" she reiterated. "It's Ronny Ralston. He was right there in the doorway. He said if he couldn't have me nobody could. That was him I saw in the airport in Omaha, but how did he know I was coming to Raindance?"

The shock was wearing off enough that she was making some headway in pulling herself together, and she realized she was just confusing everybody with what she was saying. It was only now coming back to her that she hadn't told Jake about Ronny Ralston and the way he'd been stalking her.

She also discovered that she was shivering with shock and fear. It was imperative that she calm down enough to tell a straight story and quit babbling.

As she crumpled into Jake's embrace and struggled for composure the shrill whine of a siren coming ever closer split the air until it was turned off, and the sound of car tires screeching into the parking lot below at the front of the building replaced it.

"That's the police," the manager said. "I'll go meet them."

A couple of minutes later a police officer in a blue uniform walked into the room with the manager. "What seems to be the problem here?" he asked after the manager had introduced them.

Jake's arms tightened around Brittany. "I'm not sure," he answered. "My fiancée says she saw a man who's been following her, and she's hysterical. Maybe she needs to see a doctor who can give her something to steady her nerves."

"No!" The last thing she needed was a drug to scramble her mind even more than it was now. "I'll be all right. If we can just go someplace where it's quiet—"

"I can take you down to the station," the policeman who'd been introduced as Officer Quimby said. "We'll have to go there eventually, anyway, to file the report."

Brittany was now able to recognize the fact that in all the confusion Ronny had had plenty of time to get clear out of the area. For that matter, even if the police wanted to chase him they couldn't until she was coherent enough to give them an accurate description of him and tell them what crime he had committed.

Jake was speaking to her. "Brittany, do you want to go to the police station and file a complaint against this man?"

She nodded. "Yes, I certainly do." She turned to the officer. "Oh, please, you've got to find him. He's been stalking me for months."

Half an hour later in a small room at the police station Brittany, Jake and two officers sat around a table. Someone had brought Brittany a cup of coffee, and she sipped at it as Officer Quimby questioned her.

"Now, Ms. Castle. What's this all about? Just take it easy and try to tell us what happened to upset you so."

She decided it was better to start from the beginning almost a year before, but first she established the fact that she'd lived much of her life in Raindance with her grandparents until she'd gone away to college.

It happened that the older officer had known her grandparents and remembered Brittany as an adolescent. "You were one of the cheerleaders in high school. My son played on the football team. Remember Skip Oaks?

"Of course I do," she assured him. "He was our star halfback. Where's Skip now?"

"Would you believe he's in law school?" His fatherly pride in his son beamed from his face. "He was such a hellraiser as a kid that I was afraid he'd wind up on the other side of the law."

As they reminisced Brittany relaxed. She was among old friends. They'd protect her.

A few minutes later they got back to the reason for her pressing charges against the elusive Ronny Ralston.

"I've been living in Independence, Missouri, for the past seven years, and last fall I met a man who called himself Ronny Ralston," she began.

"He's twenty-eight years old, handsome as a movie star, with curly blond hair and blue eyes. He is also well educated, charming, and he told me he was an architect with one of the well-known firms in town. The type of man every girl dreams of."

She ran her hands through her hair and sighed. "I can see now that I was a real dunderhead, but at the time I was so enchanted by his good manners, his attentiveness and his Old World courtliness that it was several weeks before I began to have the eerie feeling that he wasn't as perfect as he seemed.

"It was small things he did at first, like his childish displays of temper when denied something he wanted. He'd bang his fist, kick out at some inanimate object and sulk. Still, it was a small defect, and I shrugged off my uneasiness."

She paused, trying to get her thoughts in order. This part was going to be embarrassing, but it was important that they know everything in order to understand....

"As time went by we started kissing and caressing...uh...you know, making out, but Ronny always stopped before..."

Oh, damn! If only she'd told Jake all this before, instead of putting him in the position of hearing it as a public statement to male police officers. She couldn't look at him.

Officer Quimby spoke. "We understand, Brittany. Don't be embarrassed."

She nodded, but couldn't look at him, either. "Each time it . . . it happened he'd apologize and tell me that he knew I was a 'nice' girl and he shouldn't have taken 'liberties' with me, but his 'baser nature' was hard to control."

She slapped her hand on the table in remembered frustration. "He acted and sounded like a character out of a chaste turn-of-the-century novel instead of a man of the liberated nineties. I was flattered that he placed me on such a high pedestal, but it was also weird. I didn't . . . that is, I kept him at arm's length after that."

This time she did sneak a sideways glance at Jake. The anxious concern was gone from his expression, replaced by an inscrutable mask. A sob she hadn't known was there shook her, and she stood, knocking her chair over.

"Excuse me," she said, and hurried out the door and down the hall to the rest room.

Brittany felt a little more composed after splashing cold water on her face and replacing the lipstick she'd chewed off in her nervousness. She hated being forced to reveal the details of her love life, such as it was, to those officers, especially in front of Jake. It was degrading and embarrassing, but she wasn't going to let that creep Ronny mess up her life any more than he already had.

If Jake didn't like what he was hearing then that was his problem. There were only two ways to survive this ordeal. Either fall apart or get mad. And she opted for mad.

She was going to do everything she could to see that Ronny Ralston was caught and locked up.

When she walked back into the interrogation room one of the officers was gone, the other was going over some notes and Jake was pacing up and down. When he saw her he walked over and put his hands on her shoulders.

"Are you all right?" he asked, and there was concern in his voice, but his expression was still unreadable.

"I'm fine," she said, and pulled away from him.

"I'd like to get on with this so we can get it over with," she announced to Officer Oaks as she walked to the table and resumed her seat.

Officer Quimby arrived just then with four cans of ice-cold cola, and after they were distributed the questioning continued.

"Okay, Brittany," Officer Quimby said. "What happened after your relationship with this Ronny Ralston cooled?"

"He asked me to marry him," she answered crisply. "Earlier I'd almost convinced myself I was in love with him, but by then I wasn't so sure. I couldn't even pin down the reason for my uncertainty. He had a couple of annoying quirks, but who hasn't? At that time his good points far outweighed his less-than-desirable ones, and he still had more going for him than any other man I'd ever dated."

She shrugged. "Still, I couldn't bring myself to give him an answer. Instead I asked for time to think about it."

That was where she'd made her biggest mistake. She should have said no immediately and not let him hope.

"He was almost pathetically anxious to please," she said, "and told me to take all the time I needed. He said he loved me, needed me, and swore that he'd keep a tight rein on his 'urges' and treat me with the respect I deserved from then on.

"For the next few days he courted me with flowers and candy, delivered with sweet words and tender kisses. It was old-fashioned but very romantic, and I was strongly tempted to ignore my prickly doubts and marry him."

She shook her head. "My doubts finally won out, however, and when he pressed for an answer I told him that although I'd like to continue seeing him, I wasn't ready yet for marriage."

She shuddered and her voice turned hard and cold. "Ronny had another temper tantrum, and this time he hit me!"

Jake jumped to his feet. "When I catch up with that son of a bitch I'm going to—"

Both officers rose as one. "Whoa there, mister. If you want to stay here you'll have to sit down and be quiet while the lady tells her story," warned Officer Oaks.

For a moment Brittany was afraid Jake was going to say or do something that would get him thrown out, but he managed to get himself under control and sit back down. "Sorry," he muttered between clenched teeth.

The officers nodded and sat down, too. "How badly did Ralston hurt you?" asked Quimby.

"He didn't break any bones, but my face was quite a mess for several days, and I was fighting mad. I told him to get out and never come back or I'd call the police and file charges against him. I had the black eye and swollen jaw to prove it.

"He cried, banged his head against the wall in self-loathing and swore on his mother's grave that he'd never touch me in anger again. I picked up the telephone with every intention of calling for help, but he left quietly with tears streaming down his face."

This time it was Jake who spoke. "Did you report him?"

She shook her head regretfully. "No, I didn't. Not then. To my everlasting shame I felt sorry for him. He seemed so truly repentant, and I just wanted to be rid of him. I finally realized that what I'd thought was love was just infatuation for a man who seemed too good to be true. It turned out that he was."

Jake looked as if he were going to reprove her, but Oaks spoke first. "Didn't you say he's been stalking you?"

"Oh, God, yes." she confirmed. "It started with phone calls about a week later. The first time I told him that I didn't want him to call me or contact me in any way, but the calls continued, even though I'd hang up as soon as I heard his voice.

"Finally I got an unlisted number. Then he started sending me a white rose every day. White for purity, his first card said. My dismay built to anger and climaxed in terror when I began seeing him every day either outside my apartment or shopping in the shopping center where I traded or walking by my workplace."

Just remembering made her shiver. "He never approached me or even looked at me, but there was an aura of menace that radiated from him. That's when I knew I was being stalked, and I was terrified."

Jake swore and reached for her hand. "Surely you went to the police then," he said.

"Yes, I did, but since he hadn't broken any laws there was nothing they could do. It seems he had to maim or kill me before they could protect me. They couldn't even warn him to leave me alone, since he hadn't approached me."

Jake squeezed her hand and muttered an oath as Brittany forced herself to continue. "When word got around that Ronny and I had broken up one of the men I'd dated earlier asked me to go to dinner and a movie with him. I was tired of practically being a prisoner in my own home, and I accepted."

She took a deep breath and forced herself to speak slowly and calmly. "It was a lot of fun, but the next time I went shopping alone at night I was waylaid by a furious Ronny, who grabbed me from behind in the dark, gagged me with his hand over my mouth and dragged me into a nearby alley.

"He called me filthy names, accused me of degrading practices and beat me so severely that I spent several days in the hospital."

Jake was livid. "Why are we just sitting around here talking?" he raged, and stood up. "That scum is dangerous. If you guys can't do anything I will."

Again the other two officers jumped up. "Hold it right there, fella," Quimby said. "Let's hear the rest of Brittany's story before we go chasing shadows. We have to know who we're looking for."

Jake glared at them but stopped. He continued standing, while the officers sat down again.

"I assume the police got involved after that," Oaks said.

"Oh, yes, they put out an APB, but Ronny was nowhere to be found. They checked out his apartment and all his things were gone. When they inquired at the firm where he'd claimed to work they learned he'd never been employed there. In fact, there didn't seem to be a record of that Ronald Ralston on file anywhere."

Quimby stared at her. "You mean he'd been lying to you all along?"

She nodded. "I can't believe I was so naive! I never thought to doubt him. He said he was an only child and his parents were dead, which explained his lack of relatives. He was never short of money, and I had no reason to contact him at work.

"Actually, we seldom talked about our backgrounds. Oh, I asked questions of him, but he didn't show much interest in my past. That's why I was sure I was safe here in Raindance. I'd never told him I used to live in Nebraska. The subject never came up. I have no idea how he found me."

Jake was pacing slowly around the room, too restless to sit still. "Why did you leave Independence if he was gone?"

"But he wasn't gone," she protested. "He surfaced again a few weeks after I got out of the hospital. By the time my bruises and broken ribs were healed I'd managed to relax and convince myself that I'd seen the last of my stalker. I still took reasonable precautions, but didn't jump every time the phone pealed or the doorbell rang. I even had a couple of dates with the police officer who worked on my case."

She sighed wearily and covered her face with her hands. "Then I received the note!"

"From Ralston?" asked Oaks.

Brittany nodded. "It came in a plain, innocent-looking envelope with my name and address typed on the front. Assuming it was an advertisement, I ripped it open, pulled out a sheet of white paper and unfolded it. It was short and succinct."

Even with her eyes closed she could still see the bold black type against the white paper. "It said, 'I saw you with the cop. Just remember, if I can't have you, then nobody can.'

"There was no return address, but it was postmarked the day before from the city. My tormenter was back with a vengeance!"

Brittany's voice broke, and she rubbed at her burning eyes but forced herself to continue. "I panicked. I couldn't stay in Independence and be a sitting target for a psychopath! I had to get away.

"Leaving town was fairly easy because I'm a veterinary technician and the animal hospital where I worked had been sold. The veterinarian taking over had his own staff, so I was faced with looking for another job, anyway."

Since being warned by the officers not to interrupt, Jake had been quietly pacing around the room. Now he stopped and looked at her. His face was ashen, but his eyes burned with indignation.

"You said something about seeing him in Omaha," he reminded her gruffly. "What in hell made you think he wouldn't follow you when you left?"

Brittany was puzzled by Jake's attitude. He'd been cool and distant toward her ever since she'd started telling her story. Surely he wasn't blaming her for Ronny's behavior!

"I was sure he would," she said evenly, determined not to let him see how hurt she was by his tone. "That's why I took every precaution to make sure he didn't. The police department made arrangements for my airline ticket and transportation to the airport, and no one else knew I was leaving.

"I walked away from my job without even collecting my final paycheck, and I abandoned my apartment and everything in it except for two suitcases full of clothes."

Jake nodded. "I see. But still you said you saw him at Eppley Field?"

"I thought I saw him," Brittany corrected, then went on to finish telling her story from the time she'd landed in Omaha to the time her car had gone off the road and crashed into Jake's tree.

"So that's why you were totally freaked out that night," he said. "It wasn't just the storm."

She sighed. "No, I was 'freaked out' before it broke."

"Then why in God's name didn't you tell me that?" he raged. "Or at least you should have told me when you volunteered to stay on when Mom left."

Brittany could only stare at him in astonishment. She'd never seen Jake like this before. He was not only angry, he was outraged, but why? What had she done that was so awful?

"I . . . I don't know," she stammered, too stunned by his reaction to think straight. "I was too shocked and frightened that first night, and after that I didn't want to bother you with my problems."

"Bother me!" he shouted. "Damn it, Brittany, you knew I was an ex-cop. I could have helped. At the very least I could have taken precautions—"

"Precautions?" she interrupted. "What are you talking about?"

He jammed his hands in his pockets and turned to glare at the two officers. "Look, I need to talk to her. Could you guys get lost for a few minutes?"

Officer Oaks looked at Brittany. "Do you want us to leave you alone with him?" he asked.

She wasn't sure what she wanted, but obviously she and Jake needed to talk. "Yes, please."

He switched his gaze to Jake. "Take it easy with her," he ordered. "She's the victim, not the criminal."

When they were gone Jake turned away from her and ran his fingers through his thick dark hair. "Brittany, how could you have put my children and my mother in danger without even telling me about it?" The condemnation in his voice was chilling.

Brittany's whole body tensed. "No! You don't understand. It's me he's after. He wouldn't bother anyone else."

"The hell he wouldn't," Jake said. "I was a cop. I've had experience with these bastards. They'll do anything to get to their victim, and that includes taking their twisted, vicious anger out on anyone dear to the one they're after. If this man had found you at my house he'd probably have taken one of the children or Mother hostage to force you to go with him."

Brittany felt sick. "Oh, my God, I didn't think of that."

"No, you didn't," he snapped, "and now he knows my name and where I live. He's crafty enough to get it from the motel register whether the manager gives it to him or not."

Jake's unbridled rage and the accusation in his tone devastated Brittany. Did he really believe she'd deliberately endangered his family?

Well, why shouldn't he? Although it wasn't intentional, she'd thoughtlessly put the son and daughter who were his whole life at risk. How could she have been so selfish?

For a moment she just sat there, head lowered and hands folded in her lap, as she tried to get her scrambled thoughts in order while Jake continued to pace. The silence of the room was broken only by his booted footsteps on the uncarpeted floor.

One of her fingers pressed into the stone of her engagement ring and she shifted her gaze to it. Her eyes filled with tears, and the diamond seemed to shimmer.

It was beautiful. One carat mounted in an old-fashioned setting. She'd been so proud and happy last Sunday when they'd gone shopping for it before picking the kids up at Will and Elena's, where they'd spent the night so she and Jake could have his house all to themselves.

A tear fell and trickled down her cheek, but she blinked the others back. She'd have plenty of time to grieve later. Now she had to undo the mistake she'd unwittingly made, and there was only one way to do that.

She brushed the errant tear away with her finger and raised her head. "Jake." She swallowed to steady her voice before continuing. "I can't go back to Omaha with you now that Ronny's caught up with me. You go on home and I'll stay here and deal with him. He won't have any interest in you or your family as long as I'm not living with you—"

Jake stopped his pacing and interrupted. "Don't talk nonsense," he said dismissively. "When the police get your statement typed up you can sign it and we'll be on our way. I'll think of some way to handle the situation on the drive to Omaha."

She bit back a sob. Even though he was mad as hell at her he wasn't willing to abandon her to fend off a persistent madman. She should have known he wouldn't.

He no doubt felt that she had him boxed in, and had nothing but contempt for her for allowing this to happen, but he was too honorable a man to leave a woman unprotected. Not even if she was able to fight her own battles.

It was easy to understand why she loved him so much, but she couldn't allow him to endanger his family by letting her continue to live with them.

There was a knock on the door just before it opened, and Officer Quimby stuck his head in. "Sorry to interrupt, but we have your statement ready to sign, Brittany."

Jake motioned him in, and Brittany signed the document. The officer verified Jake's address and telephone number in Blair and promised to let them know as soon as they had anything to report.

They all said goodbye and Jake headed for the front door. Brittany had to think fast. "You go on and get in the car, Jake. I'd like to use the rest room before we leave."

He looked at her for a moment, then nodded and strode outside. She turned around and headed for the back of the building, but instead of going into the ladies' room she turned right at the connecting hall and went out the side door.

Staying close to the building so Jake wouldn't see her from the front, she edged around the corner to the back, then sprinted through the park, across the street and headed north on the sidewalk of the residential area as fast as she could run.

She'd lived in this part of town and knew all the shortcuts and alleyways. By changing directions several times and ducking behind houses and shrubbery, she managed to elude both the police and Jake, although she saw their cars several times.

It didn't take her long to get to the outskirts of town. Although there were no buildings there to hide behind, there were plenty of fields where she could lie down among the half-grown stalks of corn or wheat if anyone came by.

She spotted an ancient pickup rumbling toward her on the dirt country road and slowed her pace, not wanting to call attention to herself by running. As the vehicle approached she noticed that it was a beat-up old blue truck, faded and dirty, driven by a farmer wearing bib overalls, a wrinkled long-sleeved shirt and a cowboy hat that covered his hair.

She looked away, not wanting to encourage him to offer her a ride. The people in small midwestern towns were still friendly and hospitable to strangers, and this one was no exception. He stopped the car beside her and leaned across the seat to open the passenger door.

"Climb in, sweetheart," said a chillingly familiar voice. "We have a long way to go before dark."

Her startled gaze flew to his face, and this time she recognized it. Ronny had caught up with her again. She'd known he would, but just hadn't expected it to happen so soon.

Nor had she expected the disguise. Ordinarily nobody would mistake suave, sophisticated Ronny Ralston for a farmer. He must have been in Raindance for a while to have acquired the clothes and the truck.

Too emotionally drained to be afraid, she walked across the road and hoisted herself up into the high cab. "Hello, Ronny," she said dully as she closed the door. "I guess you won, after all."

Chapter Fourteen

Ronny smiled that charming smile that had so easily captivated Brittany at one time. "We both knew I would," he said softly. "All this chasing around was just a big waste of time, but if you like to play games I don't mind."

He patted her on the thigh, then started the truck up again. "You really gave me the slip in Omaha. I probably never would have found you if you hadn't come on to Raindance. Where have you been, and who's the dude with you?"

Brittany was relieved to see that he wasn't angry. Actually, he sounded as though he'd enjoyed the 'game,' as he called it, but he'd always been sweet natured until someone crossed him. She was willing to let him take her anywhere he wanted to if it would lead him away from Jake and his family.

"That's not important," she said in answer to his question, "but I'm curious about how you knew I was in Nebraska? I didn't tell anybody in Independence where I was going.''

He grinned happily. "I had your phone bugged, and a couple of days before you left a woman called from the police department to tell you that your seat on the airplane had been changed. You weren't home, so she left a message on your answering machine, giving date, time, flight number and destination.''

Brittany didn't believe that for a moment. "That's just not true, Ronny," she said angrily. "The police knew better than to discuss anything about my trip on the phone or in the apartment, and besides, there was no message like that on my machine.''

Ronny shrugged. "The police aren't infallible. Obviously there was a screwup somewhere, and you didn't get the message because I erased it before you got home.''

Shock rocketed through Brittany as a small forgotten incident surfaced in her memory. When she'd boarded the plane for Omaha someone was already occupying her seat, and when the flight attendant was consulted he confirmed the change and was surprised that she hadn't been notified.

Then a chilling question surfaced. "How did you get into my apartment?''

He laughed. "Honey, given enough time and a few simple tools I can open any lock. I was in and out of your apartment all the time.''

Brittany was afraid she was going to be sick. What was the use of even trying to get away from this man? She'd never be free of him! He was that fortunately rare combination of brilliance and insanity. There was probably no mischief he couldn't accomplish if he put his mind to it.

She had to humor him, to do whatever was necessary to keep his attention diverted from Jake and the children.

Looking around, she noticed that they were now headed south. While they'd been talking they'd crossed the highway and were on the narrow, twisting road filled with pot-holes that led across the large desolate area in the middle of Nebraska known as the Sandhills.

If Jake and the police were still looking for her it was doubtful they'd come this way. They didn't know she'd been picked up, and no one would attempt to walk this lonely road where it was thirty to fifty miles between tiny settle-ments that weren't even shown on the map.

The thought flashed across her mind that Ronny could kill her and her body would probably never be found, but she banished it quickly. He didn't want her dead. He wanted her for his wife. Given the choice she wasn't sure which one she'd choose.

In an effort to divert her thoughts, she decided to find out all she could about him. She was reasonably sure she'd be safe as long as she appeared friendly.

The scruffy old truck was short on beauty and shocks as they sped along the bumpy road, but the engine was smooth and in good working order. She braced herself against be-ing thrown off-balance by the deep ruts in the road.

"How did you know I was coming to Raindance?" she asked.

"It took a little doing," he admitted. He seemed proud of his exploits. "I drove to Omaha the day before you left so I could meet your plane. I saw you coming up the ramp, but just then this damned old lady distracted me by asking how she could get a wheelchair. I only glanced away for a min-ute, but when I looked up again you were nowhere in sight.

"I wasted a lot of time in the airport looking for you, and then that nasty storm came up. By the time it calmed down it was dark and I knew I'd never pick up your trail again. Luckily, I'd found a letter in your apartment weeks ago, from your old school friend, Valerie Franklin. Just a post-card, really, saying how much she was looking forward to seeing you at the reunion. I knew you'd get there eventually. So I drove out, made some discreet inquiries and then settled down and waited.''

The man was actually bragging about his duplicity and expected her to be impressed!

Brittany could almost admire the way his mind worked. What a shame to waste all that intelligence on evil, when it was so desperately needed for good.

"That was sure a smart move." Brittany almost choked on the words, but she knew that flattery was the best way to keep him talking. "But tell me, how can you afford to travel, pay motel rent and eat out when you're not working? The police said you'd quit your job."

He looked at her and cocked one eyebrow. "Aw, come on now, baby. Don't try to con a con man. The police told you I'd never worked for that architectural firm. I don't have to work. I'm independently wealthy, so to speak."

She blinked. "What do you mean?"

"I mean that my rich parents deposit a generous monthly allowance into a bank account back East in my name as long as I stay as far away from them as I can get." He spoke dispassionately, as though talking about somebody else.

Brittany caught her breath. What had he done that was so unspeakable that his own parents would pay him to disappear? "Why would they do that?"

The truck hit a pothole and bounced them around until Ronny got it back under control. "Why in hell doesn't the damn state fix these roads?" he muttered, but within seconds he'd regained his composure and smiled at her.

"I'm the black sheep in my family," he said casually. "My dad's an influential politician. You'd recognize the name if I told you. I was born when my parents were in their mid-forties and already had grown children with children. Nobody in the family really wanted me, and I was spoiled and indulged because it was too much trouble to discipline and teach me."

Again he spoke as if talking about someone else, but for some reason Brittany believed him. He'd proven to be a consummate liar, but he lied with a great deal of charm and passion so that you couldn't help but believe him. Now he was just ticking off facts in a way that indicated he didn't care whether she believed him or not.

"At least I kept things lively when I was around," he continued. "I was expelled from numerous expensive private schools for lying and stealing in elementary school, doing drugs and carrying weapons in junior high and setting fires and, uh, having sex in high school."

Brittany was appalled, but she noticed the slight hesitation and picked up on it. "Having sex isn't usually a punishable offense."

His face twisted into an ugly leer. "It is when the bitches you're doing it with call it rape."

His tone was thick with suppressed rage, and a chill ran through Brittany as she silently berated herself for challenging him. Rape! But if he was a rapist, why had he been so careful of what he perceived as her chastity?

"It cost my old man a fortune to hush up my antics and keep me out of jail," he boasted. "Boy, would that have made headlines if the newspapers had picked it up.

"But it was when I was in college that I really gave him something to complain about. I got mad when one of my fraternity brothers refused to do a boring report for me that I didn't want to be bothered with. He called me a lazy moron."

Ronny's eyes grew wide and wild, and his voice rose. "Imagine! Me! A moron? I had the highest IQ of anyone in that Ivy League ghetto."

Brittany cringed against the seat as Ronny's foot pressed on the gas pedal and the truck shot forward. For a minute she thought he was going to run it off the road, but then almost as quickly as he'd flared up he calmed down and let his foot up on the gas.

"I showed that bastard all right." Ronny was again composed and wryly insolent. "We were alone in the kitchen of the frat house, and I pulled a knife out of the wooden holder on the counter and slashed him."

He said it so offhandedly that for a moment it didn't register, and she waited for him to go on.

Then it hit. "Slashed him!" Her involuntary outcry echoed in the cab. "You mean you stabbed him with that knife?"

Ronny glanced at her and nodded. "Don't look so upset," he said, as though he'd confessed to something no more alarming than that he'd hit the man with his fist. "I didn't kill him, although I guess it was pretty much touch and go there for a while. I only spent a couple of hours in jail until my dad got his high-powered lawyers to bail me out."

A sneer twisted his handsome features. "They got me off on a plea of self-defense, but that's when my self-righteous father couldn't ignore me any longer. Instead he disowned me. He dictated the terms under which he'd still support me, and I took off. I haven't seen or heard from any of the family since."

Brittany felt drained of both emotion and energy, but still she was trembling. Was it possible that everything he'd told her was the truth? If so, he was even more seriously deranged than she'd thought.

Ronny laughed, and there was a touch of madness in the sound. "That was eight years ago, and I've seen a hell of a lot of the world since then. I've also been in trouble several times, but now my dad would be proud of me. I've become a master at eluding responsibility for my actions by my own wits, without any help from him."

Brittany leaned back, closed her eyes and felt the terror building. How had a somewhat shy, puritanical young woman such as her gotten involved with this sociopath? She'd always been careful about whom she dated, but Ronny had been so nice, so polite, so...so caring.

How could she have been fooled so easily? She wasn't stupid, but she'd sure been mistaken about this man.

She was in over her head and had no idea how to get out.

It was only a matter of time until he'd turn on her again. His mood shifts had proven quick and turbulent. From gentleman to devil and back again without skipping a beat.

Her heart pounded and she clasped her trembling hands in her lap. It was imperative that she find a way to alert the police about him, but how? Certainly not out here in the middle of the Sandhills. They'd driven by a couple of towns so small that they'd passed them before she'd realized they were just a few abandoned outbuildings.

If she remembered correctly, though, at the junction with the Interstate highway which ran east and west across the lower part of the state was a small city called North Platte. It was about one hundred thirty miles from Raindance.

She glanced at her watch and saw that it was almost five o'clock. She hadn't had anything to eat since breakfast, and although the last thing she wanted was food, it was a good excuse to stop in town.

She opened her eyes and looked at Ronny. He seemed completely relaxed behind the steering wheel, as though he didn't have a care in the world. Maybe in his world he didn't, but she had enough for both of them.

"Ron," she said as pleasantly as she could. "I haven't eaten since breakfast and I'm hungry. Could we stop for supper in North Platte?" She held her breath and prayed he wouldn't refuse.

He reached over and took her hand, and she forced herself not to pull away.

"I'm sorry, honey," he said, and there was contrition in his tone. "I should have asked if you'd had lunch. Of course we'll stop. Maybe we should get a room and spend the night. We might have trouble finding one later."

That was even better, but she was amazed at how quickly he'd agreed. It was as if he had no conscience. No conception of right and wrong. If he wanted something it was right. If he didn't want it it was wrong, and he was never to blame for anything.

North Platte was a pretty little city with green lawns, flowers and big shade trees. Ronny stopped at a restaurant called Granny's Rocker, which looked like a converted house with blue-and-white checked curtains at the windows and a rocking chair on the front porch.

"I never had a granny," he said, and there was sadness in his tone. "Mine were both dead before I was born."

After they'd been seated and given menus Brittany excused herself to go to the rest room, hoping to find another way out the back of the building, but he threw her a curve. "Good idea," he said, and pushed back his chair. "I'll go, too."

The rest rooms were side-by-side and Ronny paused to wait for her to go into the ladies'. A wave of fear swept through her. It wouldn't be as easy to get away from him as it had been to lose Jake. She should have known Ronny wouldn't trust her.

She opened the door and went in, hoping there would be a window she could crawl out of, but no such luck. She'd have to wait until they got to a motel and hope she could find a way to escape from it.

As she'd expected Ronny was waiting for her when she opened the door again.

After they'd eaten Ronny stopped at a nice-looking motel on the western outskirts of town. Before getting out of the car, he leaned across Brittany and took a gun out of the glove compartment. He dropped it into a deep pocket of his overalls, then insisted, gently but firmly, that she come in with him while he registered.

Dear Lord, she hadn't known he was armed! Would he really use that gun? Somehow she knew without doubt that he would.

Was he going to make her sleep with him? That thought drove everything else from her mind. Now that he knew she'd shared a room with Jake in Raindance would he no longer care about her chastity? Would Ronny rape her the way he'd admittedly raped other women?

Fighting back her rising panic, she used all her willpower to keep her wits about her and think. There was no telling what he'd do if she created a scene. He was violent and dangerous when crossed!

Her mind was in such a turmoil that she wasn't paying attention to the conversation between Ronny and the registrar, and she was astonished when the woman handed Ronny two keys.

"Here you are, sir," she said with a smile. "Two-nineteen and 221. Just drive around to the back and park below either room.

Brittany's head swam with relief. Apparently there was no way to predict her captor's thoughts. The mind of a madman was too devious for a rational mind to follow. No wonder he could get away with almost anything he tried.

They'd been given adjoining rooms with a door between, and as they inspected them Ronny was again the considerate companion. "Take your choice, love," he said.

It seemed that he really wasn't going to insist on sharing her bed, and for the first time it occurred to her to wonder if he'd become impotent as he'd gotten older. That would explain a lot.

The construction of the two rooms was identical, but the furnishings were a little different. Each room had a telephone. She felt a stirring of hope. Was it possible he'd overlook that detail? If he did she could wait until he was asleep, then call the police.

Both windows looked out over the town they'd just come through, but neither of them would open. The doors, however, had the standard dead-bolt locks that could be locked or unlocked from the inside with the turn of a latch without using a key. She knew he'd never give her a key, but just maybe he was too harried or tired to remember that she could open the door without one.

Both fantasies were smashed as soon as she chose the room she wanted. He immediately ripped the phone out of the wall, then used the heavy instrument to disable the lock on her door so it wouldn't open from either side.

Brittany gasped and huddled against the wall, too stunned by his casual violence to speak.

"Don't be afraid of me, sweetheart," he said with a gentleness that belied his destructiveness. "I'm not going to hurt you, but I have to restrain you until you learn that."

He walked over and put his arms around her. She shivered with revulsion but was afraid to protest. It would be foolhardy to upset him!

"Now, be a good girl and get some sleep. I have to lock the door between our rooms, but I'll be right on the other side of the wall. If you want me just call out. I'll hear you."

He left and she heard the key turn in the lock.

For a moment it all seemed so hopeless that Brittany was tempted just to sink to the floor in a puddle of fear and self-pity and cry. She was fighting a losing battle. How could she hope to outsmart a maniac with the cunning of a panther stalking its pray?

But some primal urge for self-preservation prodded her. She was only twenty-five years old, and she had a lot of living to do yet. Ronny might defeat her in the end, but she damn well wasn't going to make it easy for him.

Her hands trembled as she stripped and got under the warm bracing spray of the shower. She hoped it would soothe her screaming nerves and restore her ability to formulate a plan for escape. Also, she knew Ronny would hear the water running and assume that she'd decided to shower and go to bed.

By the time she'd finished and dressed again she had a plan of sorts. After careful inspection of the telephone and the door lock she knew there was no way she could fix them, which left only the windows as a means of breaking out.

By placing her ear against the adjoining wall she could hear the television in Ronny's room, which meant he wouldn't hear anything coming from her room unless she was unusually noisy. Quietly she took the only chair and propped it under the doorknob on that same wall. It wouldn't keep him out if he decided to come in, but it would give her time to stop whatever she was doing.

There were drapes that could be pulled across the window, but it was still twilight outside and Brittany hadn't pulled it and turned on the light yet. After taking the lamp off the bedside table, she put it on the floor, then pulled the table over to one side of the window where she wouldn't be seen through it and climbed up on top.

From that height she could easily reach the ventilator at the top of the glass. Actually, it was a piece of the window that opened and closed with a crank. At the moment it was closed.

So far so good. Now all she had to do was open it, then measure to see if she could squeeze through it.

She reaching for the crank and exerted pressure. Nothing happened. She pushed harder. Still nothing. It wouldn't budge. It had probably been shut all winter and was now stuck in place.

For twenty minutes she pushed, pulled, shoved and finally even hit it with the telephone in an effort to move the crank, although that made so much noise that she didn't dare do it again. Nothing worked. Her arms ached and her palms were blistered and bleeding, but the mechanism was immovable.

Finally she realized that it was almost totally dark and she was getting nowhere. Her nerves were shot, and nausea born of frustration and panic gnawed at her stomach.

She climbed down off the table, pulled the drapes shut and turned on the lamp. There had to be a way to get out of the room. She wasn't going to let Ronny win this time. She'd always been a resourceful woman. There had to be a solution to this puzzle and she was determined to find it.

Exhausted, she sank to the floor and sat there with her back to the dresser, her arms locked around her shins and her face buried in her raised knees. If she could just relax and clear her mind maybe she could think straight again.

In the quiet that surrounded her she could just barely hear Ronny's television. The indistinct sounds of music and laughter reminded her of her childhood when she was still very young. At night after her parents had put her to bed she'd lie in her room with the door closed and listen to the faint sounds of the television programs her parents were watching in the living room.

There was one night in particular that stuck in her memory. She'd put up a fuss about going to bed, and when her parents had insisted, she'd had a temper tantrum and hit on the door with her fists after her mother had gone out and slammed it shut.

They were living in a rented apartment on base at the time, and for some reason that bedroom had a lock on the door. In her tirade she apparently hit something that jammed the lock and—

Jammed the lock! Brittany's head jerked up and her gaze flew to the door. My God, of course! She'd accidentally locked herself in her bedroom as a child and her dad had *taken the hinges off the door and slid it open.*

She jumped up, stumbled across the room and attacked the thick brass hinges.

The pins were wedged in there, solid and forever.

Bile rose in Brittany's throat as she pushed from the bottom and pulled from the top, but to no avail. Her fingers weren't strong enough to dislodge them!

Then a thought struck her. There was a knob at the top of the hinge pin. If she could find something to wedge under it maybe she could pry it up.

A search of drawers in the room failed to produce anything but a Gideon Bible and a pen and note pad with the name of the motel chain on them. A search of her purse, the only thing she had with her except what she was wearing, was more rewarding. She found a metal nail file. It didn't look very strong, but she was desperate.

Carefully she maneuvered the round end of the file under the head of the pin and pried it up. It took a couple of tries, but finally it slowly began to move. Brittany nearly shouted for joy.

She quickly disposed of the three pins, then grabbed her purse and as quietly as possible, moved the door back far enough to get out. She slid through the opening and ran.

Fortunately she was wearing thick-soled canvas shoes that gave her plenty of traction as she headed east toward the center of town. Keeping away from the highway, she darted down dimly lighted side roads and hid behind buildings or shrubs when cars approached.

She had no idea where the police station was, and was frantically watching for a taxi, when she finally spotted one parked at the pickup window of a drive in restaurant. She flagged the cabbie down as he started to drive away, and he stopped.

"Please, take me to the police station, and hurry," she gasped, as she pulled open the door and slid in the back seat.

"Yes, ma'am," he said, and took off.

A few blocks later he pulled up in front of a lighted building and stopped. Brittany had money ready and pressed it into his hand as she jumped out of the cab.

Inside she explained to the officers on duty that she'd been kidnapped and held against her will by a man who had been stalking her for months. "He just caught up with me this morning in Raindance," she explained. "I screamed and he took off, but I notified the police there that he was wanted in Independence. Later he found me again and has been holding me prisoner ever since."

She realized she was babbling and not making too much sense. "Please, call the police in Raindance," she begged when she saw their dubious expressions. "They'll verify it. You have to arrest Ronny. He's armed and dangerous!"

"Yes, ma'am," said the portly officer with the receding hairline who was called Lester. "We'll call right away. You say this man is at the motel out on the highway?"

He picked up the phone, and Brittany paced the floor while he talked. After what seemed like an interminable length of time Lester called to her. "Miss, they want to talk to you."

She rushed across the room and took the phone. "Hello, this is Brittany Castle."

"Brittany! Sweetheart, are you all right?" It was Jake, and he sounded frantic.

"Yes. Oh, Jake, Ronny didn't hurt me, but he'll come after me when he discovers I'm gone." Her voice shook with emotion. "He's crazy! I'm so afraid..."

A sob shook her, and she heard Jake swear. "Brittany, listen to me. I'm coming after you. One of the ranchers here has a small chopper that he makes available to the police when they need it. We're leaving as soon as we can drive out to the ranch, and we should be in North Platte soon. For God's sake, don't leave the police station or let those officers out of your sight until I get there."

He hung up, leaving Brittany sputtering.

Chapter Fifteen

Brittany put the phone back in its cradle and turned around to confront the officer who'd made the call. He was talking to another policeman but looked up. "Everything okay?"

She nodded. "Yes. My fiancé will be here soon. Did you send someone to pick up Ronny?"

"Yeah, they should be here any minute. Meanwhile, you can give your statement to our secretary so she can type it up."

Brittany was taken to a small office where a woman seated behind a desk was fiddling with a computer. When Brittany and the officer walked in the woman looked up and sighed. "The damn computer's down," she grumbled. "It was fine a couple of hours ago, but now it won't even boot up."

"Must be an epidemic," the officer said. "I just talked to Raindance and theirs is down, too." He turned to Brittany. "They haven't been able to get through to Independence to confirm your charges about Ralston and tell them that he's now wanted in Nebraska, as well."

Brittany didn't know much about computers, and she was too upset to care. "Surely you can just type my report on a typewriter," she said.

"Oh, sure, no problem. You sit down here and dictate it to Dorothy. She'll ask questions as you go along to make sure you don't leave anything out. Can I get you a cup of coffee? A cola?"

Brittany declined, then sat down and started to tell her story again.

It must have been about ten minutes later when the door to the tiny office opened and the same officer strode in. "Ms. Castle," he said solemnly. "My men are back, but they didn't find Ron Ralston."

Brittany experienced a horrible sinking feeling. "You mean he got away?"

"I don't know about that. According to the men the rooms didn't look like they'd been abandoned. The lights were on in both of them, and the television was still playing in 219. I also have to tell you that the lock was jammed in 221 like you said, but the door wasn't off the hinges. It was in place, and we couldn't find any evidence that it hadn't always been."

Just then another man appeared at the door and interrupted. "Hey, Andy, you'd better come out here. You, too, Ms., uh, Castle."

Startled though she was by the interruption, Brittany still noticed the hesitation over her name but immediately dismissed it as she followed the officer called Andy into the outer office.

She gasped and swayed when she saw Ronny, cowboy hat in hand, standing in the middle of the room, looking at her with big, pain-filled blue eyes that shimmered with unshed tears.

For a moment there wasn't a sound in the room, then Ronny's voice, low and tremulous, broke the silence. "Brittany. Oh, honey, why do you keep doing this to me? Don't you know that I'm going to have to send you back to the hospital if you don't stop running away?"

"What?" Brittany hardly recognized her own raised voice. "Damn it, Ronny, what are you up to now?"

"This man walked in just now and identified himself as Ronald Ralston. He wanted to file a missing person report," said the officer.

"Mr. Ralston, suppose you tell them what you told me. Do you know this woman?"

Ronny nodded. "I sure do. She's my wife."

"Your wife!" Brittany shrieked. "Oh, no, I'm not!" She charged across the room toward him, but one of the policemen caught her.

"Just stay calm, ma'am. We'll get this all ironed out."

Calm! How could she stay calm when this maniac was telling such monstrous lies about her? On the other hand, if she didn't she'd be playing right into his little game.

She didn't fight the policeman's hold on her, but stood quietly beside him and wondered if she was the one who was crazy.

"Brittany and I live on a little farm outside Independence, Missouri," Ronny said. "About a year ago she suffered a nervous breakdown and had to be hospitalized...you know, in a mental hospital. She seemed to be getting better and they discharged her in February, but since then every time we have a quarrel she runs away and tries to file charges against me."

Brittany was both terrified and fascinated. If she didn't know better she'd believe every word he was saying. It was Ronny in action at his best. The very picture of the innocent, unworldly young husband born and raised in the country, who seldom got off the farm. A degrading stereotype, to be sure, but believable nonetheless.

"There's not a word of truth in anything he's saying," she protested, but the policemen looked confused and uncertain.

Ronny played to their hesitancy. "Aw, come on, honey, don't deny it. There's nothing shameful about having treatment for a mental problem. You can't keep running off like this. Let me take you back home where you'll be safe, and you can start your sessions with Dr. Freeman again."

Brittany's nerves were too raw, and her emotions too turbulent, to be either calm or sensible. Instead she exploded and once more charged toward him.

"You bastard!" she screamed, and raised her fists to hit him, but he grabbed her by the wrists and lowered her arms. The pressure he applied was painful, and even through the haze of fury that clouded her good sense she knew he was strong enough to hurt her badly with little effort.

"Now, now, darlin'," he said soothingly. "You haven't been taking your medicine, have you? You know the doctor said it was important that you take it every day."

He released her wrists but immediately wrapped her in what probably looked like a tender embrace, but was in fact a painful restraint. Then he lowered his head and rubbed his face in her hair, and she realized that he was actually laughing softly in her ear.

That did it! He thought he had her cornered, but there was no way she was going to leave here with him. If nothing else worked she'd do something so obnoxious that they'd have to arrest her and lock her up.

She raised her face and fastened her teeth on his earlobe. He yelled and let loose of her, then grabbed his bleeding ear. "You little hellion." His tone was harsh and his features twisted with rage.

"Don't you ever put your hands on me again," she said, her tone low and menacing. "I hate you. I'm in love with Jake. We're engaged to be married, see." She held out her hand, exposing her diamond ring to his view.

She was playing along with his game, knowing it was dangerous but unable to think of any other way to make the officers see him for what he was. She knew he didn't like to be crossed, and she was attacking his ego. Maybe that would make him lose control.

Again he was a step ahead of her. The rage in his expression disappeared, replaced by an unutterable sadness. "I know you were sharing a room with another man while you were in Raindance. Who was he, Brittany? Someone you knew when you lived there?"

She almost faltered. He was too smart, too quick with the comeback, too experienced at getting his own way for her to dare hope that she could outwit him.

It looked hopeless, but the alternative was unthinkable and she was desperate.

She tried to reason with the officers, to make them see that it was Ronny, not her, who was unbalanced, but the more she talked and was countered by him at every turn, the more hysterical she sounded and acted. She knew what was happening but couldn't stop it.

After what seemed like hours she was exhausted and in tears, while Ronny stood by with a "see what I mean" expression, looking sad and noble. She was fighting a losing battle. No matter what she did or said he made it look like the actions and ravings of an out-of-control mental patient.

When she finally excused herself to go to the rest room, Andy even sent the secretary along with her. Ronny had finally won again. Now she was the suspect and he was the victim!

She was washing her hands, when she heard someone shout her name. It was Jake! Dear God, Ronny had had her so upset that she'd forgotten he was coming.

Without even turning off the water, she pushed the secretary out of the way and tore out of the room. Jake met her halfway in the hall and caught her in his arms, crushing her against him.

"Jake! Oh, Jake!" she cried, then broke down completely. Great wracking sobs tore through her, and she clung to him, frantic with fear and frustration.

"Brittany." His voice was tight with surprise and anger. "What have they done to you?"

He turned around, still with her in his arms, and faced the policemen. "What in hell is going on here?"

Andy spoke, but with another question. "Who are you?"

Brittany had her face buried in Jake's shoulder, but she recognized the next voice with relief. "I'm Officer Quimby of the Raindance Police Department, and this man is Jakob Luther, Brittany Castle's fiancé."

"Are you sure of that?" Andy challenged. "This man claims she's his wife."

Andy apparently pointed to Ronny, and Brittany felt Jake's chest heave as he gasped. "His wife! That's a damn lie. He's been stalking her. She's scared to death of him."

"Can you prove they're not married?" Andy asked.

Jake hesitated just a moment. "No, can you prove they are?"

Now it was Andy who hesitated. Brittany raised her head and peered over Jake's shoulder as Andy turned to Ronny. "Do you have a marriage certificate?"

Ronny looked somewhat perturbed, but he hadn't lost his cool. "Of course we do, but it's home in Missouri. I don't carry it around with me."

There was just the right touch of reason and frustration in his tone as he continued, "Look, fellas, this guy—" he nodded toward Jake "—is the one she was shacked up with in Raindance. It's not likely she'd tell him she was married. Now, why don't you let me take her and go home. I promise she'll get treatment. I'll even agree to let her be institutionalized again if that's what her psychiatrist feels is best."

"Why, you son of a bitch!" Jake snarled as he put Brittany away from him and strode across the room toward Ronny.

"No, Jake," she screamed. "He has a gun!"

It was too late. Before anyone could react Ronny had the gun in his hand and pointed straight at Brittany. "Come any closer and I'll kill her." His tone was cold and devoid of emotion.

Brittany looked into the barrel of the weapon and realized that her own emotions had been so battered for the past ten or twelve hours that she was no longer capable of fear. She felt as cold and dead inside as he sounded.

At least now everybody knew who had been lying and who had been telling the truth, and for some reason at this moment that was more important to her than whether or not he pulled the trigger.

Ronny started walking slowly toward her, and everyone and everything seemed to fade but the two of them. Ronny and Brittany pitted against each other, with all the pretense and posturing stripped away.

He no longer hid behind the charming, innocent, young man persona. His face was white and twisted with hate, and madness blazed from his vacant blue eyes.

He reached her and put the gun to her head and cocked it. The metal was cold, and it amazed her that she didn't even flinch.

"I'm sorry about this, Brittany," he said, but he didn't sound sorry. "I told you that if I couldn't have you nobody could, but you wouldn't listen. Next time you'll believe me."

The only reaction she had was how could there be a next time if she was dead?

He put his other arm around her and pulled her back hard against him, the gun still pointed at her head. "I'm an expert marksman," he warned, "but even if I wasn't I couldn't miss at this distance. Just don't move until my truck pulls away."

She still wasn't aware of the others in the room, only of Ronny's arm holding her and the gun pressed against her temple.

Slowly he began backing up, forcing her along with him. If she was going to try to save herself it would have to be now, but how?

As she tried to keep up with his backward footsteps she stumbled over one of his feet, and his arm tightened as he balanced himself.

"Watch your step," he growled. "This gun has a hair trigger. Just a tad too much pressure and it'll go off whether I want it to or not."

Brittany's heart sped up. Now she knew how to stop him, but she could easily get killed in the process.

He started moving backward again, and there was no time to think. Anything was preferable to being held prisoner by this homicidal psychopath.

She moved her foot with his, but then, with a swift backward kick, she placed it in back of his and he tripped over it, loosening his hold on her. She dove away from him and heard a shot ring out, then another and another and still another as she cringed on the floor, waiting for the tearing pain of a bullet to explode somewhere inside her body.

It didn't happen, and then Jake was kneeling on the floor beside her, calling her name and lifting her into his arms. She flung her arms around his neck and he rocked back and forth on his heels.

"You're all right, sweetheart. Thank God, you're all right," he crooned as he buried his face in the moist hollow of her neck. "His bullet went into the air as he fell backward."

She was almost content to let it go with that. Jake was here. He was holding her, loving her. And she didn't care about anything else.

For a moment that was enough, but then reality intruded on her dream world and she had to ask. "But...but I heard several shots. What—"

He raised his head and looked at her, then kissed her gently on the mouth. "Those were police bullets, Brittany. Ronny is dead. He won't ever terrorize you again."

The next several hours were a blur in Brittany's fuzzy mind. All she knew for sure was that Jake had been there, touching her, holding her, talking softly to her.

She remembered being taken to a hospital, where a woman in white had given her a shot in the arm, and later a ride in an airplane that made a funny chopping noise. She'd slept during that time, curled up on Jake's lap; now that they were back in their room in Raindance she felt more alert and conscious of what was going on around her.

Jake shut the door behind them, then sat her down on the side of the bed and hunkered down in front of her to remove her shoes and socks. "I'll have you ready for bed in a few minutes, honey, and then you can sleep off that sedative."

Dear, sweet Jake. She'd put him through hell running away like that, even though she'd had only the best of intentions, but he hadn't once spoken harshly to her.

She reached out and ran her fingers through his hair. "I love you, Jake," she said simply.

His face seemed to crumple for just a moment before he brought it under control. "And I love you," he murmured, then leaned over to kiss her.

She put her arms around him and held his head against her chest. He slipped off her last shoe and, putting his arms around her waist, pulled her close. "Brittany, why?"

His voice was slightly muffled against her breast. "Why did you disappear like that? I nearly went crazy—"

"I know, darling, and I'm sorry," she murmured as she stroked his back. "But at the time I didn't know what else to do. You didn't seem to want to leave me here, and I couldn't put you and your family in certain danger by going back to Omaha with you."

His arms tightened about her, and she felt the sob that rose in his chest, only to be quickly suppressed. "Going home without you was never an option, my darling." His voice trembled. "Did you honestly believe that I'd leave you at the mercy of that maniac?"

She lowered her head and kissed the top of his. "No, I didn't. That's why I had to leave you."

He sighed, then lifted his head to pull away from her and raise himself up to sit by her on the bed. "Brittany, listen to me carefully," he said as he took her hands in his. "I love you. You are dearer to me than anyone else, so don't ever again just assume that I can live without you. Understand?"

She nodded and snuggled into his embrace.

"Now, let's get something else straight," he murmured in her ear. "I'm a flawed human being, no better and no worse than anyone else, and I tend to lose my temper when I feel strongly about something. I'll try very hard not to let it happen again with you, but it probably will because I'm not perfect. If I do you're to either yell back at me or ignore it until I've calmed down and we can talk rationally, but don't ever, *ever,* run away from me."

"I promise," she whispered against his throat, and she knew that was one promise she'd never break.

She'd found a haven in his arms and she was content.

* * * * *

Silhouette

SPECIAL EDITION™

That SPECIAL *Woman!*

SALLY JANE GOT MARRIED
Celeste Hamilton

Everyone believed Sally Jane Haskins was the town bad girl—except widowed father Cotter Graham. When a night of passion suddenly meant they were expecting, a trip down the aisle was the only choice. Sally Jane hoped that this, at last, was her chance at happily ever after....

Celebrate Sally Jane's nuptials in Celeste Hamilton's SALLY JANE GOT MARRIED, available in February.

She's friend, wife, mother—she's you! And beside each Special Woman stands a wonderfully *special* man. It's a celebration of our heroines—and the men who become part of their lives.

Don't miss **THAT SPECIAL WOMAN!** each month—from some of your special authors! Only from Silhouette Special Edition!

**Fifty red-blooded, white-hot, true-blue hunks
from every State in the Union!**

Look for MEN MADE IN AMERICA! Written by some of our most poplar authors, these stories feature fifty of the strongest, sexiest men, each from a different state in the union!

Two titles available every other month at your favorite retail outlet.

In January, look for:

DREAM COME TRUE by Ann Major (Florida)
WAY OF THE WILLOW by Linda Shaw (Georgia)

In March, look for:

TANGLED LIES by Anne Stuart (Hawaii)
ROGUE'S VALLEY by Kathleen Creighton (Idaho)

You won't be able to resist MEN MADE IN AMERICA!

WHAT EVER HAPPENED TO...?

Have you been wondering when much-loved characters will finally get their own stories? Well, have we got a lineup for you! Silhouette Special Edition is proud to present a **Spin-off Spectacular!** Be sure to catch these exciting titles from some of your favorite authors.

HARDHEARTED (SE #859 January) That Special Woman!
Chantal Robichaux's baby is in jeopardy, and only tough cop Dylan Garvey—the baby's father—can help them in *Bay Matthews*'s tie-in to WORTH WAITING FOR (SE #825, July 1993).

SUMMERTIME (SE #860 January) *Curtiss Ann Matlock* introduces another of THE BREEN MEN when Oren Breen must convince the reluctant Lorena Venable that he's her man!

FAR TO GO (SE #862 January) One of the twins, Joe Walker, has his hands full when he's hired to protect the willful Lauren Caldwell in the latest from *Gina Ferris* and her FAMILY FOUND series.

SALLY JANE GOT MARRIED (SE #865 February) That Special Woman!
Sally Jane Haskins meets Cotter Graham, the man who will change her life, in *Celeste Hamilton*'s follow-up to her CHILD OF DREAMS
(SE #827, July 1993).

HE'S MY SOLDIER BOY (SE #866 February) *Lisa Jackson*'s popular MAVERICKS series continues as returning soldier Ben Powell is determined to win back Carlie Surrett, the woman he never forgot....

**Don't miss these wonderful titles, only for our readers—
only from Silhouette Special Edition!**

SPIN3

**And now for
something completely different
from Silhouette....**

SPELLBOUND
R O M A N C E

Unique and innovative stories that take you into the world of paranormal happenings. Look for our special "Spellbound" flash—and get ready for a truly exciting reading experience!

**In February, look for
One Unbelievable Man (SR #993)
by Pat Montana.**

Was he man or myth? Cass Kohlmann's mysterious traveling companion, Michael O'Shea, had her all confused. He'd suddenly appeared, claiming she was his destiny—determined to win her heart. But could levelheaded Cass learn to believe in fairy tales...before her fantasy man disappeared forever?

Don't miss the charming, sexy and utterly mysterious
Michael O'Shea in
ONE UNBELIEVABLE MAN.
Watch for him in February—only from

Silhouette
R O M A N C E™

CONVINCING ALEX

Those Wild Ukrainians

Look who Detective Alex Stanislaski has picked up....

When soap opera writer Bess McNee hit the streets in spandex pants and a clinging tube-top in order to research the role of a prostitute, she was looking for trouble—but not too much trouble.

Then she got busted by straight-laced Detective Alex Stanislaski and found a lot more than she'd bargained for. This man wasn't buying anything she said, and Bess realized she was going to have to be a *lot* more convincing....

If you enjoyed TAMING NATASHA (SE #583), LURING A LADY (SE #709) and FALLING FOR RACHEL (SE #810), then be sure to read CONVINCING ALEX, the delightful tale of another one of THOSE WILD UKRAINIANS finding love where it's least expected.

SSENR

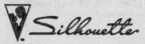